PRAISE FOR EDEN WINTERS

Readers love *Duet*

"I found myself staying up past my bed time, reading more with my first morning cup of coffee, reading even more during my breaks at work, and rushing home to finally finish reading this captivating story."

—The Novel Approach

"I'm very pleased to have been a visitor to this haunting world, where beautiful descriptions of an amazing land and people will bring to life a time gone by and bring to memory a couple destined to be."

—Mrs. Condit and Friends Read Books

"I have to recommend this to those who adore historicals, a Scotsman and Englishman falling in love, reuniting parted lovers, a haunting love story and a very happy ending."

—MM Good Book Reviews

"It's a beautiful love story woven together to make a wonderful whole and I'll be reading it again."

—Literary Nymphs Reviews Only

A
MATTER
OF WHEN

EDEN WINTERS

ROCKY RIDGE BOOKS

ALSO BY EDEN WINTERS

Duet

Naked Tails

The Wish

Consorts of the Red King

The Diversion Series

Diversion

Collusion

Corruption

Manipulation

Redemption

Reunion

Suspicion

Decision

A Matter of When

Cover Art by Rocking Book Covers

Print ISBN 978-1-62622-083-6

Printed in the United States of America

First Edition Dreamspinner Press 2014

Second Edition 2020

Rocky Ridge Books

PO Box 6922

Broomfield, CO 80021

To Z, Feliz, Pam, Will, Doug, John, and John.
Words cannot express how dear you are.

Many thanks to the wonderful Elisa Rolle
for the Italian translations and
her unwavering support of authors and our genre.

ONE

"I'VE GOT a date with a bullet, got a date with a gun...."

Every word ripped out of Henri Lafontaine, taking pieces of his soul. He pleaded with the audience, tuning out the pinch of tight leather against his knees, and knelt on the edge of the stage. Pain meant he lived, he breathed, he *felt*.

"No matter what I do, one day it's gonna come."

Frenzied fans reached for him, too far away to ease his cloying loneliness. A vise gripped Henri's innards—more than sweat poured from him with the fatalistic lyrics. One misstep, one leap from the stage, one dive into the pit of sycophants, and the arms reaching for him, the clutching, grasping hands, would hold him close.

But not close enough to melt the numbness inside.

"You say that you love me, but you only speak in lies."

He raised his voice, keeping the tempo pounded out by the quartet of musicians behind him. Not the kind of folks he wanted at his back. Hookers and Cocaine. A stellar name for a group. Most of the members lived up to the title.

1

"But I do love you, Henri! I do! I do!" A young woman with a tomato-red faux hawk shoved her way closer. Henri beckoned. Security would rip him a new one for violating protocol. Oh well, better to ask forgiveness than permission.

He crammed his whole heart and soul into belting out, "Put me down every minute, and I gotta say good-bye."

Images of his manager, his bandmates, critics, and certain members of his entourage flashed behind his closed eyelids. Pressure built in the back of his throat, sending his voice out wavering. Dampness trailed down his cheeks, accompanying a desperate plea for help, which the masses likely understood as merely the lyrics of a top-forty hit.

Aching, longing, isolation, fear—his constant companions.

He panted for a moment, letting the guitar solo wash over him, and swept a sweaty curtain of ebony out of his eyes with one hand. Damn but Ricky played like a maniac. Too bad about the "unmitigated asshole" thing. The guitar for hire coaxing ethereal melodies from a six-string bordered on miraculous, but could be better if he played from the heart and not for the money, the groupies, and the fame. Ditto the drummer, Giles, whose cocaine habit stifled true talent, and doubly so for Vince on the keyboards, "reducing his art" for the paycheck, when he'd bragged often enough of contemporary rock and roll lying far beneath his master's degree in music.

While the rest of the band wanted the trappings of rock stardom, Henri wanted one more breath. One more inhale, one more exhale. And a little less pain.

A bass beat throbbed, charmed to life by a traitor who'd sold out his brothers to a tabloid. Tomorrow's headlines would rip the band apart—if they managed to last until dawn. Serpents. He'd surrounded himself with serpents. Or rather, his manager had, someone else with dollar signs in her eyes, blinding her to the golden goose's swan song.

2

The fan fought her way forward through a sea of writhing bodies, and Henri extended his hand, signaling "come hither" with wriggling fingers, animating the image etched on his wrist. Fanciful creatures entwined with ivy trailed up his arm, disappearing under his T-shirt sleeve. Before the girl answered the call, the mob closed in, grabbing, clinging, tugging Henri half off the stage. The world turned upside down. He hung over the platform's edge. Oh shit! He grabbed at an amp and missed. Falling, falling.

"I've got you." Arms around him, but not in the way he needed. A scowling security guard clamped on tight. Great. Just what he needed.

As though he'd not been denied his greatest wish of human contact, Henri started in on the chorus while the guard shoved him back on stage.

"'Cause I've got a date with a bullet, got a date with a gun."

Rising to his feet, head bowed, he cried out for rescue, from thousands who heard the words but not the message.

"And every day that I stay with you, the closer that day comes...."

The band wound down, the drummer dropping back, the bass and keyboards quieting. The lead guitar softened to allow Henri to deliver the final words in what passed for a whisper during a live show.

"It's just a matter of when."

———

THE ENCORE, the reporter gauntlet, the picture taking and autograph signing went by in a blur. Then came the limo ride from hell.

"What's got into you tonight, Henri? You seem a little down.

Or should I be asking, 'What hasn't gotten into you?'" Ricky snickered. "Oh, maybe you *want* to *go* down."

"Did you notice that big-titted chick down front?" Giles chimed in. "Oh, wait, of course you didn't." He lowered his voice so only Henri could hear. "You would if she had a dick." He paused long enough to suck up a line of coke off a tray he'd found in the limo's bar.

Fucking assholes. Thank God their manager wasn't here. Henri could better handle their homophobic slurs than their kissing up to Marguerite and laughing behind his back when she treated Henri like a four-year-old. Lord knew she babied her moneymaker, even if her hovering did cock block him. He had to play the straight boy for the fans.

"Fuck off," he told his band. Hell, at least they hadn't invited groupies along for the ride this time. The last thing he needed was Giles pounding into some half-naked woman right next to him.

But if they dared use the n-word, by God, he'd have to kill somebody.

He stared out the window. Buildings seemed to merge together as the limo whizzed by, their features further blurred by darkness and window tint. The car slowed to a stop at a red light. What if he simply jumped out and ran? Never stopped running, never looked back? Found a place to hide where no one could ever find him?

Oh yeah. *Think of all the people depending on you,* he heard in his manager's voice. *Stop being selfish. One cancelled show cuts into a lot of paychecks. Roadies, vendors, the band....* Not to mention herself.

He squeezed his eyes shut. A hamster on a wheel. A damned moneymaking hamster. No one gave a shit about him, just the money. One more concert, one more town. *C'mon, Henri, get up on that stage. Think of your fans, Henri. Think of your family, Henri. Think of the band, Henri.*

The next time the car stopped, the band crawled out into chaos. More fans, more grasping hands. A security guard guided him into the hotel, through a crowded atrium, and into a private, invitation-only party. At least his tormenters scattered, finding better amusements than "bash the closeted lead singer."

In the background, Henri's recorded voice wailed through the playback of tonight's show, jacked up high to compete with the revelry of a crowded club. Wasn't anyone tired of hearing him yet? "Great show, man," a fan gushed, pumping his hand and grinning into his face.

"If you say so," he replied once they'd left.

His bandmates took full advantage of their A-list reputations, Ricky throwing a quick wave to the crowd before departing, a blonde clinging to his arm. Giles tossed back his and someone else's share of drinks from the open bar, occasionally rubbing his nose. Yeah, probably pretty damned numb by now. Vince held court at one end of the room, yet Henri, trained singing automaton, kept to the shadows. Maybe folks would forget him, letting him quietly sneak away. Margo, no, "Marguerite" trained eagle eyes on him. The rest of the band was free to do as they pleased, but the lead singer, the star in her eyes, had damned well better stay until she said otherwise, for once he left, the party would end, as would her evening's networking.

"Buy you a drink?"

Henri spun around. A handsome man offered a glass. "No, thanks." The pounding behind his eyes didn't need any alcohol-fueled assistance to split his brain in two, and his anxiety meds hadn't kicked in. The driving music and gyrating bodies surrounding him certainly didn't help. After parties sucked, big-time.

"Aww... c'mon. Have a drink with me."

A beguiling smile lured him in. Normally, he'd arrange a discreet meeting later in his hotel room, but something about the fan's creepy smile said, *Leave this one alone.* He had "I kiss and tell" written all over him. Henri didn't need another leaked sex tape. It had taken a lot of spin-doctoring and a look-alike claiming responsibility—for a price—to clean up the mess the last time he'd chosen the wrong bed partner.

He gave what he hoped passed for an apologetic smile. "No, really. I can't." Where was his manager when he needed her to chase off the undesirables who couldn't forward his career, or at least dispel the latest bout of gay rumors?

Tall, Dark, and Won't Leave replied, "I came all the way from New Jersey to see you. The least you can do is drink with me."

All the way from New Jersey? Where the hell were they now? Oh. Right. Anaheim. Or was Anaheim last night? They were still in California, weren't they?

Liquid swirled in a glass a few inches from Henri's nose. "It's your favorite," the guy crooned. "Jack and Ginger."

Oh, how Henri regretted letting slip such a factoid in an interview—about five years ago, when he actually *had* liked Jack and Ginger. Hell, to get rid of the moron, he'd pay any price at this point, then go back to his brooding. Floor-to-ceiling windows afforded a breathtaking view of the city—whatever its name was—his scowling manager reflected in the dark glass. Would everyone go the fuck away and leave him alone? If she wouldn't come run this asshole off, Henri would do it himself. "Fine!" He grabbed the glass and swallowed half the contents. Anything to get this fuckwad gone.

The guy's grin widened. "I'm your biggest fan."

I bet you say that to all the rockers.

"You have millions of fans, but no one understands you like I do."

Where had Henri heard that before? Oh yeah, Sacramento, LA, Portland, Seattle…. Name a town and someone there had spoken those same words.

His manager approached. Finally! "Henri, this is Lisa. Lisa, Henri." Marguerite pushed a buxom brunette his way. "Lisa here is your biggest fan."

Henri read between the lines: *You need to be seen with a woman if you ever hope to dispel those nasty rumors.* No way to dispel the truth, though.

The woman was pretty, but her maniacal grin didn't bode well for protecting Henri's privacy either. She could be the sister of the admirer he was currently attempting to fend off.

"Go away, bitch. I got here first," the would-be suitor snarled. Okay, no relation, or possibly a highly dysfunctional, competitive sibling rivalry.

The woman snapped an angry retort. Marguerite waded into the fray. Henri beat a hasty retreat. Damn but his head pounded double-time now. The world fuzzed around the edges of his vision, and whatever he'd eaten before the show threatened to reappear.

Bodies blocked his way, but he lowered his head and soldiered on. Puking in front of two hundred witnesses wouldn't win him any support from his manager. Hell, he couldn't fucking belch without making headlines.

"Sir, are you okay?"

Henri glanced up at a broad chest, the word "Security" stamped across a tightly stretched T-shirt. No use lying. "I don't feel too good." Nice, broad arms. The guy who'd broken his fall earlier. *I owe him a car or his own island or something.*

"Would you like me to escort you to your room?" Nothing sinister or even suggestive peeked out of the man's eyes. Just concern. Henri hadn't gotten concern from anyone in a long time. Too tired to come up with a smartassed retort, he merely nodded. Maybe he could fall again and earn himself another inadvertent cuddle.

The security guard tapped his earpiece, spoke a few garbled words, and wrapped a hand around Henri's biceps. "Not now, please," the man said to anyone who stepped into their path. He hustled Henri to the exit.

Henri's chest filled with lead. Why the fuck couldn't he breathe? Too many people. The air cleared a bit near the elevator. His knees buckled. What the fuck? "I'm not drunk, I swear." He grabbed at the wall and missed.

The guard steadied him. "I'm not judging, but maybe you'd better let me hold your drink."

What? Henri was still holding the damned thing?

Without realizing quite how he got there, Henri leaned back against elevator walls. The coolness felt good against his skin. "Room 1216." It was 1216, wasn't it? Or 1218?

"May I have your key, sir?" The guard released Henri's arm and held out his hand.

Shuffling, being pulled, the *snick* of the key in the door, followed by the sweet relief of his room. Hey! Room 1216! Got it in one.

Standing by the window of his penthouse suite, Henri stared out at the night. A string of red taillights marked a mass exodus from the arena down the block. His stomach rolled. Did anyone at the party downstairs miss him yet? Thank God his manager wasn't hovering over him like some overzealous fruit fly claiming dibs on a piece of rotted apple. Henri snorted. My, how well the description fit him. Something within had died long ago, leaving emptiness.

He took his glass from the guard, raised it in silent toast to his reflection, and tossed back a mouthful, a bitter brew to kill his pain. Haunted eyes blinked back at him. Tired, so tired. Concerts wiped his energy, and every song came from his heart, taking a piece of him that never regrew. A shriveled prune of a thing, his soul must be now. He needed his pills. The ones the doctor prescribed for emergencies. He hadn't already taken one yet, had he? His head pounded.

He fumbled his way to the stereo and pushed the play button. Trent Reznor moaned about hurt. "I know exactly what you mean, man."

"Would you like me to stay?" Arms folded across a well-formed chest. Bulging biceps. Blond buzz cut hair. Huh? Oh, yeah. Security guard. Asking to stay. But no invitation lurked in his eyes. Mild alarm, maybe.

"Would you? I mean, for a little while?" Henri staggered away, the need to sleep bearing down on him, an oppressive hand forcing him toward the turned-down bed. Slowly he peeled his T-shirt off, wincing at the stench of sweat. Maybe he should have taken a shower first. Too late now.

The guard's eyes widened, likely taking in the skinny torso and the ink decorating what many viewed as a rock god. Henri was merely himself. If only this man didn't know who he was and saw Henry, not Henri, the product of an imaginative manager. *Ah, I've grown maudlin in my old age.* Old at twenty-seven. Ancient.

An idea crawled to the surface of his muddled thoughts. "Sleep with me." Had Henri actually spoken those words out loud?

"Fraternization with clients goes against policy. Besides, I'm straight, and I have a girlfriend." No anger. Just business as usual. How many rock gods had propositioned the man?

Henri giggled. "So am I, if you ask my manager. No, I don't want sex." He didn't. Really. "Hold me."

"You want me to hold you?"

"I feel swimmy-headed. Need an anchor." Nice line. He

should use it again for something. Oh yeah. Maybe put it in a song.

"I could lose my job."

"No, you can't. I'm the boss, no matter what my manager says."

The crisp sheets felt cool against his heated flesh, and if his bedmate noticed his slightly sweat-ripe scent, he gave no clue. The fully clothed guard arranged himself beside Henri, the image of adorable confusion when Henri didn't attack. Henri had been fucked enough for the time being, and fucked over once too often. Tonight he'd lie in the arms of a stranger, Henri Lafontaine, a publicist's creation. Tomorrow, he'd take his fucking life back, gold record be damned.

He cuddled into the stranger's too-limp embrace. "Once I'm out, you can go."

"You really don't look too good. Is there someone I should call?"

Henri barked a humorless laugh. "No one gives a shit. Trust me."

The man grabbed Henri's wrist and raised his other arm to his face to better see his watch.

"What are you, a doctor?"

"I'm studying nursing. And your pulse is slow. Your breathing is shallow too. I think I should call somebody."

"No, really. I'm fine." Henri snuggled more firmly into his human pillow. Hell, physical contact was physical contact. He would take what he could get.

Something loosened in his chest, and he closed his eyes, imagining a lover's attention, someone who cared about Henry the man, and not Henri, the rich rock star. He conjured up his own bedtime story: they'd met at a party, fallen in love, shared a house, a life. They'd gone out to dinner, made love, and were now settling in for the night. In the morning they'd.... Well, there wouldn't be a morning for him and Nameless Guy, would there? Nameless Guy would be gone; Henri would wake alone, like he did every morning, even those mornings when he woke to find his bed filled to capacity with naked bodies.

A tear slipped beneath his eyelid, blazing a hot trail down his cheek. The aching inside flared anew, his heart bursting into a million crystalline shards.

The guard lay stiffly on the bed and wrapped an arm around Henri. Fingers stroked his forehead, brushing hair out of his face. Well, he'd be damned. One lucky woman had landed this guy.

But holy hell, was it hot in here or what? His stomach rolled. Oh shit. How much had he drunk again? He glanced around the room. Where the hell was he? On the third try he managed to hoist himself out of bed. Where was the bathroom?

"Sir, are you all right?" came from behind him.

Sir? Who the fuck had he brought home? Henri's stomach lurched again. Why wouldn't his damned legs hold him? "Oh fuck!" The floor rose up to meet him.

TWO

MARGUERITE HOVERED over the bed in Henri's hotel room, hands on her hips. "How could you do something so stupid? Think of someone other than yourself for a change! I had to call in a lot of favors to cover up your stupidity. We had to cancel shows because of you. Do you have any idea how much money we lost? How much promoters lost? How many tickets we had to refund? This little fiasco cost us—" *Whah, whah, whah, whah.*

Henri tuned out her droning. Any nosey paparazzi lounging in the hallway were getting an earful. "It's All About the Money" played in Henri's head, a song he'd written for his manager. She'd been flattered. She hadn't realized the unflattering double entendres hidden within the words.

He rolled his gaze up to the ceiling. Yeah, thank God for the small favor of Marguerite keeping his name out of the papers, though not for the reasons she believed. If word of his overdose got out, he wouldn't be considered legally competent to make certain arrangements without her knowledge, as he'd done in the scant few moments she'd allowed him alone since he'd woken up in the hospital a week ago.

"What the hell were you thinking? An overdose? Mixing drugs and alcohol? Being found drugged out in bed by a security guard? Do you have any idea what would happen to your career if a reporter found out?"

"What would happen to your career?" not *"what would happen to you?"* And *"stupidity"*? The nerve of her.

No need to point out that if the guard in question hadn't been aspiring for better things, i.e. a nursing degree, Henri wouldn't have a career to worry about. Of all the temporary employees in LA (were they in LA, or was this still Anaheim?) Henri had lucked out to OD in the presence of a trained first responder. And what better way for a creative type to come out of the closet to his fans than to end his life with a man in his room? What a way to go!

Only, the whole dying thing wasn't on the agenda.

"It was an accident. I'm telling you someone put something in my drink." He'd taken his meds. He hadn't drunk, except for the one Jack and Ginger foisted on him by the fan who wouldn't take no for an answer.

As usual, his manager had dressed herself based on TV's idea of cutting-edge chic—maybe twenty years ago. The model he'd dated last spring had pursed her surgically enhanced lips and sneered at Marguerite's lack of fashion savvy. And yet Marguerite had rallied to the woman's defense the moment Henri cut ties. *She's good for your career!* she'd said then. In the here and now, Marguerite huffed, "You can't do anything right without my help, can you?"

Apparently not went unsaid.

Another woman's much calmer voice cut in. "Margo."

"Don't call me that!" the woman who'd dubbed herself "Marguerite" hissed.

The most recent shrink in Henri's life persisted. "Given that he's recovering from a near-fatal mix of drugs and alcohol, yelling at him isn't in his best interest." The woman who'd been standing quietly by the door made her presence known.

Henri gazed with new eyes at the latest in a long string of head doctors. With her short gray haircut and trim, no-nonsense suit, she could teach Marguerite a thing or two about appearing professional. Had he found an ally? She'd seemed so impartial during their daily counseling sessions, though she'd originally raised Henri's hackles by being an old friend of Marguerite's. Perhaps she'd been listening after all.

But Marguerite wouldn't keep anyone around who didn't mindlessly echo her own shallow thoughts. How many hours had Henri spent perusing his contract, trying to find a loophole to end her hold over him? But no, if nothing else, his manager had locked on a cast-iron shackle, only to be terminated, like everything else, when she gave the word, and not a moment before. However, her temper ran hot. If he played his cards right....

He'd never realized until a few day ago how easy it'd be to block her access to his finances and other aspects of his life. Nearly dying gave a man a new perspective, apparently. Even now, the locks and security codes on his three homes were being changed, and he'd removed her name from any accounts. Phase I of the "Free Henri" project neared completion. Now for Phase II.

Not giving a damn anymore about what she might do lent him audacity, and a possible backer in the room added a boost of courage. "Sit down, *Margo*," he barked.

Midtap of spiked heeled pumps across the floor, Marguerite whirled, righteous indignation twisting her face into a mask of fury. Her blood-red lips formed an O of outrage. Henri beat her to the punch. "Sit the fuck down! I'm your client, dammit, and for once, you're gonna listen to me!"

The color drained from the woman's face, and her furious gaze darted around the room, seeking help. The doctor, appearing smugly satisfied, nodded at Henri. "You'd better do as he says, *Margo.*"

Henri hadn't met this doctor before his overdose, but once he managed to break free of his current manager, he'd keep the counselor—manager's old friend or not—because she obviously did her own thinking.

Margo sank onto the bedside chair, crimson talons gripping the padded rests. She had to wriggle in her skirt suit to sit. Years ago she'd watched soap operas to learn how to dress "rich," never realizing that her outdated styles didn't paint the successful business image she aimed for. Good thing she'd developed deafness to the snickers behind her back. Why did she insist on trying to be someone she wasn't?

The small spark of independence living inside Henri, fanned to life by really good drugs and desperation, crowed. "Since I have your attention, we need to talk. There's going to be some changes."

"Changes?" Margo snarled. "Before you get high and mighty on me, you'd better realize who's responsible for you even having a career."

Oh, hell no, she didn't go there. "You'd shoot the horse you rode in on? You may have gotten me where I am, but it's me who makes the money. Without me, you'd be waiting tables at IHOP."

"Why you ungrateful little—"

"No!" Henri held up a quelling hand, something he would never have done before he'd gotten a new lease on life. He'd taken his existence for granted before—never again.

Something about being held—and nearly losing the possibility of it ever happening again—had given him hope. He'd have love and respect for himself one day, for real this time, but to get there, he'd have to correct a few wrong things in his world. "It's my turn to talk." He sneaked a glance at the doctor, who winked, then slowly released a pent-up breath. Best not to push too far now. He'd already pressed further than he'd ever dared before.

Dressed in silken pajamas he'd never have picked out for himself, he extracted a sheath of papers from the end table drawer, delivered via courier while Margo had been out for a spa appointment. He donned a pair of glasses she'd forbidden him to wear in public, lest he tarnish his image, and proceeded to read aloud through a list. "Fifty-six thousand for a new car for my father. What's wrong with the one I bought him last year?"

"It was last year's. You want to keep your reputation up as being generous to your family, don't you?"

Henri clenched his teeth, biting back an angry retort asking why his father hadn't been to visit him since he'd woken up disoriented in a hospital emergency room. Instead, he growled, "And what about the $8,000 for my kid sister's boob job?"

"She *is* an aspiring model, and she…."

"She just turned seventeen. She doesn't need a damned boob job." Sweet little Jenni, hair in pigtails at age ten. He shuddered. "You're planning to push her like you did me, aren't you? You're gonna dress her in skimpy clothes and show her body in magazines to make a buck."

"She's a model, not a prostitute. And she won't have the surgery until after her birthday."

Only because Margo couldn't find someone to operate on a seventeen-year-old, most likely. Henri wanted to wipe the smirk off the woman's face. "Yeah, but does she want to be a model? Last I heard she wanted to study medicine and believed magazine ads exploited women. I don't mind paying for college. Or did you even consider what she, or I, wanted?" Bad enough he'd given up his late teen years to tour the country and support his family. They weren't poor anymore. Jenni deserved to be a teenager before being catapulted headfirst into adulthood.

"Henri, I...."

"It's Henry, dammit! I'm named after my great-great-uncle, and while you may now be ashamed of him, I'm not! Finding out he was a riverboat gambler and not a captain was the coolest thing ever." Oh how Margo had hung her head in shame the day a tabloid went digging and discovered the original *Henry* Lafontaine's true vocation of card shark instead of riverboat captain. He'd died by noose on the banks of the Mississippi for his sins. All her hard promoting of the namesake turned to dust in her hands. She'd changed Henry's name to "Henri" and herself to "Marguerite," promoting ties to prominent Cajun ancestors who'd probably turn them away if they showed up on the doorstep.

The truth of his Creole ancestry showed in Henri's wavy dark hair, nearly black eyes, and bronze skin. He'd spent his whole life being called black by promoters who wanted him to rap and white by promoters who couldn't accept a dark-skinned lead singer for an otherwise all-white band. Stuck in the middle somewhere.

However, in Henri's opinion, being named after the family prodigal only endeared him to his teen and twentysomething fan base. "As of today, if you want money from me, you have to ask. And I'm going to talk to Jenni. If she still wants med school, I'll pay for that, but I won't pay for you to force her into a life she doesn't want."

"Your father...," Margo began.

"My father can damned well pay for his own boob job, if he wants one! Not a cent, not one more cent, is going to a man who can't be bothered to talk to me once in a while. If he wants family privileges, he'd better damned well start acting like family." What was the use? Nobody cared. No one even saw Henri as a person anymore. He'd become a commodity, a moneymaker. Nothing more.

Voice honed to the low threatening purr designed to back Henri down, she who'd controlled his life for far too damned long declared, "You forget who you're talking to."

Henri trumped her hostility and raised the stakes. "No, I haven't... Mom!"

———

THERE'D BEEN a time when Henri had gone to school and then come home to nibble grilled cheese sandwiches while doing his homework. Mom had rushed home every afternoon to be there when the wheels of his skateboard sounded a scratch and a whir in the driveway, the scent of coffee and pancake syrup clinging to her clothing as she gave him a hug.

The woman standing in his hotel room bore little resemblance to the mother of his memories. And though he'd inherited her long nose and pointed chin, he bore little other resemblance to the tall bleach-blonde who'd become a stranger. He'd lost her, though she still lived, vastly distorted from the memory in his heart.

From the first time she'd cheered him on at a local talent competition to now, she'd changed with each new triumph. She'd been a working mother before, she and Henri's father struggling to make ends meet. A tailor-made suit hugged a figure enhanced by a personal trainer—a bit out of style, but tailor-made all the same. What Henri wouldn't give to return to a kinder, simpler time, when he'd had a family, albeit an imperfect one. Only a business deal remained, hardly a decent tradeoff.

"What did you tell the press about why you had to cancel concerts?" She wasn't exactly the best with public relations, as his stage name proved. What kind of mother lets her son perform with a band called "Hookers and Cocaine"?

"That you have the flu."

Now to test the limits of her resolve. "And if I need time to recover? Say, a month or more?" Tired, so tired. And being on the road with a bunch of backstabbers, constantly on guard, didn't allow much time to recover from his last few days in Hell.

Horror shone from eyes tinted by green contact lenses. "I'll say you're in rehab. Again."

"Why can't you tell the truth? I've had enough bullshit for one lifetime. I screwed up and nearly won a starring role in my own obituary. You can use it as a public service message." Besides, every time they lied someone always called them out anyway.

The bristling businesswoman softened somewhat, and a flash of something close to maternal affection crossed her face, gone in a heartbeat, dammit. "Because while you wallow in 'poor little me,' thinking only of yourself, I'm concerned with your career and the family, not to mention everyone counting on you for a livelihood. You've let us all down. Your fans can accept partying too hard—they expect it, even—better than your being a batshit crazy selfish little brat with no thought for anyone except himself."

Ouch! "Yes, they will, thanks to an asshole bassist who sold us out to a tabloid, calling us a bunch of drugged-out losers." And then Henri had to go and prove him right.

"He told you about his tabloid deal?" Margo snapped to attention.

"No. I found out anyway. He's not too good at being sneaky."

"And you didn't tell me?"

"What?" Henri faked stunned disbelief, adding a gasp for good measure. Maybe he should have been an actor instead of a singer. "You mean something's gone on with the band you didn't plan?" Served her right for firing anyone not pretty enough because she wanted more eye candy onstage. Eye candy usually came equipped with massive egos.

Henri's band once consisted of friends, until Margo interfered, preferring Henri to surround himself with newsworthy but shallow celebrity hanger-ons who reported his every move. Anyone close enough to influence Margo's own personal goldmine had to go. And now she planned to sink her claws into Jenni. Over Henri's dead body. Shit. If he'd died, what would have happened to his sister?

If he checked out now, the tragedy would spur headlines, lining Margo's pockets even more. He peered at the woman who'd birthed him. Did any love for him still linger in her heart, or had every ounce been driven out by greed? It'd happened gradually, his turning over his life; well, actually, it'd never been his. He'd passed into adulthood two years after gaining the public's notice on a televised competition. He hadn't won, but he'd earned enough fans to launch a career—his mother giving up her day job to act as manager. The day he'd waited in line for ten hours for a ten-second audition, Margo's hand on his shoulder had kept him from running. Back then she'd been merely supportive, if a bit aggressive. Now? Now she demanded.

He'd trade everything he owned for his family to be uncomplicated again. He glared at his mother. "Hug me."

"What?" She blanched, pulling back as far as the chair allowed. Professionally painted fingertips petted her crisp jacket.

"I told you to hug me." *Don't I mean more to you than wrinkles?*

Her wary gaze ricocheted between Henri and the doctor. The doctor tipped her head sharply toward Henri.

Henri waited. An aggrieved sigh wafted out of the woman that the little boy in Henri still wanted to idolize, and she awkwardly bent in to wrap a loose grip around his shoulders. Even begrudgingly given, Henri sought comfort from the gesture, until she warned, "Watch my hair."

He jerked back, smacking his head against the headboard. All warmth fled and he flung back the barb she'd used to hurt him. "You're my manager, something I can't change—right now. But you're not acting like my mother. You're too damned worried about the money and what people might think. Get out. I could've died, and you're more concerned with wealth and power and your fucking hair. I ask for a simple hug and you can't give it. Get the hell out.

"You can stay," Henri told the doctor.

Margo opened and closed her mouth several times, outrage bubbling to the surface of her faux-polished exterior. Exhaling a slow breath, she turned up the corners of her lips in a terrifying smirk. Shit was about to get real.

"Dr. Worthington?" she asked, voice syrupy sweet. "I believe my son may not be competent to make his own decisions. What's your professional opinion?"

The doctor, silent during the past exchange, stepped up on the opposite side of the bed. "With all due respect, ma'am, you brought me here to assess your s...."—the doctor spared a raised-brow inquiry to Henri before changing to—"client's mental state, which I have over the past week. He's competent."

Margo's grin grew positively feral. "But you could change your report, right? If he started displaying abnormal behavior again?"

"Ma'am, Henri suffers from anxiety and has a history of depression. With therapy and perhaps better adherence to medication schedules, we can get his condition under control. However, I won't fake a diagnosis for you or anyone else. You brought me here for my professional opinion and I gave it." Dr. Worthington reached into a briefcase hanging from her shoulder and extracted a tablet computer. "Besides, I've already written my report, ordered prescriptions, and scheduled appointments for this young man's therapy." The woman's hand on Henri's shoulder offered more comfort than the earlier fake hug.

Margo bolted from the chair. "Well, I suppose I'll find a new doctor."

Henri corrected her. "No, you won't."

"That's not up to you to decide!" Angry wasn't a good look for Margo.

"Mo… Margo, I'm twenty-seven. I'm filthy fucking rich, and I can damned well hire my own doctor." He slapped his hand over Dr. Worthington's. The doctor showed support with a quick squeeze, the most genuine affection to be tossed Henri's way since his sister's "Thank you for the car" squealing birthday hug. "Now, I need some time to talk with *my doctor*… alone. Would you please leave?"

Arms folded over her chest like a petulant child, Margo pouched out her lip. "Make me."

Rather than argue, Henri grinned. "Fine! If you won't leave, I will." He flung the covers back and launched himself out of the bed, coming close enough to touch, but stopping short. Storming from the suite, he turned deaf ears to her hurled insults.

Clop, clop, clop sounded in his wake, and he hurried to the elevator and punched the down button. "Please, please hurry!" he whispered to the car. Margo got there first. Henri headed for the stairs instead, clutching the handrail to keep from tumbling. His pursuer couldn't follow in her heels. Dr. Worthington, in her sensible suit and shoes, might be able to, but as long as she was on Henri's side, let her deal with Margo.

Henri beat his momager to the ground floor by a matter of seconds. The doctor dogged her heels, pleadings falling on deaf ears.

A crowd of onlookers notwithstanding, Margo caught him and jabbed a pointed nail at Henri's silk-covered chest. "You will not do this! You will not disrespect me." Spittle showered his face.

"Watch me." Henri spun on bare feet and marched across the cold marble lobby floor toward the front entrance of the hotel. He hung onto the revolving door a moment after exiting, reveling in the purple face and hateful words of someone who he would no longer let hurt him.

A few feet away a uniformed officer peered at him from over the top of mirrored shades, pausing midmotion in writing a ticket to an illegally parked Rolls-Royce. Margo's Rolls-Royce. How ironic that her car cost more than Henri's, when he'd made the money to buy the damned thing. One month's payment on the pearl-white status symbol would have bought two of the aging Chevy his mom had once shuffled him to practice in.

The officer took a step toward the commotion, and Henri let loose his hold on the door. Margo stumbled and nearly fell. Her piled-high curls lost the battle with gravity, strands sticking up at odd angles.

Henri tipped an imaginary hat at the officer and trudged off down the street in pajamas, his fluffy hair hanging down his back in a tangled mess.

Margo trotted behind, her words sweet music to his ears. "If you do one more stupid thing—"

Really? He stopped. "You'll what?"

"Then… then… you can figure your own way out of this bullshit. I've had it up to here with your irresponsible behavior."

He eyed the doctor and then the cop. "Did you hear her?" His heart thudded a mile a minute. "Did she just threaten to drop me?" Escape couldn't be this easy.

"Sounded like it to me," the doctor replied, followed by the conveniently placed officer's quiet, "Yes."

Henri faced Margo, tamping down the part of him longing to bend to her will, do anything, say anything, for her approval. She glared.

Although famed for his creative song lyrics, when asked to produce bad behavior out of thin air, nothing immediate came to mind. Several bystanders stood on the sidelines, snapping pictures with cellphones. *May each benefit properly from their cold-hearted nosiness into someone else's meltdown.*

He had to do something, anything, outrageous. Beyond rehab stints, trashed hotel rooms, or drunken brawls in seedy clubs. What to do? What to do? Escape lay at his fingertips if he could push his mother a fraction of an inch further. What the hell could he do to piss her off?

Gaze falling on the cop, Henri muttered, "Sorry, man. But it's for a good cause." He brought both hands up to hold the officer's head and slammed his lips down, initiating a game of tonsil hockey with a surprised opposing team.

THREE

Nurse Attitude made a hasty retreat. Amazing how quickly she fled from so simple a gesture. Henri had only licked his arm twice before she bounded out of the room to report to the higher-ups. Ah, and that's what he paid for every time he checked himself into rehab—quality entertainment.

A five-foot-nothing human dynamo bounded through the door before he'd even gotten his tongue back in his mouth. Ms. Perky, also known as Tessa Eklund, meditation therapist, merely smiled and quipped, "Let me guess. Tastes like chicken, right?", thus taking all the fun out of his crazy act. "How are you feeling today, Henri?" She deposited a large bronze bowl and an even larger purse on his coffee table, and removed three nested bowls from the larger one. Funny how someone who couldn't be still for even a moment intended to teach him how to calm the fuck down.

He wouldn't pass up an opportunity to rattle her seemingly unflappable cage. "Why don't you be the judge? Come on over and check for feathers. Or better yet, have a taste of chicken." He held out his arm.

Henri sat sprawled across an armchair by the window in the luxury quarters of his favorite Los Angeles rehab facility, where he'd been hiding from the world since his "kiss the cop" incident. So far he'd managed to shirk all responsibilities for a full three weeks. He owned houses he'd spent less time in.

"I'm afraid I'll have to pass—I'm vegan." The woman giggled and sauntered over to pat his head, pushing his arm out of the way. She stooped to pick up a drink cup from the floor. "Hmmm, you're feeling like a temperamental rock god, right?"

"How'd you guess?"

"You always feel like a temperamental rock god." She balled up the cup and slam-dunked it into the trash can. "She shoots, she scores!"

He'd been waiting for a visit from this woman all afternoon. Therapist Tessa was the closest thing he had to a true friend. How pathetic was that? "I'd kill for a joint."

"And I'd be killed for giving you one." She flitted around the room, plumping the pillows on his bed, hanging up a jacket he'd deliberately left on the floor.

Yanking her chain about his drug use had become a ritual for them. "Pul-eeze. Have a heart." Henri gave her puppy dog eyes. "Everybody knows you health care types have the best shit."

"Only because we confiscate it from our temperamental rock god clients." She shoved his tennis shoes into the closet. Twice daily housekeeping cleaned his room, and yet his meditation coach recleaned every day. Of course, he made sure to leave plenty of debris lying around. Lord knew what Perky Girl would do with her nervous energy if not put to good use. Spontaneously combust, maybe? That'd be messy.

Henri deserved an Academy Award for his put-upon sigh. He added a pout for effect. "That's a no, isn't it?"

"Yes, it is." Tessa straightened the blinds he'd left at an angle.

"But... but.... I'm in here to relax and create music. I can't relax and create music without a big fat joint."

"Sure you can. What you need is meditation, not medication. You don't need drugs." Her scowl would have been scary if she'd managed to be a little taller. Five foot with her skinny frame gave her the appearance of a pixie. A pixie who, at the moment, was rearranging the magazines on his coffee table —alphabetically.

"Prove it!" Ha, had her there.

"That's why I'm here. Meditating on your own puts you to sleep, yoga inspires inappropriate comments, and you don't play well with others, which leaves out group therapy. I'm your last hope before you're shuffled into arts and crafts as the de-stress portion of your stay. Trust me, you don't want arts and crafts." She plopped down onto the floor by the coffee table. "Now, I want you to clear your mind."

A little digging in a handbag nearly bigger than Tessa produced a fat wooden peg, tipped with rubber. She closed her eyes and took a deep breath before letting it out in a controlled exhale. The cleansing. Eyes still closed, she tapped the peg against the side of the first bowl. The sweetest, purest note emerged, sending cold chills along Henri's arms. At one time she'd have insisted on him joining her on the floor. She'd learned to pick her battles and not waste a precious moment of their half hour together. Henri remained in the chair, but he listened as she wound the mallet around the top of the bowl, creating a soothing hum.

"Inhale deeply, now breathe out. Let go of the pressures, let go of the pain. Push them out of your body. Slow, steady breaths. Feel the tension drain, all of your stresses, all of your cares."

The first bowl still sang, and she added notes from the second and fourth; the smaller the bowl, the higher the pitch. When notes from the others faded, she tapped the third, the first, and the second and fourth again, then slowly wound the mallet around the edges of each bowl.

The created harmony soothed his nerves as much as her friendly presence. Henri's failures taunted him before reality kicked in. Reflection was the last thing he needed, the first being a band, a stage, and an audience. He'd lost his band—everyone but him belonged to Margo. Not that the other members of Hookers and Cocaine were his friends, but he'd earned one hell of a lot of money with them, not to mention fame. For a moment he struggled to breathe. What the hell had he done?

He might have won his independence from his mother, but he'd paid a heavy price. He'd barely managed to maintain status quo while with his old band; now his recent mad dash for freedom meant starting over. Starting over took energy. The mere thought had Henri ready to curl up for a nap. And then mad panic set in again. Pills. He needed pills. Or a joint. Booze would do in a pinch—the reason he was in rehab and not at home, where five minutes and a few bills could get him whatever he wanted. At the very least, somebody hand him some chocolate!

Fuck it all. "This isn't the kind of music I need. Got any rock and roll or heavy metal hiding in that bowl?" Words always formed in his head while she played, but sappy, sunshine-and-roses stuff, not anything Henri Lafontaine could put his name on. He needed pounding rhythms, a primal scream, some way to release the darkness within. "The Darkness Within." That'd make one hell of a song title.

"These are delicate instruments, meant for calming, soothing, and meditation. They're not gongs." Tessa lifted her chin into the air.

A gong. Hmmm.... What if he introduced a gong to the new tune he'd been working on? Sure, Queen had ended

"Bohemian Rhapsody" with a gong, but how many of his current fans knew of the seventies hit? And those who did might enjoy the touch of nostalgia and homage to a group who'd influenced a young Henri. Still, a gong. Different. Different was good. "What else do you play? Piccolo? Flute?" He pictured Tessa with fairy wings, sitting in a tree while serenading birds.

Narrowed eyes and pursed lips announced an acceptance of his challenge, a very different image from "Fairy Tessa." "Name a song, any song, and I'll play it, using just what I find in this room."

She was supposed to get adorably flustered, not accept. Still, a slim chance beat none. "You're on. If you can't, I get a joint." Might as well make the most of the situation.

"And if I win?" *Shwoosh* went an empty tissue box into the trash. *Please don't let her ask why I go through so many tissues.* Isolation meant no warm bedmates and pending calluses on Henri's palms. Sooner or later she'd find the empty lotion bottle under the bed—and likely order a replacement.

"Front-row concert tickets, if and when I ever have a band again."

"I will, you will, and you're on." Tessa lifted her pointy little chin another fraction of an inch. Stubborn woman. Henri liked her. A lot.

She scrounged through the room again, gathering up a variety of items: two glasses, which she filled to different levels of water in the sink, an empty soda can, a book, the tissue box, and "Aha! You owe me, mister!" She turned around, sheer triumph on her face. She held aloft a Chinese takeout box and set of chopsticks. Damn. Busted. "Someone's been sneaking contraband in."

"How much do you want to keep quiet?" Henri reached for his billfold. A guy couldn't survive on the healthy meals provided by the center, and so far no one had figured out that "Cousin Joe" who faithfully visited every day worked for a delivery service.

Tessa skewered him with blasts of pure fury from her frosty green eyes. Oh hell. With Henri's luck she'd live up the reputation of fiery redheads. "You swear to me it's only food, no drugs, and we're good."

Henri held two fingers aloft, in a symbol for "scout's honor" that he hadn't used in fifteen years. "The nurses have a full list of everything I take. It's on my chart."

"Good." She washed the chopsticks off in the sink. "Now, what song do you want?"

"I don't care, you pick." She'd never manage a decent rhythm with her assorted pile of junk.

"How about Sheila E.'s 'The Glamorous Life'?"

"Works for me." An oldie but a goodie.

Her malevolent grin put the evil day nurse to shame. Tessa took a deep breath and closed her eyes, chopsticks in hand. *Tap, tap, rap, rap, bibbity bop, bop, bop.*

Henri managed to slough off some of his lethargic stupor. Damn. In a good way. "How'd you learn to play?"

"Sheila E. was my idol growing up. A kickass woman who played drums? Awesome. I practiced on my desk at school with pencils, kept getting into trouble." Her rhythm didn't falter throughout the conversation. "Finally my dad gave in and sent me to lessons." All grin and bright green eyes, it was easy to imagine her as a hyperactive kid. "I started in junior high band as a percussionist, went through high school and on to college."

Hell, Henri pitied the woman's teachers. Keeping her still must have been like trying to rope a cyclone. Unless they'd been the ones to discover the mighty power of setting a bronze bowl in front of her—the only thing he'd ever seen hold her attention for longer than five minutes.

Bip, bip, bip, bop. "At State I met a group of exchange students who introduced me to new instruments. They suggested Tibetan bowls for their calming effects."

Heh. No need to wonder why.

She nodded toward the coffee table. "I've got a cool setup in my garage. Come by for a private concert sometime." *Thwack, thwack, boppity bop.*

Here she was, a therapist, chatting with a so-called rock god about music. Her face nearly glowed. She wasn't trying to sell him anything. She wasn't asking him to make her famous. All she wanted was to share her passion—and maybe teach him to meditate.

Once upon a time Henri had felt the same way about his songs, before every single note became a commercial endeavor, words written to impress fans and earn money. What he wouldn't give to have a bit of the old fire back. "Do you still play drums? Have you ever played in a band?"

"Only in college. Now I'm teaching my nephew, and occasionally entertain at parties with my bowls. I put away my rock star dreams a long time ago." She gave a halfhearted smile. "My dad advised me to find a safer career option. Or demanded, rather."

Dad had a point. "Yeah. Look at me. You might have turned into a drugged-out, rock has-been."

She darted her tongue out, giving her the momentary appearance of a bratty twelve-year-old. "And wouldn't that have been awful? They'd put me in the next room and we'd be neighbors."

Somehow, except for the drugged-out part, Henri could imagine a lot less pleasant things than being Tessa's neighbor. He'd simply send her to the rec room to play the pool table with cue sticks when she grew annoying.

Henri hadn't told her he was gay from long habit of keeping

things hidden that might affect ticket sales, and she didn't ask. She also didn't flirt or throw herself at him. She wanted nothing personal from him but conversation, his mental well-being, and a chance to clean up his room. And she didn't scurry off, duty done, the moment she'd scribbled on his clipboard at the end of their sessions. She cared. What a rare gift. Nobody in LA cared anymore. They must have imported her from Iowa or somewhere.

She stopped dead still—for about three heartbeats. "Oh, crap! I'm gonna be late for my next appointment!" In a flurry of motion she disassembled her makeshift drums and shot out the door, enormous purse slamming against the bowls in her hands with every step.

Damn, but Henri needed to sleep now. She'd never have given him a joint, even if he'd won the bet, but she probably hadn't doubted her abilities for a moment. Henri'd been her level of cocky once.

He added "Hear Tessa play drums" to his to-do list. Next time he'd bet for chocolate.

"MR. LAFONTAINE? I'm Detective Shepard of the Los Angeles Police Department. I'd like to ask you a few questions." A suit and tie couldn't disguise one of LA's finest. He screamed cop from the moment Henri entered the private sitting room designated for talking with guests. Couldn't have the general public romping around in patients' rooms. Not that Henri lived in a cell by any means. His suite rivaled a five-star hotel. It should, for what he paid.

"I didn't do it." Hee. The title to one of his songs, actually, about a man pleading innocent and being guilty as sin.

LA wiseasses being a dime a dozen, the cop didn't comment on the lame attempt at humor. Maybe he wasn't familiar with the song. "Your toxicology report shows your blood-alcohol level was well below the legal driving limit, and there was evidence of venlafaxine hydrochloride, in keeping with the prescription you provided. It checks out. However, we also found GHB in your system, as well as in the glass you left by the bed."

"I was drugged?" He knew it! A chill ran up his spine.

"Unless you like playing Russian roulette by mixing alcohol with sedatives, yes. Bad enough you drank with your prescription."

Drugged. "Fuck. Oops, sorry, Officer."

"Detective."

"Sorry, Detective."

"Under the circumstances, I believe 'fuck' is appropriate." The guy never cracked a smile, but his stiff manner softened. "Tell me, do you recall anyone near your drink at any time?"

"The guy who gave it to me. He tried to talk me up, but was too friendly, like, creepy-stalker friendly. I figured he was safe enough—he couldn't have gotten past security without an invitation." At least, not to Henri's knowledge. Of course, a pretty face and a smile went a long way in winning favors.

"Can you describe him?"

"Not really. About my height and weight, dark hair, which describes about half the guys there. Oh, I believe he said he'd come from New Jersey."

"We found concealed cameras in your hotel room, and rope and duct tape in the closet. Housekeeping insists they weren't there the last time you were in your room, as they cleaned shortly after you left for your concert. Feel free to say 'fuck' again. It appears you were set up. Do you have any idea who'd do such a thing?"

Holy shit! Really? *Really?* Straining his brain didn't help to bring a face into focus. Some of Henri's band members might have a grudge, but why shoot the cash cow? "I have no idea.

Could have been anybody. I'm in a pretty cutthroat business." Shit. Another problem and another reason to watch his back. "Not to mention how damned obsessed with viral videos people are these days." Fuck, fuck, fuck, fuck, fuck. No telling what the guy intended.

"You're safe enough here, but I'd recommend additional security before you go back out in the world."

Yeah. Made sense. "Can I ask you a question?"

"Sure."

"I can't get papers in here and they censor my magazines"— Henri added air quotes—"*for my own good.* What happened to the cop I kissed?" Not one of his finer moments, for sure.

A slight upturn of lips might have been all the smile the detective could manage. "He caught hell at the precinct, took a few days off, and has been getting requests from your fans to sign their 'I kissed Henri Lafontaine' T-shirts."

Henri slapped his hand over his face. "I'm sorry."

"Don't be. To be honest, it gave us something to talk about besides homicides, domestic violence, and budget cuts."

"Go easy on the guy, will ya? I feel bad enough already." Henri peeked out from between his splayed fingers.

The detective winked. "At the station, if we're not picking on you, it's because we don't like you. Officer Reyes is none the worse for the wear, I can assure you."

"Oh crap. He has a name!" Henri slapped both hands over his face. "Next, you're gonna tell me he has a wife and two kids."

"No, he's single. But I'm told his fourteen-year-old sister is jealous. He won major cool-brother points for meeting her idol."

Henri dropped his hands in time to witness Shepard's eyes crinkling at the corners. "Tell him I'm sorry."

Any humor left the man's face. "Mr. Lafontaine, you're the victim of assault. It may not have gone as far as the perpetrator intended, but you were violated. We don't blame victims for acting out of character. Stress does funny things to people. Now, if you recall anything else helpful, please give us a call. We've spoken to a few people at the party and questioned the hotel staff, but no one had anything else to add."

"Did you talk to my manager?" Margo had spoken to the guy. Would her fear of gay rumors keep her from cooperating?

"Yes. She gave the same description you did."

"Did you tell her why you wanted to know?"

"Until we know otherwise, everyone in the club could be a suspect. She simply knows we wanted to question anyone you'd come into contact with that night."

"What about video? There were cameras everywhere."

"A security camera showed someone entering your room while you were out, but a hooded sweatshirt hid their face. The party guest list didn't turn up anything suspicious. And it seems the video at the party had been turned off to preserve your privacy."

What the hell? Oh. So no one could see who he left with. That had to be Margo's idea. Fuck. "What should I do now?" Bad enough his band hated him. At least he knew where those guys lived. But a total stranger? He could be anywhere.

"Now we continue our investigation. In the meantime, be careful what you say to the press."

"Can I tell them what happened?"

"Yes, but leave out details and descriptions until we have the suspect in custody."

Margo. She'd stood toe to toe with a crazed fan, had talked to him, even. If she believed him to be an intended hookup, though, she might not have been forthcoming. And no video? Really? Without consulting him? Sometime soon, if Henri ever talked to her again, they'd have a long heart-to-heart about priorities.

Now, he didn't have a family, he didn't have a band, and he

did have someone out to get him. And recreational drugs were no longer an option—unless he wanted to burn out young and join the 27 Club. Great, just great. Walking a tightrope without a net. Hey, that might be a good song title, if he lived to write the words.

FOUR

MANAGER PROSPECT number one wasn't winning any points. "First, we'll tell your fans the stress got to you and you snapped. Not only will you be admitting your failures, you'll win sympathy points."

"I was drugged." Henri tore his gaze away from the window and the fat robin sitting on a branch outside. He'd been in rehab long enough. Soon it would be time to join the bird out in the world again. Did he have to?

"Do you really want your fans to know the truth? I mean, they haven't found the culprit yet. Now, I can set up negotiations to get you back into Hookers and Cocaine, with me as your manager, of course."

Margo wouldn't go for such an arrangement, and neither would Henri. "I don't want to go back. I want to move on." He wasn't sure of much these days, but making all the same mistakes over again wasn't an option.

"You'd give up your place as front man for a successful group to go solo?" The dollar signs flashing in the man's eyes were getting pretty annoying.

"They're called Hookers and Cocaine. How much worse can it get?"

The man cocked a brow, adding a smug little smile. "A lot worse. Trust me."

Trusting the bastard would never happen. "Fuck you and get out."

———

"DENY EVERYTHING." Manager prospect number two looked the part of a smarmy spin doctor—down to his shark smile and snake oil salesman vibe.

"People will think I'm guilty. Can't I hold a press conference and tell my side of the story?" God, what Henri wouldn't give for a joint or a drink. Perhaps both.

"I can assure you that honesty isn't in your best interest here. I also suggest you patch things up with your band and move on."

"Why is everyone hung up on me getting back with a bunch of two-faced losers? Fuck you and fuck them. Without me they'd be nothing, and not a one of them has so much as called me. No, they couldn't wait to spill their damned guts to the press. I'm done with them." Assholes. They'd said every-thing in the gossip rags from "We always knew it was only a matter of time 'til he OD'd" to "I tried to get him to stop. He wouldn't listen." Bastard! Giles had no room to talk about drug use.

At least no one had outed Henri—yet. But then again, Margo would have their balls if they did. He might not be her client anymore, but she wouldn't allow anyone to hurt royalties. As a manager, she had her uses, however misguided.

"Henri, I don't believe you fully realize what's at stake."

"My band, my livelihood, my family, my fans, and my pride?"

"Well, I think—"

"I think you need to go back to my mother and say, 'No deal.'"

––––––––––

Dr. Worthington sat next to Henri, legs crossed and arms hanging loosely over the sides of her chair. A restful pose. She always appeared unrushed, and never once consulted her watch during their visits. "Have you considered what you'd like to do next, when you leave here?"

Henri sprawled on the floor on his back, hands tucked behind his head. Hey, he got three square meals a day, nobody bothered him, and his room beat most hotels he'd stayed in. Why leave rehab? "I haven't figured that out yet. I'm having a hard time finding a manager who'll let me do anything but perpetuate the insanity of doing the same old thing. I want to make a clean break. There's no one in my band I called friend or remotely trusted."

The doctor nodded. "Whatever happened the night of your concert was only the final straw. From what you've told me, the pressure had been building for some time. Sooner or later, you were headed for a breakdown. And you should have disclosed your suicidal ideation to your past doctor."

"But I didn't try to kill myself."

Henri's shout didn't penetrate Dr. Worthington's unnerving calm—something Henri both loved and hated about the woman. Sometimes a guy needed a good fight, and the doctor wasn't inclined to deliver. "I know that, you know that, but you did entertain suicidal thoughts, a possible side effect of your medication. I've changed your prescription, but at the first sign of trouble, I want to know. And you have to take your medicines as prescribed. I can't help you if you won't let me. Under no circumstances are you to use recreational drugs or alcohol. If you run into problems, I've prescribed a limited number of lorazepam, to be used only in emergencies."

Henri forced a smile. "Gee, take the fun out of my life why don't you? I'm still allowed hookers, right?"

Without so much as a flinch, she replied, "Only if you practice safe sex."

"Jeez, lady! I'm kidding! I'm part of Hookers and Cocaine. Or was. I have a reputation to uphold."

"Henri, no one's trying to control you or keep you from having fun. We're trying to show you how to enjoy life in a non-self-destructive way. You've got a lot on you at the moment. You don't need added burdens."

Damn. Why'd she have to talk sense? It was much easier to ignore the shrinks who quoted text-book psychobabble. "What should I do?"

"Get away for a while. Clear your head. Decide what it is you want from life. Not your mother, not your band, but what you, Henri Lafontaine, want to do."

Henri stared at the ceiling. "I wish it were that easy."

"Nothing worthwhile is ever easy, Henri."

"If I paid you more, would you start telling me what I want to hear instead of talking sense?" Henri shot her a glare, meant to be intimidating.

"As you say on your *Shark Infested Waters* album: 'No Way in Hell.'"

———

HENRI LOGGED into his e-mail. Only five thousand today. He

checked the folder marked "Shit I'll Actually Read." Hot damn! He clicked open the e-mail from his sister.

Henri,

I'm sending this from Vivian's house, 'cause Mom's told me not to talk to you. She said you're into drugs and that you're a bad influence. That's not true, is it? Henri, how could you?

Jenni

Damn. Margo had gotten to her. And there wasn't much use in denials. He had been into drugs, but why had his mother waited until now to share the info with Jenni? Oh yeah. With Henri gone, the manager in her needed someone else to control.

How he'd love to move Jenni out of the family nest, or at least spend some time with her, find out if she really wanted the future Margo planned. But no. Here he sat in rehab, his future a hazy blur. How could he save Jenni if he couldn't even save himself?

Henri had no idea how a mugger got in, or where he'd found the dull rusty knife, but it sure hurt like hell to get his heart carved out. Oh wait. Who needed a thug with a knife? He had the world's most dysfunctional family—and he was the star of the show.

Time to take back his life. If only he knew how.

He picked up the center-approved magazine he'd been reading and opened to an article about a former star who'd made a comeback, thanks to his incredible "miracle-working" manager. Henri could sure use a miracle or two. He circled the name "Lucas Honeycutt."

———

"You have a visitor." Henri glanced up from his crossword puzzle, interrupting his quest for a six-letter word meaning "deranged." "A Six-Letter Word for Deranged" might be a good song title. If only he'd gotten his stalker's name, and if it contained six letters. The day nurse smiled sweetly at him. Her business casual attire, designed to hide her true vocation, suited her well. Any who met her outside of work probably wouldn't guess the light sweater and dress pants cleverly disguised the key holder to the loony bin. Right, *rehab*, not crazy house. "Safe haven" more summed it up.

Here he'd been quite enjoying his isolation. No screaming fans, no screaming managers, no one with a hand out, no one making demands, and best of all, no one trying to drug him up and film him doing whatever scary-party-creep had planned. At least the detective hadn't mentioned having found a goat in the closet, or chicken blood. Brr....

For a time, Henri had even begun thinking of himself as Henry again, shucking off the industry-created Henri persona for one slightly more comfortable and infinitely less high maintenance. He rubbed his knuckles against a scruffy chin. Was it Tuesday yet? He only shaved on Tuesdays.

"You checked them against the list, didn't you?" His admittance paperwork contained a long listing of people he'd rather not deal with. Margo's name topped the list, followed by any family members except for Jenni. Margo added too much stress to his life. Dr. Worthington had recommended he take this time out of his busy schedule to de-stress, relax, and consider the life he truly wanted.

Somewhat of an underachiever on all matters personal, Henri focused on the relaxing and de-stressing instructions, avoiding plans for the future. Margo had slipped a letter in, admonishing him for "neglecting his duties," but Henri wasn't Margo's problem anymore, and every time the woman crossed his mind he found himself performing the good doctor's grounding techniques to slow his pounding heart and hyperventilation. He'd sent a reply, using her own words to terminate their contract. Damn, but he wanted his mother back. Not "Marguerite," not "Margo," but "Mom."

"They're not on the list, Mr. Lafontaine."

"Who is it? Did they give a name?"

"Lucas Honeycutt."

Lucas Honeycutt? Henri rolled through a mental index, finding no memory matches for the name. "Doesn't ring a bell."

"He says you asked for him."

Oh.... *Lucas.* Holy shit! His one final hope at salvaging his career. "Send him in."

———

HENRI STUDIED the man in the chair across from him, who appeared quite different from other managers of his experience. And handsome, in a rode-hard-and-put-up-wet kind of way. His bio put his age at fifty-seven. His craggy face and thinning, reddish-brown hair told a story of high mileage. His blue jeans and button-down shirt said he hadn't come to intimidate. Point in his favor. A spark of intelligence shone from brown eyes that met Henri's gaze head-on.

"Why did you call me? There are plenty of more prestigious managers out there who'd love to represent you. Why me?" The man's dark-eyed regard dared Henri to lie.

Henri could try flattery and stroke the man's ego, or tell the truth and risk losing his last hope. No way would he admit *because you take on hopeless cases and give them fresh starts.* "Because you're the only manager I've talked to who didn't advise me to lie, cheat, or steal my way back into my old band."

"They were choking the life out of you and turning your

talent to rubbish. Why would I tell you to go back?" Lucas leaned forward in his chair, staring eye to eye with Henri. "Those other managers are fools."

Really? "Mr. Honeycutt? We're gonna get along fine."

"I'll warn you upfront: I won't tell you what to do. I think you've had enough of other people's manipulation. I will, however, make recommendations. And I absolutely insist that you meet me halfway. If you're not willing to work hard, I'm not wasting my time on you." Lucas sat back in his chair, one foot crossed over his knee and iPad in hand. "First off, you're leaving the band, but what about the songs? You wrote most of the lyrics, didn't you?"

"Yeah, but they're listed as collaborations. My m... manager kept up with the copyrights."

Calm and cool, the man who might become Henri's new manager didn't miss a beat. "Then write more. Some of those are old, and I'm sure you learned a bit along the way." He winked and added, "Songs can be copyrighted. Titles can't. Also, I want you to take a good, hard look at yourself. For the last few years you've been coasting. You've lost some of your sparkle, and your own band didn't seem a good fit for you anymore. Now's your chance to decide who you are, what kind of music you want to perform, and make it happen. Our spin will be you're leaving the band voluntarily to pursue a new direction."

Reinvent himself? And had Henri lost some of his drive? Well, coming to a concert stoned or hungover might count as showing a bit of disinterest, though he'd given up hard drugs two years ago in favor of pot and booze. The heavy stuff sapped his creativity. "What do you want me to do?"

"First thing, you're going to take time off, write new material while I lay the groundwork for your return." Lucas punched away on his iPad for a minute.

"Do you really believe this will work?" Could Henri drop the fake and finally be himself?

"I wouldn't waste my time if I didn't."

So cool, so confident. And yet so down to earth. Different from Margo in a million ways. Trusting anyone at this point might be beyond Henri's abilities. He snorted. Look where trusting family had gotten him. "I'm taking time off here."

Lucas wrinkled his nose. "No offense, but this environment isn't conducive to the creative process."

True. But the public knew where Henri's houses were, and his usual haunts. "Where can I go?"

"I'll work out the details and get back to you."

"Let me see the contract."

Lucas reached into his briefcase and extracted a sheaf of papers. Old-fashioned, despite the iPad. Nice.

Extremely straightforward, nothing out of the ordinary. "I'd like my lawyer to look this over."

"But of course."

In the end Henry signed on the dotted line, one step closer to getting his life back.

———

"You had a visitor, but he wasn't on the list and wouldn't tell us his name so we turned him away," Nurse Cranky announced.

"He?" Dare Henri hope his dad had come by? "What did he look like?"

"How should I know? Fred was on shift."

"Can I talk to Fred?"

"In about two weeks, when he gets back from Cancun."

Fuck. Henri wouldn't be here in two weeks.

"Oh, I do remember one thing. He told Fred he's your biggest fan."

Oh shit, oh shit, oh shit. He'd been found. Henri held his breath to keep panic at bay.

The moment the woman left the room, he dialed Detective Shepherd. Then he called Lucas. "Get me the fuck out of here."

———

LUCAS RETURNED three days later. "I have just the place. I know someone I'd like you to spend time with, though his style of music is vastly different from yours. If you don't mind my saying, vocally, you need a bit of discipline. You've never taken the first voice lesson, have you?"

Voice lessons? Really? A bit late for vocal training. "I've got a gold album. What do I need with voice lessons?"

"The man who thinks he knows everything is a fool." Lucas displayed no smirk, no smugness, merely a matter-of-factness Henri couldn't deny. Damn the man for being right. "And wouldn't you like to add a platinum album to your collection one day? If you want to up the rewards you have to up the stakes and, to be totally honest, your current version of 'A Matter of When' won't get you there."

Finally, someone said what Henri always believed, instead of "You'll get it next time." "I hang out with this guy, he teaches me a few things, I write some songs, and then what?" Maybe the guy smoked good shit. And shared.

"You'll need backup, a name, a little exposure. We'll go into the studio, leak a few tracks to incite interest, and you start touring again."

"You make it sound easy." The doctor's words came back to Henri: *Nothing worthwhile is easy.*

"It's my job to make it easy." Reared-back shoulders and a determined gleam in his eyes said Lucas meant business.

Okay, Henri could play along. It wasn't like he was doing

anything else useful at the moment. "Who is this guy I'm supposed to learn from?" Was it too much to ask for a gorgeous Greek god of a man? A horny one? Damn, but Henri needed to get laid, but the mere idea of inviting someone into his bed who'd sell him out five minutes later deflated his libido.

"Sebastian Unger, an opera tenor, and the son of a good friend of mine, so be on your best behavior."

Opera? Well, Henri could make a deal. Let this Sebastian guy keep whatever he'd been offered, as long as he left Henri alone and gave Lucas good reports. Bonus for drugs provided. No way in hell would the creative juices flow without a bribe for the muses, despite what Dr. Worthington said.

"Where does he live?"

"Evergreen, Colorado."

Colorado? Woot! Legal pot! "When can I leave?"

———

"Now, I know you're leaving and aren't my client anymore, but if you ever need me..." Tessa pulled out a business card and scribbled on the back.

Oh. So now she'd show her true colors, with a wink and a "Call me." Henri should have known.

Instead, she said, "That's my personal e-mail. If you're stressed, feel yourself slipping, either call or e-mail." Her crystal green eyes bored into his. "If not my help, though, please ask someone. A family member, a friend. You've come too far to go back now." She hugged him as tears glittered in her eyes. "Take care of yourself."

So this was what it felt like to have someone truly care. Strange, but nice. Henri kept the card.

47

FIVE

WELL, HELL. Lucas had promised Henri would get away from it all, but did the sprawling log and stone two-story even have running water or air-conditioning? Old house for old owner? Maybe this wasn't such a good idea after all. Who wanted to spend the next month in a technological sinkhole with a grandfatherly curmudgeon who devoted every waking moment to reliving old glory days? *When I was your age I was a star!* Born in 1951 was all Henri had learned of his tutor.

Henri parked his Harley in front of the house and unhooked the trailer. If he had to travel out into the wilds, at least he went in style. Besides, from the looks of things, there were plenty of places around here to ride whenever he needed to escape the phantom of the opera hiding within the creepy old house. Helmet in one hand, duffel in the other, laptop bag slung over his shoulder, Henri clomped up to the door. He set the bag down to ring the doorbell.

With the house set back from the road down a long drive, at least he'd see his stalker coming if the guy drove up. And although trees bordered the property on three sides, open fields provided a buffer. With any luck, though, Detective Shepard would soon have the maniac behind bars. Henri slipped one of Dr. Worthington's "emergency pills" out of his pocket and swallowed it dry. Damn, but he had the headache from hell.

He admired the view while waiting, the gorgeous green of the Colorado Rockies, and sucked in air totally devoid of car exhaust, even if breathing did take a bit more effort up here. Quiet. No passing cars, no human sounds. A bird chirped in a nearby tree, and gladiolas of every color thrived in well-tended beds. The garden needed roses.

The door opened. Henri peered inside, but a broad chest blocked his view. "Can I help you?"

Smooth as silk and rich as chocolate, the man's voice washed over Henri. Wow. Henri glanced up, and up some more. The guy had to be every bit of six three, with russet corkscrew ringlets giving him an angelic air. Linebacker shoulders topped a body that appeared naturally stocky, and while not gorgeous in an airbrushed magazine-cover kind of way, Henri certainly wouldn't kick him out of bed. He reminded Henri of someone else. Hmm....

"I'm here to see Sebastian Unger. I'm staying for a while." Henri had gotten the correct house, right? Though he wouldn't mind spending a month in the glass and chrome creation down the street, a real party place from the looks of things. This rustic home stuck out among the neighbors' newer, architectural marvels. They spoke of wealth; this house whispered of days gone by.

Chestnut-colored eyes took Henri in. Large men normally didn't appeal to Henri. "Skinny at all costs" types inhabited his circles—and his bed, on the occasions when he managed to sneak one past the ever watchful eyes of his band and manager. This guy topped him by a good few inches and exuded sexy in an unfamiliar way. Comfort. He appeared comfortable in his own skin, unlike Henri, who at the moment had no clue who he actually was. With his soothing tenor, maybe Mr. Sexy Voice was a student too. This could prove interesting.

The man extended his hand. "You must be Henri."

Henri removed a leather glove and locked palms. Firm grip. Nice. Especially depending on which body part benefitted from the grip. He might not be groupie material, but Mr. Smooth-As-Silk-Voice might do to warm up a bed at night. What happened in Colorado had better the hell not follow Henri back to California.

"I'm Sebastian Unger, but please, call me Seb. Sebastian's too formal." The foreign expression on Sebastian's face took Henri a moment to work out. An openness, and genuine lack of guile. Creases formed on Sebastian's cheeks, extending all the way up to his twinkling eyes. What do you know? A sincere person. In the music business.

But wait. This wasn't the guy from online. "Aren't you supposed to be old?"

Sebastian barked out a laugh. Damn, what a voice. It might not be a good fit for a rock band, but Henri would pay the guy to read to him—or talk dirty. "Fuck me harder" would work. "I'm twenty-five. I take it you looked up Sebastian Unger on the Internet and got my father. I'm 'Unger the Younger,' as they say."

Heat rushed Henri's face. Hell, he hadn't blushed in years, having lost the ability after about the fiftieth time someone threw underwear onstage and offered him free use of the orifice of his choice. "Is your father here, or are you the one I'm supposed to meet with?" Oh, please, please, please, let it be this guy. If he spoke dirty, Henri might get off on his voice alone. Hell, if he read his grocery list, Henri would likely sprout wood.

"As my father died before I was born, I'm afraid you're stuck with me." Sebastian stepped aside and opened the door wider. "Please, come in."

First chance he got, Henri would send off scathing words to the online site he'd gotten his misinformation from.

He followed his host into the house that time forgot. From his vantage point in the foyer Henri spotted what appeared to be a sitting room, completely furnished in antiques, unless he missed his guess. Margo had gone through an antique phase about the time Henri had earned his first big record deal. A spiral staircase led upward, and Henri dogged Sebastian's heels up bare, wooden planks, worn from hundreds of footsteps. Wow! What an ass! Nice, solid handfuls. And the man's sturdy build meant he wouldn't break from a good pounding.

The silence seemed awkward, and ogling his host's posterior probably wasn't good manners. In LA among his old crowd, maybe, where an ass like Sebastian's probably cost about seventeen thou in surgery. Homegrown ass. Who'd have thought? "How do you know Lucas?" Henri asked. Though he hadn't learned much about his manager yet, he'd didn't peg the man as the type to hang out at opera houses. Dive bars, maybe.

"He's an old friend of my mother's. We lost touch over the years and reconnected after she died."

He'd lost his father and his mother. Poor guy. Then again, if Sebastian's parents were anything like Henri's....

"Here's where you'll be staying." Seb opened a door and led the way into a spacious room. White curtains covered the windows, and through the lace Henri spotted mountains dotted with tall trees. What a view. "Put your things here and I'll show you the rest of the house." Sebastian eyed Henri's bag. "Is that all you brought?"

"I've got more out in the trailer, but I'll go get them later." Henri stripped off his leather jacket, chaps, and other glove, and placed them on a chair, keeping his back turned to his host—

offering a prime view of his ass, were the man interested in looking.

The room, like the rest of the house he'd seen thus far, was furnished in a style of days gone by. A double four-poster bed provided the focal point, with a dresser, mirror, and a chest in a matching pattern of carved wheat.

Over the bed hung a canvas of a sunlit meadow in full bloom with wildflowers. Simple, elegant, and homey. "My grandmother's work." Sebastian stepped up beside Henri. "She was a gifted artist, but only painted for pleasure. She never sold her paintings."

Okay, something was expected of Henri, possibly compliments, most assuredly agreement. "It's… nice."

Sebastian gave him a cocked-brow perusal that seemed to find him lacking. Oh yeah. Opera guy. Cultured. His grandmother had probably taken him to art galleries and museum openings. Henri's grandma had taken him to tractor pulls and dirt track races. God rest her soul.

The rest of the house maintained the same bygone feel. Thank God the kitchen had been updated and the bathroom sported indoor plumbing. They neared the last room on the first level. "Here's the music room. Feel free to spend all the time you like here." With dramatic flair, Sebastian pushed back a pocket door and ducked his head to enter the room.

Well, damn. A polished wooden floor gleamed in the sunlight streaming in from windows every bit as tall as the door. A bay window overlooked the grounds, and the end of the room was an obvious modern extension, with three glassed-in sides. In the middle of the extension sat a grand piano. An old-fashioned velvet settee sat opposite, matching chair in front, with cables, recording equipment and a stereo to make the average rock fan cry filling the remaining space. Twelve-foot ceilings would make for some hellacious acoustics.

"Do you play?" Sebastian swept a hand toward the piano.

"A little. Not concert-worthy or anything, but enough to work on my music." Truth be told, Henri created melodies in his head, pecked out a basic draft on the piano, then relied on others to bring his visions to life. Try as he might, he'd never mastered any instruments.

"We'll work out a schedule to suit us both. Through the week I'm often gone. You'll have plenty of privacy."

Gone? "You're supposed to be here, helping me." Why did having an audience suddenly matter?

"I am. But on Mondays I have acting lessons. On Wednesdays, dance. My languages classes are online, to be taken anytime."

"Acting? Dance? You're a singer, not an actor or dancer."

Sebastian must have possessed the air capacity of a blimp, for he sighed deeper than Henri had ever heard. "Let me guess. You know absolutely nothing about opera."

"Not true." Hmm.... What had Henri read? Oh yeah, he kept getting distracted. "I know you sing."

"In four different languages. And act. And dance. One doesn't merely sing *The Barber of Seville,* one *is* the Barber of Seville. "

Margo had forced Henri to take dance lessons once. They didn't take. He had no sense of body rhythm at all—the reason he'd turned down a stint on a reality show where he'd be paired with a professional dancer. His career wouldn't have survived the embarrassment. Wild, drugged-out binges ending in rehab? Fans expected those. Tripping over his own feet while trying out a routine he couldn't even pronounce? Career suicide.

A man of Sebastian's size might need a lot of lessons.

"Why languages?" Hell, some days, Henri barely managed English, though Margo insisted he learn enough French to perpetuate the image of a Cajun heritage and charm reporters.

"Have you ever sung in Italian?" Again a brow arched over one of Seb's eyes. Henri used to try for raised-eyebrow glares, but never mastered moving his brows independently.

"No." Henri had plenty of Italian fans, but had never felt the need to connect with them on a more personal level. Besides, then he'd have to do the same for his Spanish, German, etcetera fans. His grandmother had spoken Cajun French, but he'd never learned enough to qualify as fluent, just a few well-practiced phrases. Until she'd tried to capitalize on his ancestry, his mother hadn't encouraged embracing the familial roots. She and Grandma Lafontaine hadn't seen eye to eye.

"It's not enough to babble sounds. You have to understand the words to bring them to life." Sebastian's chest swelled, and he released a melody Henri couldn't understand. The words sounded damned good, though, and even without grasping the full meaning, the sorrow behind them clearly shone. Sebastian finished, offering a challenge with his eyes.

Holy fuck, the guy owned one hell of a set of pipes. Not that Henri would tell him and feed another singer's overgrown ego. "I suppose I can amuse myself while you're gone." It wasn't like he could fire up a joint anyway until he found out the guy's views on recreational drugs. And Henri's being here to learn "discipline" didn't bode well for Sebastian joining in.

"Good. Get settled, make yourself at home. Feel free to clean up before dinner."

Was that a hint?

The hell with Sebastian Unger and his arrogant opinions. How could anyone expect Henri to be squeaky clean after riding a thousand miles? Of course, his stop in Vegas didn't help. At least the one-nighter he'd picked up didn't seem to realize he'd slept with the real Henri Lafontaine and not an impersonator. Hell, Henri had encountered three look-alikes himself while on his hunt for a willing body. Sex with someone who looked like him? Too disturbing, even for him.

He settled for picking at his helmet-hair and headed downstairs, following a soft tenor melody into the kitchen. He sniffed but didn't smell cooking. His stomach rumbled anyway.

"Do you eat seafood? Lucas didn't say."

Because Lucas didn't know, having only recently entered Henri's life. "I'm starving. I'll take anything." Maybe he should have given Lucas a list of food favorites to have on hand. He had no intention of giving up pizza, burgers, and fries while hiding from the world. And who knew what kind of delivery service he might find.

"Have a seat." Sebastian pointed with a knife to a rustic wooden table that might have been handmade. "I'm making tuna salad."

Henri plopped down in one of six mismatched chairs. Tuna salad. He hadn't eaten a tuna salad sandwich since high school. "Wait! What?" Henri stared down at the plate and glass of tea Sebastian set before him. "This isn't a tuna salad sandwich."

"Of course it is." Sebastian took a seat opposite of Henri. Real wood paneling gave the room a homey feel, unlike the marble and granite of Henri's primary home—pretty, but uninviting. "Anything worth doing is worth doing with style." Sebastian sounded like Dr. Worthington, with her "Nothing worthwhile is easy."

Instead of the usual loaf bread his mother had used, the creation on Henri's plate involved a sesame-seeded Kaiser roll. Bits of green that weren't iceberg lettuce peeked from between the bread. He lifted the top of the bun to find the brownish bits he expected, mixed with tomato, onion, and chopped celery. "You don't half do anything, do you?" At least the creation wasn't meticulously prepared for maximum nutrition and minimum flavor, like the stuff at the rehab facility.

"Some people live, others live well, even in the simple things." Sebastian bowed his head and folded his hands before biting into his sandwich. Uh-oh. Henri didn't have much experience with believers beyond the ones who wrote him to inform him he was headed for Hell. Non-news. If Hell existed for sinners, he'd already paid for his ticket, though to be honest, Heaven and Hell hadn't recently crossed his mind. "Heaven and Hell," now there was a good song title.

Take me to Heaven,
Send me to Hell,
Something, something, something, something.

He'd work on the lyrics later. His sandwich waited. He took a bite and chewed. Wow! Damned good for a simple meal.

Sebastian polished off his sandwich and made another. "More?" he asked.

"No thanks. I'm good." Henri's late night caught up to him and he yawned. "I think I'll turn in early, if that's all right with you."

"Sure. I'll clean up down here and see you in the morning. By the way, I provide meals, but don't expect maid service. I'm a singer, not a servant."

Hell, the guy had to be hard up to take a total stranger into his home. For all he knew, Henri was an ax murderer. He gave no sign of recognition. Surely Lucas had told the man who'd be sharing his roof. While Henri hadn't counted on five-star treatment here, he had at least expected his host to be impressed. He was Henri Fucking Lafontaine for fuck's sake!

It was going to be a long month.

"Loo, loo, loo, loo, loo, loo, loo, loo."

The loo-loos traveled from high to low and back up the scale. Henri lay awake, staring at the ceiling. *Make it stop!* Every note pounded through his skull.

"Loo, loo, loo, loo, loo, loo, loo, loo."

Sebastian had a great voice, but did he have to have a great voice at... Henri checked his phone... 7:00 a.m.? A pillow over his head didn't help much. If he'd known he'd entered the lair of an early riser he wouldn't have stayed up until two. He flipped the covers back, nearly knocking his MacBook to the floor. For three full hours he'd stared at the screen, typing a few words and later deleting them. "Heaven and Hell" lived up to its name, promising one and then giving the other.

At one point in time, words and ideas flowed from his brain to his fingers. Now, the injustice of abandoning his brainchildren to somebody else pissed him off so badly he couldn't write. Still, Lucas had made a good point. Best to start anew. New band, new music, new attitude. Only, please, could he do it at a later hour?

He pulled on yesterday's jeans while mulling over the matter of a new band name. He struggled into his T-shirt. Henri Lafontaine was the largest part of Hookers and Cocaine. Any publicity he gained in the future would inadvertently boost them as well. Oh hell no. No freebies. They'd made their last dime off of old Henri.

He followed the loo-loos down the stairs. Going back to the name Henry was out of the question. Who'd buy a rock album from Henry? He stopped in his tracks at the kitchen door. Sebastian danced around the sun-lit space, loo-looing away while periodically checking pans on the stove. The scent of coffee teased Henri's nose. Coffee. Beans of the gods. His stomach growled from whatever burbled in a pot. Sebastian glanced up, smiling when he noticed Henri. "I hope I didn't wake you. I'm one of those annoying morning people. This is my favorite time of day."

Oh. One of those. They should come with warning labels. Well, it was only for a month. Hopefully by then Lucas would have worked his magic and redirected Henri's career. Henri decided on honesty. "Actually you did." Sebastian's smile fell. It returned with Henri's, "But if some of what's cooking is for me, you're forgiven." Might as well be nice—at least until after breakfast.

"Breakfast is the most important meal of the day. Now, what would you like to drink? I have coffee, tea, and orange juice."

"Coffee works."

"Help yourself." Seb nodded toward a nearly full pot. A cup tree like Henri's grandma used to have held a trio of cups. Another sat near Sebastian's elbow by the stove. "Oh, and since you're not used to the altitude, you might get a headache." He handed Henri a bottle of ibuprofen and returned to his cooking and loo-looing.

Henri swallowed two pills and washed them down with orange juice. "What are you doing?"

Seb brandished a spatula. "What does it look like I'm doing?"

"I meant the singing."

Both auburn-colored eyebrows rose toward Sebastian's rather high hairline. "Don't you do vocal exercises to keep your voice in shape?"

"Vocal exercises?" He was kidding, right?

"Didn't you learn drills from your teacher?"

"Teacher?"

Confusion flashed across Sebastian's face and settled into disbelief. "You're a world-famous singer and you've never had lessons?"

Henri shrugged. "No. I just sing. It's a gift."

Sebastian slapped his free palm over his face. "This is going to be a long month."

"Got milk?" Henri stared into the refrigerator—one of the few new-looking items in the home.

"Milk? You drink milk?" Seb drew back as though from a rather nasty bug.

"What's wrong with milk?"

"Nothing, if you want to clog your throat with phlegm. There's *almond* milk on the second shelf."

It was going to be a long month.

———

Tessa,
   I'm stressed, help!
   Henri

Henri,
   Follow this link, and remember—meditation, not medication!
   Tessa

Henri clicked on the provided link and rolled his eyes when he landed at "The Eternal Fairy Queen's Mystical Bower." Heh. Had she read his mind, or did others see her the same way Henri did? He clicked again on an embedded video. There sat Tessa, behind her bowls. "For my friend, Henri," the Tessa onscreen said. He closed his eyes and whooshed out a breath to Tessa's murmured, "Let go of the stress…."

He might survive after all. Even if it was going to be a very long month.

SIX

"WHERE ARE we going?" Henri stared out the window of the tiny Volkswagen Beetle, the car seeming much smaller for being filled with Sebastian's broad shoulders.

"You'll see." Sebastian hummed to himself with the radio off. If he wasn't speaking, he sang; if not speaking or singing, he hummed. Chances were, he sang in his sleep. Oh, that'd be interesting.

The trees, the mountains. How tranquil... until they merged onto I-70. Both hands gripping the steering wheel, Sebastian stared with single-minded determination through the windshield. His gentle humming took on an urgent quality. Was that the soundtrack to the big battle scene from *Apocalypse Now*? "I'd hold on if I were you," he advised. He hit the gas, neatly inserting the car between two eighteen-wheelers.

They were so close to the rig in front of them that Henri could count the scratches on the bumper. A quick glance in the side mirror showed the truck behind them close enough to reach out and touch.

A sign appeared on the right: "Runaway truck ramp 2000 feet." Runaway truck? Oh shit!

Seb veered again, hauling them out of the right lane and into the middle one. Henri glanced at the space they'd just left. Too fucking small. A quick turn had him grabbing the "oh shit" handle to keep from crashing into Seb.

He glanced at the speedometer. Eighty? Normally, on the bike, Henri loved speed, but.... "Could you fucking slow down?"

"Slow down out here at your own risk." With a lot of glancing back and forth between his mirrors, Sebastian maneuvered them into the left lane with mostly passenger vehicles and a few trucks.

May this particular bug not wind up on anyone's windshield.

Down and down they traveled, Seb's knuckles turning white. And then....

"Oh dear God!" An eighteen-wheeler appeared over a rise in Henri's side mirror, heading straight for them.

Sebastian stopped humming. "Is something wrong?"

Henri peered through his fingers while a bright red, two-ton missile rumbled by with what seemed inches to spare. The Beetle swayed in the passing breeze. He let out a sigh of relief.

And then another truck appeared.

"I'd recommend you close your eyes and trust me." Did Sebastian have to sound so smug?

After three more of what appeared to be near misses, Henri took the man's advice. The humming turned to chuckling. Asshole. Henri clutched his seat belt with both hands. Please, please, let them not get plowed by a Peterbilt.

The road hadn't been this winding and steep when he'd driven up on his Harley, had it? The Hollywood Hills didn't even come close to this asphalt nightmare.

He opened his eyes when they slowed and exited the road from Hell. Hallelujah! A stoplight!

"Are you all right?" Sebastian asked, darting a quick glance to Henri before the light changed to green.

"Sure, fine," Henri lied. "What makes you think anything's wrong?"

Sebastian entered a mall parking lot. Was he out of his mind? They couldn't go in there. He'd be recognized. Seb drove around the mall and parked in front of a movie theater.

The car stopped! Finally! Would kissing the ground be overly dramatic? Henri peeled his fingers off the seat belt. "Isn't it a bit early for a movie?"

"Movies don't start until one. They allow me to use an empty theater to practice."

Henri followed Sebastian in through a side door, trying to hide the tremor in his legs. How often had Sebastian driven the hellish road? And how much money would it take to keep him from doing it again with Henri in the car?

"Hey, Seb," a smiling woman said. "You can have seven." She pulled the door closed behind them.

Sebastian hummed his way down the hall and underneath a banner for an action-adventure film. Cool! Henri had been waiting for the show's release. Must have happened while he'd been in rehab. Maybe they should stay and watch. A raised platform stood in front of the floor-to-ceiling screen. The room must serve double duty as an auditorium.

"You stand here." Seb pointed to a spot dead center of the stage. "I want you to sing something that shows me both your upper and lower limit so we can work on your range. Breathing might be a bit harder than you're used to because of the elevation, but not as bad as at the house."

Yeah, his range. The weakness preventing Henri from performing some of the songs that sounded better in his brain than coming out of his mouth. He climbed up on stage. "Hey! Where's the microphone?"

"What microphone?"

"I'm gonna sing, aren't I?"

"In a room this size, you need a microphone?" Sebastian crossed his arms across his chest.

It was a pretty large room. "Never mind."

Seb stalked off toward the back. What the hell? How was he supposed to hear back there? He took a seat on the last row, dead center. "You may begin."

Henri started in on "A Matter of When."

Sebastian popped out of his seat. Had his ass even touched the plastic? "Wait! Stop! You can't simply start singing. You'll strain your voice. Warm up first."

"Warm up?"

"Loo, loo, loo, loo, loo…," Seb began.

I feel like a fucking idiot. Henri joined in on the third set of loo-loos.

Apparently satisfied after fifteen rounds of varying pitches, Seb relented. "Try now."

Henri started out low and built toward the chorus of a song he no longer planned to perform in public.

Seb moved forward. Twice. "Good for lower scale. Now let me hear upper."

"Umm… that was it."

Seb didn't comment, but his cheek sank in on one side like he was chewing the inside of his mouth. He marched down front, pointed Henri toward the back, and took his place on stage. Even from a distance Henri saw the man's chest swell as he seemingly sucked every bit of the air from the room. He threw back his head.

Deep, resonant, filling the entire space but never once overpowering, Seb's voice drew prickles up Henri's neck. He sang in another language. Italian, maybe. The melody took him from low notes to high, and never once did Seb waver.

Henri's jeans grew tight, cold chills not the only thing rising. The song took a sad turn. Though the words weren't in English, there was no mistaking the sheer pain, the crushing darkness of the notes. Henri wiped moisture from his eyes. Crying? Over a song he couldn't even understand?

Seb reached the song's climax and held the final note an impossibly long time. Impressive. And also unnecessary for a rock singer. A gold album on the wall said so.

But, damn, the expression on Seb's face, full of longing. When he sang, Seb turned into a sensuous creature, one who whispered sexy promises into Henri's ear and then surpassed every one. Women must throw themselves at the guy after every performance.

If only Henri could capture some of the man's magic for himself.

———

"WHAT ARE you doing?" Seb folded his arms across his chest, reminding Henri of the time one of his teachers had caught him smoking behind the gym.

"It's just a cigarette." This time.

"There is no such thing as just a cigarette." Sebastian snatched Henri's Marlboro and dropped it to the ground, then stomped on the cherry until the glow died. "Your breath control is atrocious, you're probably already suffering from a lack of oxygen at altitude, and you inhale smoke to help that along."

"Hey!"

"For the next month you're under my care. You can kill your-self on your own time. Now, pick that up. I'm not your servant." Sebastian whirled and stalked off.

What right did he have to dictate Henri's actions? Henri was a paying customer, and wasn't the customer always right? He headed back inside for another cigarette. The stench of burning leaves from around the front of the house stopped him. Crap! He'd parked his bike out front.

He dashed into the front yard to find Seb gleefully tossing leaves on a fire, close enough for smoke to engulf his Harley. He charged. "What the hell are you doing to my bike?" He wrestled Sebastian to the ground, their fall broken by leaves.

"It's just a bit of smoke." Seb pinned Henri beneath him.

"Do you have any idea what smoke'll do to the finish?" Henri squirmed but Seb didn't budge.

Instead, he stared down, locking glowers with Henri. "You worry about a machine, but not your voice. If I set the thing on fire, you could get a new one tomorrow." He trapped both of Henri's hands above his head, securing them with one large paw. He lightly wrapped the other paw around Henri's neck. "But if this goes, it's gone for good." Seb rolled away.

By the time Henri regained his feet, Seb was busy spraying the fire with a water hose. He rubbed his throat where Seb had touched him. "Point taken."

———

SEB AND Henri sat on the settee, listening to a playback of Henri singing. "What is that?" Seb point a damning finger at the stereo.

"I dunno. A Bose?"

Seb didn't need knives in the kitchen. His cutting glare could chop through steel. "There! Right there!" He jabbed a remote button and played the chorus again.

"Me breathing?"

"Yes! Breathing! In the middle of a line! Can't you wait until the end?"

"Well, no."

"Stand up."

Henri rose. Oh hell, what was the guy gonna set on fire this time? Seb slapped his hand against Henri's middle. "This is your diaphragm." He raised his fingers to Henri's throat. "This is your voice box. Air must come from here—" He patted Henri's stomach again. "—travel up here—" He traced his fingers up Henri's sternum. "—and come out here. Now, take a deep breath."

Henri complied.

"No, no, no. Again! Watch how only the top of your chest rises. You're not breathing deeply enough. Pull the air in all the way down here." Again he touched Henri's middle.

Henri reared his shoulders back and inhaled, trying to visualize taking the air into his belly. How stupid. Besides, Seb was bigger. Much bigger. Henri gasped, imagining Seb pinning him to a bed, taking control, wrapping his fingers around Henri's wrists....

"Good, good. Now sing the line again."

"What?" Oh fuck. The line. Henri sang, but ran out of air before reaching the end of the sentence. How could he possibly manage breath control when visions of a naked Sebastian left him breathless? If he left right now he could be in Vegas tonight, scratch a few Seb-inspired itches, and be back tomorrow.

"You need to learn to let your air out at a controlled rate." Seb launched into a note Henri might reach with a stepladder. He held it, and held it. Never once did he fade before ending the note on a crisp cutoff. "I have an assignment for you. Practice until you can sing inhaling only after every second line. When I come back, I expect you to be able to hold your notes."

Henri had had enough. "I've got gold albums." Or one, at any rate. "I've been nominated for a Grammy."

Seb released Henri like he burned. "You're lucky none of

your fans appreciate good music. Any opera lover in the house would cover their ears every time you inhaled." Seb exaggerated an inhale, sucking in air like a drowning man. "Got a date with a bullet." He whooshed out the breath, then sucked in another equally noisily. "Got a date with a gun." *Whoosh.*

"I do *not* sound like that!" *Do I?* Henri squared off against Seb, hands braced on his hips.

"Yes, you do!" Seb huffed out another 'roaring bull' breath. "And you have a lovely singing voice."

A compliment? From Seb?

Seb gave back any points he'd won by adding, "Too bad you insist on screeching."

"I don't screech." Technically, Henri preferred the term *wailing*.

"Yes, you do."

"Lucky me. My fans don't care." And the band stayed too stoned to notice.

"Very lucky. You rock stars are all the same." Sebastian shook his head, sending his curls bouncing. "You sing, you flop around the stage like a dead fish." He flapped his arms like a seagull taking flight. "And how much money do you make? Houses, cars, jets. The world is your plaything, and you treat your gift, the one thing enabling you to live your lavish lifestyle, as less important than your stupid motorcycle." Sebastian clomped around the room, hands in the air. "Meanwhile, I practice six hours a day, study dance, acting, and languages, to make no more than the average high school teacher." His nostrils flared, and a crazed look appeared in his eyes. "And most of that goes toward lessons to improve my performance!"

Henri didn't know how much teachers made, but it couldn't be much. "But you own this nice house, lots of prime real estate. If you need money, why don't you sell…?"

Sebastian's face shaded to scarlet. "Sell my home? Sell my

home, he says, he who has three or four and doesn't worry for a roof over his head. Here I am, trying to help you be a better vocalist, and Mr. I've-got-gold-records-who-the-fuck-needs-you tells me to sell my home." Sebastian stalked over to Henri, leaning down to put them nose to nose. "I'm doing this for Lucas, not for you. I made a promise to a friend and I intend to keep my word. Now, I'm leaving. You have two choices. Do as I say and practice your breathing, or pack your things and go back to LA, to bellow like a wounded animal until someone more willing to listen to reason topples you from the charts."

Wow. Talk about righteous indignation. And Sebastian had gotten all that out without a noticeable breath. It really could be done. "Where are you going?"

"It's Monday. I have a class." Sebastian slammed the music room door so hard the windows shook.

The nerve of the guy. How dare he scold Henri like a spoiled child? Did he have any idea who Henri was? Fans waited hours in the rain for a glimpse of him. Women ripped off their shirts for him to sign their breasts, for Christ's sake. And a little nobody opera tenor spoke down to a rock legend. Well, Henri hoped to be a legend one day, if he survived long enough in the music industry. Therein lay Henri's problem. He'd gotten his first recording contract at seventeen. At twenty-seven, he'd enjoyed a successful career, but he'd never won a Grammy or an American Music Award.

Some bands lasted seemingly forever, keeping their existing fans and gaining new ones, but Hookers and Cocaine wasn't the Stones or Aerosmith. Before "the incident" their record sales had begun to dwindle. If Henri was to succeed, he'd have to try harder, be smarter, and write songs that touched hearts—or keep himself in the headlines through bad behavior, an exhausting proposition. Without the music he'd be nothing. Unacceptable.

Every day a barrage of younger, hungrier lead singers

appeared on the scene. If he didn't constantly struggle to survive, he'd be left behind. And therein lay the key: he'd stay hungry, and surround himself with equally hungry musicians who'd go the extra mile.

He ran upstairs and logged into his computer to call up a video from this year's Grammy-winning band. Damn but the guy could sing, and even in his wildest dreams, Henri's vocal range couldn't compare. Though he strained to hear, never once did the guy pull in a breath midsentence. Maybe Sebastian had a point. "Loo, loo, loo, loo, loo, loo, loo, loo." Down the stairs Henri sang. If he looked and sounded ridiculous—so be it. After warming up, he attempted his song again, focusing on his breathing.

It took four hours, but by the time Seb returned, Henri managed two lines without pausing. Not well, but he'd improved.

The worry in Seb's eyes faded to relief. "Good. Now try another song." Had he really thought Henri might leave? And was he more concerned with the money he'd forfeit, letting a friend down, or the possibility of Henri leaving angry?

"Can I stop now?"

"I said 'good,' not 'perfect.' Is 'good' good enough for you?" Sebastian arched a brow. Showoff.

What the fuck! "Hey! You've got home field advantage. I'm fighting altitude here!"

"Excuses, excuses."

"Well...." Gold records. Younger singers.

Sebastian glared, arms folded over his chest. "Will 'good' win you a Grammy?"

"Well...."

"I've got a date with a bullet...." Sebastian gave an audible gasp. "See, you even write your songs to allow for pitiful breath control."

"Hey—" The caring in a pair of soulful brown eyes cut off what Henri might have said next.

Sebastian dropped his voice to a beguiling croon. "Why limit yourself? Being a better singer costs you nothing but your lessons, which you've already paid for." Before Henri could reply, Sebastian added, "Keep practicing while I fix dinner."

Limit himself? Sebastian believed Henri limited himself? The nerve. Lucas's words came back to him: *write more*. Whatever Henri wrote had to beat any Hookers and Cocaine song. Damn but he needed some greasy fast food, a joint, and a beer. And not necessarily in that order.

"Dinner's ready," Sebastian called a short while later.

The spicy aroma from the kitchen didn't bode well for burgers and fries.

"Grilled chicken breast with baba ghanoush, pita chips, and green salad."

So much for Henri's fast-food craving. "You're going to feed me healthy every day I'm here, aren't you?"

"If I filled your motorcycle's tank with trash, would it run?"

"No."

"Then why do you expect more from your body? Optimum performance calls for optimum fuel."

A pretty ironic statement from a guy who appeared blessed by genetics and didn't need gym visits to stayed toned. Then again, all the dance lessons probably helped. Seb wasn't bulky or ripped, but… perfect. Without even trying! Damn him.

———

A SLAVE driver, that's what Seb was, with his "you will sing this" and "you will do that." Henri would kill for a smoke. Or a bowl of ice cream. Or milk. Hell, he'd settle for one measly Hersey's Kiss.

He ticked off another day on the calendar. Four down, twenty-six to go. Thank God June was a short month. What he wouldn't give for a night out on the town. Seb wasn't too shabby in the kitchen, if you liked healthy food, but Henri thrived on grease and fat, burning off the extra calories onstage.

The man in question poked his head through the music room door. "I'm going for a walk. Care to join me?"

"Where are you going?"

"Just for a walk. I must exercise to stay in shape on days when I'm not dancing."

Bored with practicing the same song over and over, Henri donned tennis shoes and followed Seb out the door. The late spring sunshine beat down, but this high up in the mountains the day held a bit of cool. Pine and sunshine. Not a hint of smog. Henri could get used to this.

Seb hummed and loo-looed to the edge of the tree line Henri had noticed from his bedroom window. Surely he wouldn't have to put up with *that* during their walk. "Do you constantly warm up?"

"Yes, I do."

"Why?"

"My tour group's season ended in May and starts again in September. I begin rehearsals in late July. However, the Central City Opera here in Colorado has a lively summer season, and they've called me to fill in for sick performers. And I guarantee you, every member of my company is practicing as much as I do. You wouldn't want me to fall behind, would you?" He exaggerated a pout, with lips a shade too full for the rest of his face. Kissable lips, or lips made to wrap around a cock. The anonymous fuck in Vegas had happened too long ago. Henri needed some action.

But "fall behind"? Damn, opera singers were more competitive than rockers. "You take your singing seriously."

"Why wouldn't I? It's my life, my livelihood. All I've ever wanted to do." Seb picked his way around a boulder, following a meandering path up a short rise. Wildflowers created a riot of blue, pink, yellow, and lavender amidst green grass, and the sweet scent of blossoms rode the breeze.

Henri followed a few steps behind. "Really? Even when you were a kid? Didn't you want to be a fireman when you grew up?" The Henri of today snickered at his younger self having once aspired to be a cop. As if.

"No. My mother was a soprano. My whole life I've been surrounded by music. I was even born in Modena." Sebastian's voice held a note of pride.

Modena. "Is that in Wisconsin?"

Sebastian snorted. "Modena, Italy. Where Pavarotti was born. I toured with my mother, and some of the greatest voices in the world sang me to sleep at night." He launched into an, "ahhhh-*ahhhh*" that echoed off the mountains. A half smile erased years from Seb's face, allowing Henri to glimpse how he might have looked during childhood.

"I bet you were a handful." He imagined a little Seb wandering around backstage, getting into mischief.

"I was. But many of the performers missed their families while touring. They adopted me. And they taught me their native tongues."

"If you already speak them, why do you study languages?"

"It's not enough to merely mouth the words. You must understand them, feel them, live them." Seb launched into one of the more soulful pieces in his vast repertoire, the one that had gotten Henri misty-eyed in the theater.

Puzzle pieces from Seb's life slipped into place. In the few short days they'd known each other, Seb had never sounded like a man in his twenties. His philosophies, his outlook on life, even his speech at times, seemed much older. "Were there ever any other kids to play with?"

"Who needed other kids? I had music." This time the smile didn't reach Seb's eyes.

Henri only toured in his late teens and as an adult, partying into the night, surrounded by willing bodies to keep him company. Or at least at first. Now, no matter how many people tagged along, he still felt alone. Was that how Seb had felt, the only child in an adult world?

"Occasionally I stayed here with my grandmother, but she died when I was twelve." Seb stopped to examine a flowering vine.

"How old were you when your mother passed, if you don't mind my asking?"

"Not at all. I was six months shy of my seventeenth birthday. She dedicated herself to her craft, ignoring her own health. And found out too late about her breast cancer."

Seventeen, his sister's age. Damn. As independent as he was, and as angry at his folks, Henri still couldn't imagine being alone in the world so young, or his mother dying. "Where did you go?"

A shadow flitted across Sebastian's face, gone as quickly as it had come. He averted his gaze and resumed his hike through the trees. "A family friend took me in and continued on as my patron."

A tightening of Sebastian's lips said there was more to the story. "What does a patron do?"

"He backed me financially until I began drawing an income, helped me apply to the Met's young artist program, and ensures I have everything I need."

Yes, definitely more here than met the eyes. No one did something for nothing, not in Henri's world, anyway. "What does he get out of it?"

"Why, the pleasure of being a part of my success." Seb's laugh held a bitter edge. "Actually, he's a huge supporter of not only me, but the opera itself. He's extremely generous with the Met, as well as some smaller companies. If he or a friend throws a private party, I'll attend and give a concert."

Wow! Must be a pretty rich guy to have his own pet opera star. Henri kept the words to himself.

"This way." Sebastian veered down a path to the left. "I've neglected my walking while you've been here. I need to get five miles in today. Are you game?"

"Five miles? You walk five miles a day?" The farthest Henri had trekked lately was from a tour bus to a stage door, running a gauntlet of grabby fans.

"Every other, but yes, I must stay in shape."

Henri bit down on a too-easy retort. Sex burned lots of calories, and if done right, worked all the major muscles groups, including those firm glutes hidden beneath Seb's pants. "Why don't you lift weights?" With a house the size of Seb's, it'd be easy to turn an unused room into a gym.

"If you change the contour of the instrument, you change the pitch. I walk, I lift light weights, but nothing designed to change my shape." Seb patted his chest. "When someone casts me in a production, they expect a certain sound. I work hard to make sure they get their money's worth."

Jeez. The only time Henri worried about weight was if his jeans got too tight, then it was all about being thin. Seb worried about losing weight, rather than gaining. A first, in Henri's book.

The path took them up an incline. Seb loo-loo'd the rest of the way. Henri huffed and puffed a few paces behind him. Damned high altitude! He'd kill for a walking stick to either help him climb or to whack the guy currently bounding up the trail like he had springs for legs.

How the fuck did he do that?

Just when Henri thought his chest might explode, Sebastian quieted and stopped. "Look there." He stepped back and let Henri have the view. "Have you ever seen anything more beautiful?"

Henri caught movement below and managed to steady his breathing enough to focus. A herd of deer grazed among wild-flowers below them.... A hawk circled overhead. A light breeze kissed Henri's cheek. Quiet. So quiet. "I understand why you like it here."

"This land has been in my family for four generations." A touch of sorrow stained the words. "We're on the edge of the goldfields. My great-grandfather's family used to own much of the valley, too, before they fell on hard times. Come on, we need to be getting home."

Seb said not a word, nor did he hum, on the way back to the house.

SEVEN

"Dammit!" Henri slammed his hand down on the piano.

"What is it?" Sebastian poked his head through the door.

"Have you ever worked your ass off for something, only to have it taken away from you?"

Seb paused before replying, "Yes. What are we talking about here?" He held a dishcloth in his hand. The man cleaned more than anyone else Henri ever met, though Tessa the meditation guru came in a close second.

"My songs. I did most of the work, but since I shared credits, Lucas believes I should write more and forget the old ones." His former band might as well have taken possession of his right arm.

One side of Seb's mouth lifted. "I tend to agree."

"What?"

"You're Henri Lafontaine, former lead singer. Every time your old band advertises, they're advertising you too."

It worked both ways. "Yeah."

"What do you know about passive aggression?"

Hmmm.... Seemed like Dr. Worthington used the term. "That it's a bad thing?"

Seb laughed. "Useful sometimes. My mother called it 'getting revenge and coming out smelling like a rose.' Now, the song you sang the other day is called...?"

"A Matter of When."

"And it's a depressing piece about a man leaving a smothering lover by way of suicide, right?"

No one had ever summed up the song in quite the same way before. "You're not helping, Seb."

"I'm getting there. From what I understand, songs can be copyrighted, titles cannot."

Lucas had said the same thing. "So? As you said, if I advertise a new song with the same name, I'm giving a bunch of douchebags free publicity." No way in hell.

"Write a completely opposite new song, with the same name."

"What's that supposed to do?"

"Henri Lafontaine performs a song entitled 'A Matter of When.' It's fresh, it's cutting edge, it pushes boundaries you've never dreamed possible. Your former band performs a completely different song, very dark, and also five years old. Nothing says, 'I'm over those losers and their morose lyrics' like an in-your-face, tongue-in-cheek comeuppance." Seb winked.

Easier said than done. "There's only one little problem."

"What?"

"Those are the best lyrics I've ever written. I'm not sure I can do better." "Sober" and "songwriting" might be mutually exclusive, in Henri's case.

"Sure, you can. You've been in love before, right? The butterflies in the stomach. The 'will she call or won't she?' Your heart skipping a beat when a certain young lady enters the room."

Okay, somebody didn't get the memo, or read the tabloids.

While he said grace before every meal, Sebastian had yet to go off on any homophobic rants. Besides, technically he was a paid employee—his opinions shouldn't count. How odd that they did. "Sebastian, how much did you know about me before I got here?"

"Only what Lucas told me. You're a rock vocalist preparing for a midcareer makeover. You need some coaching, and a quiet place to write."

"You didn't once look me up online or read any of those tabloid articles?" The next words out of Henri's mouth could destroy their growing-more-comfortable-by-the-day relationship. Of the many restrictions Margo enforced, the one that chafed the most was having to be someone else, showing up at social events with a woman clinging to his arm, answering questions about his personal life with, "I'm too busy now with the band to have much of a social life." What a lie. The rest of the guys had girlfriends or wives, a couple had both. Henri was alone because of Margo's iron will. No more. With this new start, the mask must fall. Yet revealing his true self might cost him friends and fans.

Who was he kidding? What friends? And who wanted bigoted homophobes for fans?

"Sebastian, I can honestly and truly say I've never gotten butterflies in my stomach when a woman entered the room, unless you count the time Sister Mary-Agnes caught me composing dirty limericks in the school music room." Henri shuddered. "That woman had no qualms about taking a ruler to my knuckles."

"What? You've never been in love?" Seb stopped talking, but his sympathetic frown continued the conversation. *Oh you poor thing.*

"I didn't say I'd never been in love." In junior high school, each week had brought a new crush, sometimes on a guy in class, sometimes an idol from one of Henri's numerous rock magazines, once a substitute teacher. He took a deep breath and disclosed what would soon be public knowledge, and damn the consequences. "I've never been in love with a woman."

Confusion, shock, disbelief, revulsion. No telling how Sebastian would react. He never batted an eyelash. "But you've still been in love. Draw from your own personal knowledge. Use the pleasure, the pain. In my experience, audiences crave strong emotion of any kind: love, triumph, sorrow, heartbreak. Make them feel what you're feeling and they'll eat from your hand." Without another word Seb left the room, la-la-la-la-la-ing all the way.

Damn. That had gone well.

After dinner Henri called his new manager. "Is there a reporter you trust to tell the truth and not embellish?"

Lucas didn't hesitate. "I know a few."

"When I get back in town I want to tell my side of the story. The drugs, the band, the drugged drink. And Lucas?"

"Yes?"

"I'm giving you a heads-up. I plan on coming out."

"To LA? But you're not due back for three more weeks."

Henri let silence answer for him.

"Oh. Tabloids got it right for once, did they?" Lucas's laugh carried no derision.

Well, damn. The tabloids. How Henri hated proving those bastards right. "Do we have a problem?"

"No. But I have to ask you something on a personal note." Lucas took on a businesslike tone.

"Go ahead."

"Has something happened between you and Sebastian? You're my client, but he's the son of a dear friend, with his own career to worry about. If you hurt him, you'll answer to me."

Fathers of sixteen-year-old daughters never sounded so fierce to defend virtue.

Did Lucas just out Sebastian?

———

"How's IT going?" Sebastian eased down onto the settee, facing the piano where Henri had spent a fruitless few hours.

"Not good."

"Why not?"

"I heard what you said about emotions, but saying and doing is a lot different." Most of Henri's recent emotions conjured the same kind of angry, depressing songs Hookers and Cocaine thrived on.

"What do you have so far?"

"Come here." Henri patted the bench next to him and scooted over.

Sebastian sat. Before Lucas had dropped his bomb, Henri had no problem sitting close to Seb. Now, proximity added fuel to the fire of thoughts he shouldn't be having about a man his manager would kill him for seducing. He didn't usually go for intellectual guys, yet the warmth of Seb's body summoned him closer. A hint of cologne teased his nose. Huh? He'd never noticed Seb wearing cologne before. Then again, quitting smoking might have contributed to there currently being more smells in the world. And never had Henri's fingers been more awkward on a keyboard. Hands as graceful as hammers, he banged out the basic opening for his new version of "A Matter of When." With a too thick tongue, he launched into the vocals.

"From the moment I saw you."

"Nope. Not feeling it." Sebastian placed his hands over Henri's to still their frantic pounding.

"But I just started."

"And already your audience is yawning. Grab their attention with the very first note. Now, the original song starts, 'I've got a date with a bullet,' right? All dreary and depressing."

"Hey!" It'd been catchy enough to warrant Grammy attention.

"Well, it is. If you want to remove the previous image from people's minds, you're going to have to think big. Maybe you should put this one away and find something easier to work on."

Like hell would Henri give up. He dug his heels in. "I like this one."

Sebastian squared his shoulders. "Try another."

Henri would show him. "How about 'Whores and More'?"

Seb's sigh ruffled Henri's scrawled-on music sheets. "Guns and bullets it is."

Henri shifted on the bench to begin again, his thigh rubbing against Sebastian's. Sebastian stood abruptly. "Time to fix dinner." He fled the room. Henri stopped playing and pressed his hand against his leg where Seb's had been. A bit of tingle remained, and his cock began to rise at the recollection of Seb's nearness.

And Seb ran. He'd felt their connection too, had he? Henri smiled, humming a new song and conjuring lyrics.

"The spark is there, let's fan the flames."

Seb had a certain quality that spoke to Henri. He wasn't the type Henri usually went for, but maybe, like his music, Henri had simply gone for what was available without giving much thought to what he really wanted. Sure, Seb chewed Henri out on occasion, but only when Henri deserved or needed the scolding to strengthen his resolve. There was something to be said for a man who could hold his own, and who cared about more than fame and money.

Seb provided meals and training, but didn't stop at the bare minimum. He truly cared about everything more than

Henri'd ever cared about anything. In time, could he care about Henri?

But what did it matter? They'd be together for a short while and then go their separate ways. In a year, would either of them recall the single month spent in each other's company?

Henri stopped playing, stroking his fingers silently on the piano keys. What secrets lurked beneath Sebastian's clothes? Henri imagined them both naked, moving in unison in the four-poster bed upstairs. He unzipped his fly and slipped his hand inside to stroke his growing erection. "Loo-looing" from the kitchen meant he'd be safe for a while. Heh. What would Mr. Perfect think about what the big, bad rocker did to him mentally?

Would Sebastian want Henri inside of him, or roll Henri onto his belly and do what he wanted? How reserved he was in the light of day. At night, would he take control, make demands of his lover? Or would he worship Henri's body, take him to new heights of arousal?

Henri moved his hand faster up and down his shaft, cupping his balls through his jeans with the other hand. Oh, damn. His breath hitched. "Oh, oh, oh!" Harsh breathing filled his ears, his heart hammered. "Yes, yes, yes, yes, yes!" he hissed.

The Sebastian in his mind invaded his body, stretching him, making him burn. "Oh, God!" He vaguely heard the loo-loo-loos drifting in from the kitchen, almost caressing him. His stomach muscles tightened and lightning zinged through his groin from the raw power of Seb's imagined thrusts.

Henri shot, one hand tugging a faltering rhythm, the other catching a rain of droplets. Eyes tightly closed, he breathed through his climax, hissing out "Sebastian!" from between clenched teeth. He opened his eyes to find Sebastian standing speechless in the doorway.

"I... um...." Someone needed to call the fire department to put out the flames in Sebastian's cheeks.

"Dinner's ready?" Henri should be embarrassed. He wasn't.

Did Sebastian realize he'd licked his lips? "Err... yes." He spun on his heel and tromped off down the hall.

Henri stared down at his cupped palm. Oh yes. Seb could run, but he couldn't hide.

———

"Can you pass the salad, please? I want *more*." Henri added a hint of innuendo.

Sebastian didn't take the bait. "Sure."

One-word answers, that was all Henri had gotten since his arrival at the table. Sebastian passed the salad bowl. Henri made sure their hands connected. Sebastian jerked his fingers back and sat rubbing them on his side of the table, keeping his eyes firmly on his plate. This wouldn't do.

"Sebastian, we might as well clear the air here. You caught me jerking off. I didn't intend for that to happen. We're both men—these things happen. I don't want you uncomfortable around me."

"I'm not." Seb sat ramrod straight, muscles bunched to flee at any moment.

Oh, really? "Are you worried I might try to seduce you?" Sebastian's reserve added an element of excitement to their meal. Why shouldn't Henri and Sebastian entertain each other? They were here, the two of them, with no witnesses. Seb was hot, in a quiet, take-a-minute-to-notice way.

"No. Not at all."

Henri reached across the table, lifting Seb's face with two fingers under his chin. "You should be."

Far from the backpedaling Henri expected, Sebastian met his

challenge full-on. "I'm your teacher, you're my student. I also refuse to be another notch on your bedpost. Now, if you'll excuse me, I have work to do."

Well, damn if the man's refusal didn't make him the most desirable fuck on the planet.

———

The next morning Sebastian prepared breakfast and left early for lessons. He kept out of Henri's way all day. Henri spotted him through the window, walking the wooded trail alone. Fuck. He'd been looking forward to their walk. Oh hell, they needed to clear the air. Again. However, Sebastian only put in a brief appearance at dinner, not allowing enough time for conversation.

Henri hadn't noticed how much Sebastian's company meant to him until he lost it. Time to apologize—if he remembered how. He knocked on Seb's bedroom door.

"What is it?" Seb had never sounded so annoyed before, no matter how badly Henri goaded him.

"I'd like to talk."

"Go ahead. I'm listening."

Not good enough. Spilling one's guts required eye contact. Henri dropped his usual cockiness. "Please open the door, Seb."

The door slipped open a crack. "What do you want?"

"I'm out of practice with admitting I'm wrong, since I haven't been allowed to make my own decisions since kindergarten, but I admit that I messed up. You're not someone to fuck and forget." He swallowed hard. His admission didn't wipe away his guilt.

"Go on."

Oh crap. Full disclosure. He hated full disclosure. "I'm not going to lie and say I don't find you attractive. I do, even if I don't understand it. You're not the kind of man I normally go for."

Seb's face darkened. "And what kind do you go for? Thin? Gorgeous? Rich?"

"More like shallow, vain, and clingy. I'm not used to being around men who tell me no." The tiny space in the door started to close. Henri placed his hand in the way, not forcing the door farther, but not letting it shut. "I'd welcome you into my bed, but realize I value your friendship too much to lose it because I did my thinking with my dick. Can we call a truce?"

Silence. Henri readied himself to snatch his hand back if need be. "A truce? Name your terms."

"I'll not try to seduce you if you'll forget what an ass I made of myself."

One side of Seb's mouth quirked up. "You do make an impressive ass. Have you ever considered auditioning for *A Midsummer Night's Dream*? It's a starring role."

Was that a chuckle? "So I've been told. Look, Seb, I like you. And I'm sorry. Can we go back to the way we were?"

The moments ticked away, Henri holding his breath. Hell, if he kept this up, he'd be able to sing three lines without breathing at all.

Sebastian let him off the hook. "I suppose I should be flattered."

"Not really. Trust me, I'm not that great. Just a drugged-out rocker who put his foot in his mouth."

The door opened a bit more, revealing Sebastian dressed in a robe, holding a book in his hand. "I'm all for pretending it never happened."

"Thank you, Seb. Good night."

The stiff set of Sebastian's shoulders relaxed. "Good night. I'll see you in the morning."

Henri let out his breath once the door closed. He'd fully meant his apology, so Seb should have invited him in. "You're incorrigible," he muttered to himself. He hummed all the way back to his room, words forming in his head.

"Incorrigible, there's no hope for you...."

Lucas had been right about one thing: Henri found plenty of song inspiration while staying with Sebastian.

———

"STRETCH YOUR neck." Seb lifted Henri's chin with two fingers. "Stretch, stretch. Feel the muscles pulling."

Henri had to look stupid as all hell. Still, Sebastian spoke to him, actually *touched* him. Stupidity well spent.

"Now," Seb continued, his quiet murmur as soothing as Tessa's bowls, "imagine you're picking apples. There's one way up high over your head, nearly out of reach. Loo, loo, loo, loo...." He ran up the scale. Henri joined him on the second "loo."

"Nice, now keep going, stretch, stretch, reach for it." Seb pushed Henri's chin up higher, so far he almost couldn't swallow. "Breathe from your diaphragm. Take a deep breath, let it out slowly."

Seb circled. Henri followed each movement with his eyes. "Loo, loo, loo, loo...." Henri hit his limit. Seb kept going.

He made a full circuit and returned to stand in front of Henri. "I have lessons this afternoon. I want you to practice while I'm gone. Keep thinking of picking apples, reaching for something on a high shelf. Believe it or not, it works." Without another word he swept out of the house. A few moments later the VW rumbled down the driveway, fading from Henri's hearing.

"Damn. I thought he'd never leave." Henri dashed into the kitchen and flung the pantry door open. Spices, dried lentils, a bag of potatoes, canned soup, canned tuna, spaghetti noodles, a bottle of wine. Aha! There! Way in the back, on the top shelf. There all the time, and Seb didn't share. "Mr. Healthy, my ass.

"Loo, loo, loo…," Henri sang, standing on tiptoes and wriggling his fingers. Almost there! "Loo, loo, loo…." He bounced on his toes. Just one more half inch and…. "Gotcha!"

He snagged the chocolate bar and danced away with his prize. Junk food! Finally! Chocolate goodness exploded on his tongue the moment he peeled the bar open and bit down. Oh damn. Now that was good.

Holy shit! Had he actually bypassed wine for chocolate? Huh. Must be some kind of breakthrough. Wait! He stopped nibbling and reached into the pantry again, stretching for all he was worth. "Loo, loo, loo, loo, loo, loo… loo!" Hot damn! Chocolate and a high C. Wait until he told Seb. Well, not about the chocolate. His throat felt a bit sore, but… a high C!

Seb would be so proud. Wait a minute. Why? Why was the man so concerned? Sure, Lucas paid him for lessons, but Henri's dance teacher certainly hadn't put so much effort into seeing him succeed. And Henri wanted Seb to be proud of him. What the hell?

He sank down onto the kitchen floor, munching his pilfered treat.

Now if Sebastian rewarded Henri with chocolate, he might do better with his vocal training. He grinned. What if Sebastian rewarded him with kisses? Or maybe more. Oh yeah. What if, instead of running the other day, Sebastian had fallen to his knees and taken Henri into his mouth? Oh hell yeah!

But… Sebastian cared. He acted like a friend. Fucks were easy to find, friends weren't, and fucking a friend was a damned good way to lose the friend. And yet, just conjuring the man's satiny smooth tenor crying out in ecstasy had Henri hard and throbbing.

Was it wrong to want a man he considered a friend? Or did he want the man *because* he was a friend? Safe. Sebastian made him feel safe, and like he was worth more than his bank account or fame. Then again, exactly how much was Lucas paying him? Probably enough for a helluva lot of chocolate bars.

Henri's elation crashed and burned. Sebastian had told the truth. Henri was a student, nothing more. A fat wallet full of cash, like he was to everyone else. He picked himself up off the floor and marched to his room for his keys. Might as well make Sebastian earn the money, and learn to keep his hands to himself. But first, time to ride to town and replace Sebastian's chocolate stash.

Never let it be said that Henri Lafontaine owed anyone anything.

"Have you ever danced close to someone?" Sebastian strolled into the room, swaying to the smooth jazz Henri had playing on the stereo.

Henri shot a glance to the grandfather clock. Wow! He'd been wrapped up in composing and hadn't noticed the time. His newly acquired high C had called for some revisions. "Not really. There was an awkward high school prom thing my mother insisted I go to." He'd been photographed a million times with the school homecoming queen on his arm. He'd have preferred her brother.

"You don't talk about your family much. Are your parents still alive?" The question from anyone else might have seemed nosy. Sebastian wasn't nosy, merely interested. He'd get an answer.

Henri fought off a sigh. "Yeah. We're on the outs right now."

A wrinkle appeared between Sebastian's brows. "Make amends."

What? "But...."

"But nothing. I have no family. It's just me. Christmas, Thanksgiving, I'm alone. I'd give everything I have to be able to sit down at dinner with my parents, or call them, share my good days, get their advice. Don't take your family for granted, or one day they'll be gone, leaving you with nothing but regret for things you did or didn't do. Now, come here." Seb jabbed a button on the stereo. Music too slow to dance to wafted from the speakers.

"Why?" And what did this have to do with singing?

"We're going to dance."

Dancing? With Henri's two left feet? No, Seb would dance, Henri would make a fool of himself. "Why?"

"I need the practice, and you need the experience. Why do you think so many songs mention dancing? It's the most intimate thing two people can do outside the bedroom." Was this Seb's version of a come-on?

Henri's cock accepted the perceived invitation. Not now! Visions of the girl who'd posed as his high school sweetheart filled his head, allowing him to dampen down his urges. She'd kept him laughing the whole time at prom by whispering naughty things into his ear, like, "See that guy over there. I'd do him, would you?" She'd been one of the few people he'd been honest with. And one of the last people he'd trusted completely. Imagining Seb in her pink taffeta dress didn't help him reel in his libido. The man would look good in anything.

Or nothing.

"Follow my lead." Seb offered his hands.

"Why do you get to lead?" Henri placed his hands in Seb's larger ones. Electricity raced up his arms and straight to his groin.

"Because I've taken years of lessons and you haven't."

"Good answer."

Henri had never watched Seb dance, but imagined anyone that tall, with feet large enough to provide a firm foundation, must be awkward. But Seb didn't dance—he floated, gliding effortlessly across the floor, Henri in tow. Every movement, every touch of skin against skin, sent Henri's senses hyperaware. Even the brush of Sebastian's fingers ignited a fire Henri didn't understand. It was all he could do to keep his erection away from Sebastian's thigh. He'd sworn to leave the man alone and intended to keep his word.

He was there, and it had been a long time. Nothing more. Henri was merely being a guy. Any attraction meant nothing. Yet when Seb's breath wafted over Henri's ear, Henri stumbled. Seb caught him. Good, dependable Seb never once misstepped.

The music ended and Seb dipped Henri backward. Only inches of space separated their lips. Henri stared up into Seb's eyes. Something clicked. They moved as one, lips connecting with lips, a brief meeting, and then apart again. One moment Seb held him, the next minute he dashed toward the door. "I need to start dinner."

Henri stood in the middle of the room, running his fingers over his mouth. Sebastian had kissed him. A sweet, haven't-seen-since-grade-school innocent gesture. The smile was on his face long before Henri realized it. He returned to the piano an enlightened man.

While he'd never sing such sappiness in public, the settee wasn't likely to tell.

"He kissed me...."

———

OVER THE next few days, Henri studied Sebastian. His every precise move. Lucas had sent him here to learn discipline. Seb needed to unlearn discipline. After the first surprise kiss, no more followed. No way was the kiss coerced. If Seb loosened up once, maybe it would happen again. "I need to go to town. I'll be back in a bit." Henri trotted down the stairs, past Seb, helmet in hand.

"Want me to come with you? I could drive my car."

And ruin the surprise? Nope. Not happening. "Nah, that's all right. When I get back you can go with me." On Henri's bike.

EIGHT

"No, no, no, no, no! Do you have any idea what the wind does to vocal chords?" Sebastian gripped the porch railing, as though Henri might try to drag him into the yard by force.

"It's got a face shield." He held up the present he'd driven into town for.

Seb scowled at the helmet Henri handed over. "But what about underneath? Air will get in."

An easy enough problem to solve, thanks to Henri's sister, who had no idea what to get him one Christmas. "I have some Turtle Fur."

"Turtle fur? Turtles don't have fur." Sebastian lowered one brow while raising the other. How the hell did he do that?

Henri marched over to the Harley's saddle bag and pulled out the Christmas present he'd gotten from his sister two years ago and had never worn. Fuzzy and purple, the object looked like the love child of a knit hat and the "turtle" part of a turtle-neck sweater, worn outlaw fashion to cover the neck and mouth.

"Here." He ripped the tags off and brought the soft material back to Seb.

Seb eyed the garment with suspicion. "And this keeps the wind out?"

"Yes."

His anger softened, a touch of anxiety taking its place. "I've never ridden a motorcycle before."

"You're in for a treat. But you have to trust me. If you feel me lean, lean with me. If you fight, you'll throw the balance off." His sister had nearly toppled the bike a time or two. "Have you ever ridden a horse?"

"Yes."

"Same principle. Be one with the animal."

Sebastian held his ground.

"Come on! Loosen up a little. Have some fun." Had the man ever done a spontaneous thing in his life?

"Oh, all right. If it'll make you happy." Seb pulled on the Turtle Fur and managed the helmet with Henri's help.

Henri tied his hair back and slipped his own helmet on. He'd heard enough complaints from previous passengers about his unruly locks whipping them in the face.

"Now, it's kinda like dancing, but this time you have to follow my lead." Several wonderfully windy roads awaited, but for Seb's first outing, Henri would take a fairly straight path.

Seb climbed on the back of the bike and wrapped his arms around Henri, clinging more tightly than was comfortable.

"Ease up there, big guy. You won't fall."

Seb relaxed his hold.

Henri fired up the Harley Road King and coasted down the driveway and onto asphalt, getting a feel for his passenger. Seb's thighs were warm against his butt, and having the man's arms around him added a bonus to the ride. Now to teach him a thing or two about trust—and freedom.

They'd gone nearly ten miles when Henri recognized the vibrations coming through his back: Sebastian's laughter.

————

"Why do you take those?" Sebastian watched Henri swallow a pill.

"Because I have anxiety and depression. These help me get by."

"You're masking the problem. Why not tackle your issues head-on?"

Said the man who lived on a mountaintop far from civilization. "It's not that easy."

"What causes you anxiety? What causes you to be depressed?"

Let him count the ways. Henri settled for, "Many things. Worrying about what other people think, mostly." Not to mention crazed psychotics with rope and duct tape. Though, so far he'd not noticed any strange cars driving by. With any luck loony-boy had hightailed it back to New Jersey.

"Why do they matter?"

"Because they can make or break my career." Or kidnap him and hold him for ransom.

"You give them too much power."

"Well, it isn't easy being the great Henri Lafontaine." Henri barked a cynical laugh. If people only took the time to learn the real him, they'd run screaming.

————

"Open wide." Sebastian formed an O with his mouth.

Dear Lord, the man shouldn't do that! It'd been way too long since the Vegas one-night stand.

"Relax your muscles and open your throat." Sebastian belted out a note.

He probably gave amazing blowjobs. Henri did as he was told, fighting off the image of what he'd like Sebastian to use to fill his mouth. Just like deep-throating.

"Now sing. La-la-la-la-la-la."

Damn but Henri made it through their drills this time without the least bit of soreness or hoarseness. But he still wanted a blowjob.

NINE

THEY SETTLED into a routine. Every morning they breakfasted together. They took walks on clear days before Sebastian led Henri through warm-up drills. On Mondays and Wednesdays Sebastian disappeared for a few hours for lessons, and occasionally holed up with his laptop to recite non-English words. Sometimes he joined Henri in the music room; other times Henri worked alone. The room seemed empty without Sebastian.

Sebastian burst in, belting out what might have been French. Henri stopped pecking on the piano keys, mesmerized by the sheer power of the man's voice. Longing filled him, and despair. Without understanding the words, he felt the pain of loss. Tears gathered behind his eyelids. Damn, how he'd love to be able to affect listeners with the tone of his voice alone.

Sebastian ended the tune and started teaching while Henri swiped his eyes with the back of his hand. "I don't suppose I need to explain your lesson."

"No."

"Sometimes words move an audience, other times, mood. Set

the mood. Don't tell them what to feel with words—make them feel it clear down to their souls with music."TENSION BUILT in the room so strong a knife could slice it in two. Henri stopped playing, but didn't turn to face Seb, sitting on the bench beside him. "Why won't you kiss me again?"

Sebastian answered too quickly. "Because it's not my place to."

"Why not? We're grown men. You don't have someone who'll object, do you?"

"My patron...."

"Surely he doesn't control your love life." Something about the way Sebastian said "patron" caused unease to stir to life in Henri's belly, like the way Henri used to say "my manager," with an added shiver for good measure.

"I was hired to help you improve your technique. It'd be unprofessional to get involved with a student." For all of the man's acting lessons, the words came out forced, unnatural.

"I'm only going to be your student for another week." Yeah, then what?

"Then I'll miss you." Sebastian toyed with the piano keys, no real tune emerging. The set of his jaw belied his indifference.

"I'm not asking for involvement. I want a kiss." Henri exaggerated a pucker. "One little kiss, then I'll shut up."

Sebastian huffed out a sigh and laid on the drama, hand splayed against his chest. "If that's the price I have to pay. The things I do for my art."

As before, he brought their lips together for minimal contact. Henri would have no evasion. Lacing his fingers in Sebastian's curls and using his grip as leverage, he brought their mouths firmly together, ignoring Seb's "Mmmmmph!" of surprise.

Taking advantage, Henri coaxed Sebastian's lips open with the tip of his tongue. Sebastian stiffened, keeping his mouth firmly closed. After a moment his resolve and rigid stance melted. He parted his lips to allow Henri's tongue inside.

Tentative at first, Sebastian grew bolder, and while not matching Henri's fervor, he became a willing participant in their intimacy. Sebastian pulled away first. Henri didn't stop him.

"I…. I suppose you can tell I haven't been kissed much."

Telling someone they kissed like an amateur? Even if they asked? No, not happening. "Really? You could have fooled me."

"Really." Sebastian stared straight ahead, his face and ears flushed a deep crimson.

"As you said before, I'm only here for a little while. I could teach you if you like." Boy, could Henri teach him.

The offer hung in the air while the grandfather clock in the corner ticked off the minutes. "Lead on."

Henri held out his hand and stood, waiting long moments until Seb joined their palms. He led the way to the settee and settled on the overstuffed seat. Seb sat down beside him. Henri placed his palms on either side of Sebastian's face. When Sebastian would have brought their lips together, Henri held him still. "Today it's me teaching the lesson. Follow my lead." He nuzzled noses, then skimmed his lips across Seb's eyelids, his forehead, and down his nose. He captured Seb's full lower lip between his teeth and lightly tugged.

To the tempo of one of Seb's waltzes, he slid his tongue against Sebastian's, and though the contact left him wanting, he didn't push for more. The kiss went on forever, Henri allowing the novice to explore to his heart's content. They ended the kiss and held each other, saying nothing. Henri's heart pounded out a staccato beat. The sun sank and the room darkened, but still they sat, Henri rubbing his hand lightly over Sebastian's back. If Sebastian gave any indication of wanting more, Henri might come in his pants.

At last Sebastian murmured, "I guess we should be getting to bed." He gave Henri a final, brief kiss. To his credit, he didn't run, he ambled away at an unhurried pace.

Henri went to bed so hard he ached. No way could Sebastian be a virgin. No fucking way. In his dreams Henri laid Sebastian out on his bed and worshipped every nook and cranny of the man's body with his tongue. His sheets needed washing the next morning.

———

"Seb?" Henri approached Seb's room to peek through the partially open door. The man kept his room as neat as the rest of the house. Unable to resist, after tapping and calling, "Seb?" again, Henri tiptoed into the room. No personal effects littered the dressers. The whole place screamed "museum." From the white comforter and curtains to the lace doilies on the table, nothing in the room captured Sebastian's warmth. How could he stand being in here? Henri's room back home was his comfort zone, filled with books, magazines, his favorite chocolates, and a porn collection to die for. Where were Seb's dirty little secrets? A cabinet beckoned. Henri opened the door to find a stereo, CD cases stacked neatly underneath. Pavarotti shared space with Judy Garland, Yanni, Domingo, and every single Hookers and Cocaine CD, cases well-kept but worn.

Why had Seb lied about knowing who Henri was? Ice water froze in Henri's veins. Damn, Sebastian was another fan, out to make money off the down-and-out rocker.

Give him a chance, why don't you? Maybe Lucas sent those CDs to familiarize Sebastian with Henri's work. Made perfect sense. Or perhaps Sebastian didn't want to come across all fan boy. What if he didn't like the CDs?

Honesty. If Henri wanted honesty, he had to give it. He put

the CDs back and slipped from the room. If Sebastian wanted to tell him, he would.

———————

HENRI STARED at his "might read" e-mail folder. After weeding out the hundred or so he had no intention of opening, only a few remained: twenty-two from his mother, several from the rejected managers, and only one worthy of his attention.

Hi, Henri,

I really wish you and Mom would patch things up. I miss you and I'm tired of us not getting to talk.

Love,

Jenni

DAMN. SEB was right. Sooner or later, Henri would have to work things out with his folks, for his sister's sake. He whooshed out a sigh and opened an e-mail from his mother long enough to read the words "selfish" and "spoiled." He deleted the message and its twenty-one brothers and sisters.

Fuck, but he couldn't get his life back together fast enough.

He tiptoed downstairs to get a drink, not wanting to disturb Seb if he was sleeping.

"Put me down every minute, and I gotta say good-bye."

What the hell? Henri crept to the kitchen and peered through a crack in the door. Sebastian alternately swept the floor and used the broom handle for a microphone.

"I've got a date with a bullet, got a date with a gun."

Well, that solved the mystery of whether Seb liked Henri's music. And damn did the man know how to sing.

Henri ducked when Sebastian turned around. Oh shit. Maybe he didn't like the song.

Tears streamed down his face.

———

THE MOUNTAIN path seemed lonely without Sebastian, but Henri needed to clear his head. For all they'd shared a house and much time together in the past three weeks, he still knew very little about the guy. Parents gone, grew up in opera, yet listened to Henri's music. He knew Lucas, but they couldn't be close—Sebastian didn't talk about him much—or anyone else. No personal photos adorned the walls of his home, and quite frankly, the pictures Henri found on the Internet of Sebastian Senior didn't resemble Junior. The man had inherited his mother's curls and eyes, though. He still reminded Henri of someone. But who?

And last night he'd been crying alone in the kitchen. Not going in and finding out what was wrong was possibly the hardest thing Henri had ever done. Even harder than giving up cocaine. And hookers. But Sebastian was a private man and likely would have clammed up and not shared what bothered him. Hell, Henri'd been there.

Sebastian Unger remained an enigma. And isolated. In the past three weeks, Henri's voice mail would have chimed constantly if he hadn't set his cell phone to silent. And each evening he triaged hundreds of e-mails. To Henri's knowledge, the house phone had only rung twice, and Sebastian didn't often carry a cell phone. What kind of desolate life did he lead?

Control. He kept a tight fist on control. The only time he let loose was when Henri coaxed him to go for a ride. On the Harley the man was free, and never more beautiful than in those moments glimpsed in the Harley's rearview mirrors: tousled hair peeking out from under the helmet, smile as wide as the Colorado sky.

It dawned on Henri—here he was free too. Here he'd been just himself, not Henri the rock god. Except for a few investments made online in the wee hours, he'd not touched his money. He'd been a mere man, enjoying time with another man who wanted nothing but to help him perfect his craft. Sure, Sebastian got paid, but the attention he gave to Henri, the extra touches, couldn't be for hire. And certainly not the kisses.

Time to show some appreciation.

Sebastian was known in town—Henri might be recognized as well, meaning a night in public wasn't going to happen. Especially since Lucas's warning. If Sebastian hadn't been kissed much, chances were he'd not been properly romanced either. Before Henri left to return to LA, he'd remedy the lack. He never wanted to see tears in the man's eyes again.

———

"How's THINGS going, Henri?"

"Fine, Doc." Henri stretched out on his bed to gaze at the mountains. So serene. Life moved at a slower pace here, which suited him fine. "I haven't had to take any emergency pills, just my normal meds."

"Good. Have you thought about your future?"

Henri pictured his counselor, back home in LA, with the noise, the traffic, the smog. Much better to stare out the window at the blue Colorado sky. "You know I'm gay, right?" Might as well lay the cards on the table.

"Your sexuality is none of my concern, unless it affects your emotional well-being. Does it?"

"I'm tired of living in the closet. In order to be me, I need to let the world in on who I am. Besides, I don't like pretending a stranger my mom found is my date." Henri imagined Dr. Worthington pecking away on her computer, filling in the pieces for the puzzle named Henri Lafontaine.

"Are you saying you want to form a relationship with a man?"

Was he? "I suppose I am. Maybe. Someday."

"There may be backlash if you come out, on you, on your family, and on your career."

Normally, "the family" comment would have pissed him off, but Dr. Worthington had proven time and again that Henri had her full consideration, not the family. She'd made Henri her primary concern—the reason Henri still called. "My parents don't much care for me whether I'm gay or not, and I survived an overdose and years of just being me. My fans have stuck with me through stints in rehab, infighting with the band, picketing from right-wingers, and a scandal or five hundred. If they, and my family, can't deal with who I really am, fuck 'em." The only one who mattered was Jenni, and she'd want Henri to be happy. Besides, her favorite TV show starred a gay teen. She'd be cool.

Now that wasn't quite right. Seb mattered too.

"Are you sure you're doing what's right for you?" Ah, the voice of reason. Why Henri paid the big bucks.

"As sure as I've ever been about anything."

"Henri?"

"Yes?"

"For what it's worth, I believe you've always known what you wanted, you just weren't allowed to have it. Now, how about drugs? Alcohol?"

Damn. Henri hadn't even thought about drinking or smoking a joint in days. "I haven't even been tempted. Aren't you proud?"

"The only one who needs to be proud of you is you."

The good doctor had no idea how wrong she was.

———

"I'll be coming back soon. Any leads on the guy at the party?" No way in hell did Henri want to return to LA and face the jackass who'd drugged him.

Detective Shepard's sigh wafted through the phone, as negative as any of Henri's former songs. "Without much to go on, I'm afraid we've reached a dead end."

Oh shit. The nut job waited, rope, duct tape, and drugs in hand. Was it too much to hope that he'd picked up a new hobby? Maybe comic books? Or returned to New Jersey?

"As we discussed before, I recommend heightened security. If you ever see him again, keep us informed."

Henri reined in the fury growing inside. Yelling at the detective wouldn't solve anything. He had his hands too full of homicides and domestic violence to worry about one puny rocker.

"Thanks, I will." Was even being here putting Seb in danger? God, Henri hoped not.

TEN

"Where are we going?"

"You'll see." Henri bypassed his Harley in favor of Seb's car. The night would turn cool by the time they returned.

Henri wore jeans and a T-shirt, all he'd brought with him, and had tried to tame his fluffy, cotton-candy hair into a somewhat neat braid down his back. He'd even shaved. On a Friday.

Seb wore khakis and a button-down shirt. Based on evidence given, he didn't even own jeans. He was a fiftysomething man living in a twentysomething body. Henri hoped to narrow the gap.

The restaurant he'd chosen had started life as the dwelling of a wealthy family, and perched on the edge of a mountainside. Over the phone they'd stated their dress code. Money changed everything. A private dining room, free from prying eyes, offered the best view on the whole mountain, so the manager said. Good. In years to come, Henri wanted Sebastian to remember this night.

"We're not dressed for this," Sebastian hissed when Henri pulled the car into the parking lot.

"You worry too much."

Instead of entering through the main door, they were met by a young woman and escorted around back and up the stairs to a secluded balcony. "Good evening," she said, "your server will be with you shortly."

"Wow!" Sebastian's eyes widened as he took in the vista below. At the bottom of the valley a river snaked through the trees, while houses, made tiny by distance, lined the banks.

"You like?" Henri breathed out a sigh of relief. Never had he wanted to please someone so badly. Maybe Sebastian's gentle nature brought out his protective instincts. Then again, maybe wanting to share something special won out over caution. Either way, tonight had to be perfect.

A bouquet of gladiolas graced the table. Seb raised a brow when Henri pulled out his chair for him, but sat quietly. The brow rose again, joined by its twin, when Henri reached out to squeeze Seb's hand.

Seb cleared his throat. "I love gladiolas."

Henri smiled. "I sorta figured, with about a zillion of them growing in front of the house."

"My grandmother tended the gardens when she was alive." A faraway look momentarily appeared in Seb's eyes. "They were her favorite flower too. I'm afraid I can't match her green thumb, but I try."

"My gran grew roses." Henri pulled down the top of his T-shirt to show the long-stemmed red rose bud over his left nipple.

Henri expected a laugh—Seb didn't disappoint. "Isn't a rose a bit soft for a hardassed rocker?"

Sebastian had stepped right into his trap. Henri stood and pulled his T-shirt up to reveal the rose stem, sharpened to a dagger point, piercing a life-sized human heart inked into the skin over Henri's own heart. A drop of blood clung to the point.

"I take that back. It's not soft in the least."

Henri smoothed his shirt down and rejoined Sebastian at the table.

"Do you mind me asking about your tattoos? Some are kinda... scary."

"Which ones?"

Sebastian wrinkled his face and pursed his lips a moment, finally deciding on, "All of them."

Henri held out his arm. "Most people call this a demon. It's not. It's a gargoyle. You know what a gargoyle is, don't you?"

"Of course I do. Many opera houses and cathedrals have them. They're supposed to ward off evil spirits. What about the rose through the heart?" Understanding crossed Sebastian's face. "'Rose Through the Heart' is one of your songs."

"Yes, and here...." Henri showed his other arm, bearing the image of a .38 Special and bullets. "This symbolizes 'A Matter of When.' It's from the cover."

"You've inked your career into your skin. Tell me, what happens when you run out of skin?"

How many more albums would it take for Henri to run out of space? "I guess I'll have to recycle concepts."

"I have one more question."

"Ask away."

"Why are you doing this?"

"Why am I doing what?"

Sebastian swept his hand out to indicate the table.

A smartassed answer wouldn't get Henri off the hook this time. Best to stick to the truth. "Because I want to." Here came the part where Sebastian jumped up and stormed back to the car, wanting no part of anything with Henri besides a working relationship. Maybe.

Sebastian surprised him. "Would it be selfish of me to throw out all arguments about right and wrong and enjoy a nice evening with you?"

Turning dinner into an actual date couldn't be that easy, could it? "Not in the least."

A waiter stepped through the door, bottle in hand. "Good evening, gentlemen." He didn't ask, he merely filled their wine glasses from the vintage Henri had ordered earlier and sat the remainder of the bottle in ice. He didn't take their orders either.

A moment later two women joined him, one with a tray of assorted breads, the other with a bowl of mixed greens salad. One quietly filled their salad bowls while the other placed her burden on the table. When they retreated, Henri said, "I hope you don't mind, but I took the liberty of ordering for us. I believe you like trout?"

"Love it."

Good. It seemed easier to simply preorder and minimize talking with the staff. He'd made sure each dish steered clear of dairy, in keeping with Sebastian's diet. Several times the man and women reappeared, bringing out their meal, clearing plates, refilling Seb's wine glass—Henri merely toyed with his, sipping water instead. His doctor would be so proud. Each time the attendants made an appearance, Henri stopped talking until they departed, leaving no stray words to be swept up and reused. He'd learned his lesson long ago—if people wanted dirt, they'd dig it up. He wouldn't supply the shovel.

"What will you do when you get back to LA?" Seb asked between bites.

"Lucas has some musicians lined up for me to talk to. I'll be choosing a new band. I also have a few ideas of my own." Inspiration struck. "Any suggestions?"

"Choose only those you trust. You don't need a band, you need a team. Mutual respect is crucial."

Henri'd had enough suspicions and mistrust with his last band. "Really?"

"Certainly. If I give my all during a performance and another player gives nothing, no one will say he or she ruined the show. They'll say the show was awful, which reflects on everyone in the company."

Oh, yeah. Definitely no two-bit guitar slingers who'd sell Henri out to a tabloid. Still, there were no guarantees whoever he hired would be trustworthy. The best he could hope for was a crew of competent musicians who would coalesce into a working organism rather than a manufactured band. "What about you? What will you do?"

A barely perceptible chill settled over the table. "My patron is vacationing in Europe with his family. He'll visit me after he returns, checking up on his investment before I begin rehearsals." A touch of bitterness tinged Seb's words.

"If you don't like him, why not get a new patron?"

Seb stared into his wineglass. "I can't. He's been generous with me. I should be grateful."

"And you're not?"

"Can we not talk about this? The things we want in life come with a cost." Seb's forced smile was as fake as Henri's trumped up bio. "He's a perfectionist, and demands perfection of me. Wanting perfection isn't a bad thing, is it?"

Henri didn't push. If Seb wanted to say more, he would. Henri changed the subject. "I didn't know what you might want for dessert and ordered one of each—or rather, everything without dairy. They make vegan cheesecake here." The door opened and the servers reappeared, the man pushing a laden cart and the women fussing over the table, removing dirty dishes and resetting the plates.

Over coffee, vegan cheesecake, and apple crumble, they watched the sun dip below the tree line. Seb surprised Henri by taking his hand. "I know what you're doing, and I don't need your pity, but thank you anyway for a lovely evening."

What the fuck? "Pity?"

Seb smile lacked humor. "If you met me in LA, would you wine me, dine me, dance with me? Kiss me?"

Henri hesitated.

"Of course you wouldn't. I'm the man of the moment, nothing more. In a week you'll be back where you belong, and I'll be here. Never again will our worlds meet."

What? Henri snatched his hand back. "I thought we were friends. You're gonna write me off when I leave here?"

"You mean... you mean you'd still talk to me after this?" Why did Sebastian appear so incredulous? Who had done a number on this man, to make him think he was "the man of the moment"?

Was Henri wanting to hang on to their blossoming relationship so hard to believe? He reclaimed Sebastian's hand. "I've come to trust you. You give advice, solid advice, without trying to manipulate me. I've got a lot of serious decisions ahead. I'd love your input."

"But how?"

"I can e-mail you tracks, send demos of anyone I'm considering for the band. Sometimes I might want to talk about nothing. Or about the tuna sandwich I had for lunch that doesn't come close to yours. Who else will put up with me prattling on about nonsense?" He shifted his chair closer and stared into Sebastian's eyes. "Everyone out there wants a piece of Henri Lafontaine. They see the money, the fame, and they want their share of the pie. They don't see me." Actually, Henri wouldn't mind Seb wanting more of him. Where had such a thought come from?

The curtains ruffled on the window to their left. Henri nodded and the door opened. A lone violinist stepped out onto the balcony, now shadowed by dusk settling over the mountains. Henri stood and bowed to Sebastian. "May I have this dance?"

For a moment Seb hesitated, and Henri feared being turned down. Then Sebastian shook his head, a rueful grin on his face. "You know me too well. I can't resist dancing."

As before at the house, Sebastian took the lead, sweeping Henri a bit closer to his chest than he'd done in the music room. No matter how shy he appeared while dining, when singing or dancing he came into his own. Henri rested his head against Sebastian's shoulder, swaying to something sultry and slow. Seb hummed along with the melody, his voice rumbling through his chest and into Henri's ear.

Keeping their bodies tightly together shielded their rising erections from the violinist, and tantalized Henri with the brush of his cock against Seb's. Still Seb kept rhythm, never faltering as Henri did, and never abandoning the dance to hump Henri's thigh like Henri wanted desperately for him to do.

The song faded, and Henri pulled back. Seb stared down at him, eyes aglow and lips curled up the edges. If ever a moment cried out for kiss, this one did. If they were man and woman, nothing would stop them.

Oh screw it. Henri reached up, placed his hand against Seb's cheek, and brought their lips together.

The violinist missed a note.

Just one.

———

"WHERE DO you want these?" Henri carried the vase of gladiolas into the house.

In true Sebastian Unger fashion, Seb grew humble. "I still can't believe you bought me flowers."

"Don't tell me you've never gotten flowers from a man before."

Seb's face shaded to match the crimson of the blooms. "On some nights my dressing room is filled with bouquets from fans —some men, some women. These are special."

Henri sat the vase down on the entryway table and swept a humming Seb into his arms to whirl him around the foyer. He'd gotten much better at avoiding toes. Sebastian kept time as they stepped through the hall, turning lights on and off along the way. They reached the bottom of the stairs. "I guess this is good night." Damn, but Henri wanted to dance, and more, until dawn.

Sebastian studied the floor for a minute and slowly released a loud exhale. He lifted their joined hands and kissed Henri's fingers. "It doesn't have to be."

Henri's heart hammered against his ribs. "Are you sure?"

"How else will I get to see the rest of your body art?" Sebastian led the way to his room and closed the door behind them, keeping his eyes firmly fixed on the floor. What was he afraid of? After a moment he recovered, resuming his humming and their dance. He lost his awkwardness while dancing, or singing, his former confidence returning. For a man who made the masses swoon, Seb seemed a novice at romance.

"I don't do pity fucks," Sebastian said.

An answer rolled readily off of Henri's tongue: "Neither do I."

Seb backed away, fumbling with the buttons on his shirt. Henri batted his hands away and took control, making short work of the closures. The shirt rustled to the floor. When Seb bent to pick up the garment, Henri stopped him. "Let it lie. We'll worry about cleanup later." Henri's T joined Seb's shirt on the floor, soon followed by khakis and jeans. Seb wore nothing under his pants. And Henri hadn't noticed? Damn, he'd lost his touch.

Sebastian peeled the tie out of Henri's hair, unraveling the braid until Henri's hair brushed free over his shoulders.

Henri kicked off the designer briefs he'd been paid to endorse before his meltdown. At last they stood naked, Henri self-conscious about his skinny frame, multicolored ink etched into his skin: dragons, demons, warrior princes, and, carefully hidden in the midst of flame, the image of a man, sword in hand. Henri had never before told anyone the meaning, hinted at in one of his earlier, lesser known songs: "Walk Through Fire." He'd gotten the piece during one of his sappier moments, back when he'd still lived and breathed music and hadn't yet become a commodity. He'd screamed out the words, "I'd walk through fire for love," and young women had screamed them back at his concerts.

Seb was beautiful without adornment. And solid. A thick coat of reddish-brown curls covered his chest, a lighter coating on his belly, arms and legs. His semi-hard cock matched the rest of him, tall and thick, rising from the only trimmed hair below Sebastian's neckline.

Henri rose up on his toes to enjoy one of Sebastian's kisses and press his own hardening flesh against a furred thigh. For a man who professed to not having been kissed much, Sebastian learned fast.

He caressed Henri's tongue with his own, unhurried, arms held stiffly by his sides. When Henri ran his fingers up Sebastian's spine to grip his shoulders, Sebastian responded, timidly at first, then more assured in his exploration of Henri's back, never venturing below the waist until Henri did.

The curls on Sebastian's chest were interesting to touch, and most of the guys Henri had been with in the last few years trimmed or shaved their body hair. Henri's patch of roughly three dozen chest hairs didn't require much maintenance, though he did trim the dark pelt around his groin. Shaving wasn't happening. A "hmmm" sneaked out.

"What?" Sebastian craned his neck to peer down his chest to where Henri now slithered his fingers though silky swirls.

"I like your fur. It's sexy."

Seb barked a laugh. "It's just hair. Nothing special."

"It is special. It's yours." Oh shit. When had Henri grown so sappy? At least Seb hadn't laughed at him. He rubbed his fingers across Seb's chest. He'd take the roughness over smooth any day.

The more natural look suited Sebastian, making a larger-than-life man more approachable. Henri buried his face in Sebastian's chest hair and inhaled the scent he'd noticed on the piano bench—subtle, not overpowering, and mingling with Sebastian's own natural scent to create an enticing, masculine blend.

He swiped at one of Seb's nipples with his tongue. The puckered skin formed a peak before he treated the other to some attention. Next, he lapped at the skin beneath Seb's ear and was rewarded by a chuckle. Nipping Seb's earlobe earned him a groan. His hand on Seb's chest sent a silent command, and Seb sat on the bed. Henri settled on the floor between his knees.

His scant five o'clock shadow rasped against Sebastian's inner thighs, the strands of his hair inky black against Seb's pale skin. A squeaking bedspring when Sebastian shifted broke the silence. For the first time in nearly a month, Seb was completely quiet, no humming, no vocal drills, no groans. Time to make a change.

Henri flattened his tongue and lapped up the underside of Seb's cock. A gasp sounded above him. If inexperience in kissing meant inexperience in loving, Henri would make this night memorable. They lived very different lives. Sooner or later, reality would crash down and they'd be swept up in their separate worlds. Despite what he'd said at the restaurant, time and distance didn't make for lasting friendships. He'd have to make each moment together count.

He took one of Seb's balls, then the other, into his mouth to gently roll them with his tongue before returning his attention to Seb's shaft. The broad head stretched his lips. He wrapped a hand around the base, stroking the part he couldn't lick. Seb moaned and flopped back onto the bed.

A hand against his face slowed Henri's movements, and he stilled, reveling in Sebastian's panting. Yeah, someone liked this —a lot. When Sebastian relaxed, Henri started again. He slipped a hand down and stroked his own shaft. This might be as much as Sebastian would allow. No sense pushing for more and ending things before they'd properly begun.

Seb had other ideas. He reached down, grabbed Henri beneath the arms, and pulled, scooting back until he lay completely on the bed with Henri resting on top. Seb's saliva-slick cock rubbed Henri's. Damn, that felt good. Seb closed his fist around them both and bucked his hips, driving their shafts together.

Oh, yeah. Good. Really good. Sebastian's warm breath teased Henri's ear. "I… I want you to fuck me."

Oh, hell. Henri clamped his muscles down tight, fighting the urge to come. "I don't have any supplies." Damn the luck.

"I have them." Seb slid a drawer open in the bedside table and fished out lube and condoms. "Not that I use them much."

Not the blushing virgin he seemed like at times, then. Henri slicked his fingers and circled Sebastian's hole. Seb's quick flinch spoke volumes. "I'll go slow," Henri assured him.

He kissed Seb again, easing a fingertip inside. Slender fingers didn't help much against being unused to such invasion. Sebastian kept condoms and lube handy, flinched with the lightest attention, and certainly wasn't well practiced. Yet, he met and matched Henri's exploration, less shy now than during their first kiss.

Seb spread his legs wide, his breath whooshing out as he

relaxed. Henri pushed his fingertip past Seb's ring, working him loose before adding a second finger. He nibbled Seb's neck and lightly humped his thigh.

At last Seb thrust back against Henri's hand, sighing when Henri removed his fingers. A little fumbling got Henri covered, slicked, and ready for action, and he lined himself up with Seb's hole. Slowly he pushed inside. Tight heat gripped him, pulling him in. Ah, damn. So fucking good. Seb's cock dragged against Henri's belly, leaving a trail of dampness from the leaking tip. Henri braced his weight on his arms and took a few cautious thrusts, eyes on Seb's face.

Seb bit his lower lip, face a mask of concentration. He breathed out deeply and gave a little smile while lifting his knees to frame Henri's skinny body. Henri bent for a quick kiss before establishing a rhythm. His brain fuzzed out. Faster and faster he worked in and out, Seb's hands on his hips and lower back guiding the pace. His hair formed a dark curtain, slithering over their skin.

The bed complained. Henri ignored the squeaky cries, focusing on the "Oh, yeah," breathy little grunts and nonwords of his lover. Sweat beaded on Henri's brow. He stopped, fighting the urge to let go. Not yet.

He bit at Seb's nipples, lowering down to give Seb's cock plenty of belly friction. They moved together slowly, languidly, until Seb's bucking kicked the heat up a notch. Urgent thrusting gentled when Henri paused to stare down at Sebastian's face and his kiss-swollen lips. He kissed him again while trailing his fingers down Sebastian's arm.

Sebastian squirmed and Henri smiled. The man was so easy to read. He angled to hit Seb's prostate, writhing his abs against Seb's cock.

The familiar sizzle began in his groin, and he chased ecstasy, picking up the pace. "Ahhh...," he exclaimed, stilling and pumping burst after burst into the condom. His internal muscles spasmed, and he stilled, pleasure washing over him with hurricane force.

Seb rooted a hand between them, stroking himself in earnest. Henri fought valiantly with a too-sensitized cock, resuming his thrusting to push his lover over the edge. Once, twice, three times.

Sebastian cried out, eyes scrunched tightly closed and mouth wide open. "Ah, ah, ah" turned to a jubilant "ha!"—a grimace to a grin.

Henri slowly withdrew and flopped down beside Sebastian, issuing an invitation with wide-open arms. Seb rolled over into the embrace, both of them laughing at the sheer joy of the moment. They fell asleep, a sticky mess. For once Seb didn't seem to mind disorder.

If this was a pity fuck, then whose pity?

ELEVEN

"Need some help?" Henri rose on his toes to kiss the back of Seb's neck. He'd slept like a log and awoken to an empty bed. Now to ensure hunger led Seb away and nothing more.

Seb paused mid-flip of an egg. "Umm... isn't there a law stating this morning is supposed to be incredibly uncomfortable as we both try to pretend last night never happened?" Maybe he expected the eggs to do flips on their own or something, as hard as he stared at the pan.

"You want to forget it happened? I don't." Henri nuzzled Seb's neck. Surely the guy couldn't be serious. After last night?

"Don't you want to?" An unmistakable tension had Seb's shoulders as tight as bowstrings.

Mouth close enough to gust breath over Seb's ear, Henri whispered, "No. And I should be polite here, I suppose, and say, 'Only if you do,' but to be honest, I don't care if you want to pretend or not. I'm not ashamed of last night, and will try to convince you of the need for a do-over at the first opportunity." His heart hammered as he waited for an answer.

Seb clicked the stove off. They had their eggs for lunch.

———

Seb's fingers danced on the piano keys. He sang three words of something Italian and hit a third of the keyboard in a resounding crash. "You, you—" he sputtered, and he started the run up to his entrance again. "You're distracting me."

"Hope so." The piano hummed softly when Henri thunked the underside of the keyboard with his head. "You'll just have to establish your priorities." He couldn't say a word after that: his mouth was full.

Seb leaned back on the bench, offering a helping hand behind Henri's head to speed him up and the other on top to cushion against more blows. The occasional odd notes sounded —played by Seb squirming against the keys.

He gave up all pretext of singing, yet his breathy moans made the sweetest music. A lick brought forth a gasp; sucking his balls made Seb groan. And when Henri took him deep, Seb chanted "Oh, God" in a least three languages.

Henri would never look at a grand piano the same way again.

———

"Loo, loo, loo, loo, loo, loo, loo, loo," Henri sang from the movie theater's stage.

"Again." Sebastian sat in the last row. "A bit louder."

Henri filled his lungs to capacity and repeated the exercise.

"I think you've got it." Seb grinned. "Now get up here and kiss me."

———

"Okay. Deep breath, relax your throat." Sebastian conducted their morning lesson from the comfort of his bed.

"Are we practicing or giving blowjobs?" Not that Henri would complain, mind you, having often fantasized about this very thing.

"Henri?"

"Yes?"

"Is all you think about sex?"

"Only when a hot hunk is close by." He meant it too.

Three days. How short the month had been. Soon Henri would pack up, reattach his trailer to the bike, and head back to... nothing. An invisible hand squeezed his heart. If only he could take Seb with him. But soon Seb would leave to tour with his company. Would he even think of Henri at all? Henri had three short days to ensure he did.

———

Henri sat side by side with Sebastian at the piano, putting the finishing touches on his latest creation. He sang the first line.

"Where have you been?"

Sebastian silenced Henri with a restraining hand on his arm, his voice, his beautiful tenor, mimicking the melody with foreign words.

"Dove sei?"

Henri smiled and sang the second line. "All my life spent lonely."

Again, Sebastian answered in Italian. *"Tutta la mia vita in solitudine."*

"I know you're out there."

"Lo so che sei là fuori da qualche parte."

Sebastian's soulful rendition encouraged Henri's own efforts, and he poured his heart and soul into, "The one I've waited for."

He played the line again on the piano for Seb's, "*La persona che aspettavo.*"

They sang the final two lines in unison, Henri swearing, "I know I'll find you," while Seb harmonized, "*Lo so che ti troverò.*"

They ended with Henri's, "It's just a matter of when," and Sebastian's, "*E' solo una questione di tempo.*"

Beautiful. Fucking gorgeous. If only Seb would give up opera to tour with Henri....

"We could always perform together, like Pavarotti and Friends." The twinkle in Seb's eyes said he was joking.

If only.

———

HENRI SAT on a chair by the window, glasses pulled down on his nose.

"I love a man in glasses," Sebastian commented from his perch on the settee. He held a copy of *Hitchhiker's Guide to the Galaxy* in one large paw. Henri clutched his iPad and would never admit to losing himself in the pages of *The Hunger Games*. Die-hard rocker gods were supposed to read die-hard rocker books, right? Yet he'd snuck a peek at Jenni's copy of the popular young adult novel and had lost himself in Katniss Everdeen's heroics.

"Yeah. Well, feel privileged. You're probably the only person outside my immediate family to see me wearing them."

"Ah, vain, are we?"

Ouch! "I don't give a damn about my appearance—I don't have to see me." The fight slowly leaked out of Henri. "My m... my old manager insisted I not tarnish my image by being a human with poor eyesight." Like anything could possibly be worse than the hard-partying, hard-drinking, hotel-room-smashing hellion tabloids said he was.

"You don't even wear your glasses while driving?"

"I only need glasses to read. It's hell signing autographs without them, but I hate contacts."

"Keeping up appearances? You?"

Henri shrugged. "They weren't my rules."

Sebastian set his book aside, focusing totally on Henri. "You don't strike me as a man who lives by others' rules."

No. No, he wasn't. Took him damned long enough to figure it out. Sebastian returned to reading and Henri settled back, engrossed in another's adventures. Seb laughed out loud. For a moment Henri feared he'd somehow figured out what Henri was reading, and was poking a bit of fun. But no, his gaze traveled back and forth, back and forth, until Seb paused to turn a page. How quaint. An actual, turn-the-pages book.

"Do you always read sci-fi, or is the humor what you read for?" Henri had read *Hitchhiker's Guide* while in his teens.

"Both. I read to de-stress. Humor, sci-fi, and fantasy take me away from the world. I can be the hero, be everything I'm not."

Oh, Seb would surely love *The Hunger Games*. That is, if Henri would ever admit to reading the story. "Reading gives me song ideas." "You're Beautiful When You Read" popped into Henri's head. Nah, no one would play something so sappy but a children's show. Hell, he'd never make the suggestion to Lucas. He might try to sell it, and the last thing Henri's wavering reputation needed was for him to serenade a bunch of puppets. After a few minutes, he glanced up to find Seb watching him. "What?"

"Oh, nothing."

A few minutes later, he caught Seb staring again. "What?"

"Nothing." Seb hastily returned his attention to his own book.

Henri put aside his iPad and stalked across the floor to snatch the book from Seb's hand. "It's not nothing, and you're going to tell me what's bothering you."

"You really want to know?" A flush swept up Seb's face.

"I wouldn't ask if I didn't."

"Well, as long as you remember you asked for it."

"What?"

"You're beautiful when you read."

Oh hell. Now Henri would never get the song out of his head. Seb must pay. "Just for that…." Henri cast the book aside and dug his fingers into Sebastian's ribs.

Sebastian guffawed. "Stop! Stop! I'm ticklish!" He jerked this way and that, but Henri was faster. Seb grabbed Henri's hands, rolling into a ball on the floor to protect his ticklish belly. Henri followed him down.

"Two can play that game." Sebastian traded defense for offense, pinning Henri beneath him. He gouged Henri's sides with his fingers. Henri didn't flinch. "No fair! You're not ticklish!"

"Never said I was."

Their eyes met. All humor fled Sebastian's face. Hovering above Henri, inches separating their lips, in slow motion Sebastian descended, touching, pulling away, then returning to delve deeper.

Their tongues entwined in a slow waltz. The waltz deepened into a tango. Sebastian braced his hands on either side of Henri's head. His lips were soft, his kisses filled with the same passion he put into his singing.

He rolled to his side, taking Henri with him and freeing his hands to slide under Henri's shirt. Fingertips against Henri's nipples, Sebastian blazed a trail over Henri's neck with his tongue.

A little fumbling and Henri managed to get Sebastian's pants open and wriggle his hand inside.

He wrapped his legs around Sebastian's thigh. Supplies were upstairs and damn if Henri intended to stop long enough to go get them. Good, so good. Slickness formed on his palm from Sebastian's leaking cock.

Sebastian's breath came out in little pants. Thrilling tingles started deep inside Henri. Holy hell! He was gonna blow in his pants like some horny teenager. And he didn't fucking care. He kissed Sebastian with all his might, driving his denim-covered cock against Seb's thigh.

Seb's mouth muffled his whimpers and Henri let go, ramming hard one more time and then stilling, his cock pulsing again and again. His hand slipped more easily over Sebastian's flesh, a moan of completion joining Henri's throaty groan.

Every muscle in Henri's body seized and relaxed. His forehead smacked against Sebastian's, and he laughed. When was the last time he'd let go? Played with a lover? Taken such joy from a hand job... well, a hand job for Sebastian, not even a hand job for Henri. And he'd loved every single minute.

"Why are you laughing?" Seb asked.

Henri planted a kiss on his lover's nose. "Because I'm happy."

Sebastian studied him for a minute, his concerned frown melting into something more resembling acceptance. He held Henri close. Henri sucked up affection like a sponge. Who knew when he might find it again?

———

"WHAT'S GOING on?" Henri stood in the doorway, watching a whirling dervish of an opera singer dusting a bookcase he'd already dusted four times.

In a near panic, Sebastian paused long enough to blurt, "I've neglected my housekeeping."

"Seb, calm down. The place is spotless." Henri took the duster and laid it aside. Seb's excuse to put distance between them wouldn't fool anyone. Tomorrow Henri had to go. "Spend the day with me. Tonight, I'll help you get the place in order."

"What do you want to do?" A wrinkle appeared between Seb's brows.

Henri wanted to kiss the worry line smooth again. "Let's go riding."

The most gorgeous of days waited outside, bright blue skies punctuated here and there by puffy clouds. Henri helped Sebastian bundle up, as he insisted on. "If I catch a cold, you have to stay here and nurse me back to health."

"If you catch a cold, I'll spoon-feed you chicken noodle soup." Like Henri's mother had done, many years ago before fame and wealth tore them apart. Now wasn't the time to dwell on the past.

Seb faked a cough. They both laughed.

"You just want to get me into bed."

Seb's beautiful smile gave the summer sunshine a bit of competition. "Anything wrong with that?"

"Nothing at all."

Seb no longer clung when they rode together, though he kept his hands on Henri's waist. Down the winding curves they rode, curves Henri had avoided at first. Seb leaned left and right, keeping pace with Henri, his laughter ringing in Henri's ear.

How could he leave here? He'd felt more at home in Sebastian's old house than in his marvel of glass and marble back in LA. And certainly more so than at the parental home he vowed never to set foot in again.

He leaned back, resting against Sebastian. With helmets on, passing motorists couldn't tell they were both male. And besides, this was Colorado. Maybe not as open-minded as California, but damned close.

The ride wiped away Henri's fears for tomorrow. He relaxed

in the moment, being king of the world, with his Harley, his Sebastian, and millions of miles of open road.

He'd worry about tomorrow tomorrow.

TWELVE

ONE, TWO, three, four, five. Yep, jeans accounted for. Shirts packed. Henri lifted a prescription bottle from the dresser—still half full. He hadn't taken a single emergency pill since Sebastian had challenged him to address the issues and not merely mask the symptoms.

Now to do a quick e-mail check before shutting down his computer.

Tessa had sent him a link to a YouTube video of her playing her bowls. The caption read: "For H." When he got back to LA he owed her dinner, flowers, or something. Or maybe he'd cough up those concert tickets. If he ever found another band to have a concert with. He didn't even notice his own smile at her closed-eyed playing until his lips turned down as he searched through his other e-mails.

Nothing from his sister. Whatever happened to the sweet little girl who'd wanted to be a doctor and save people? Had Margo succeeded in corrupting her? He Googled "Jenni

Lafontaine." Nothing. Ahh…. Too simple, and surely Mom would capitalize on her famous son's name.

Henri clicked a link for "Genevieve Lafontaine," a listing offering an icon resembling Jenni. Holy crap! A barely dressed young woman appeared onscreen in a provocative pose. Take away the makeup and teased-up hair, which added ten years, and the model would be his kid sister.

Henri closed the browser. No, no, no, no, no. As much as he enjoyed making music, doing what he wanted to do, why did he have to pay so heavy a price? Most of his friends had sold him out—except for the one his mother ditched for not being pretty enough. His family had their hands out. Why couldn't life be simple, like it used to be? Oh, yeah, *his* life had stopped being simple the day he'd invaded America's living rooms via a talent show. Before then the highlight of his weekend had been hanging out in the garage with his friends, trying to be a band. Sometimes his lyrics had sucked, other times they hadn't, but he'd thrown himself into the creation. Like Seb did his singing.

He powered down and stashed his laptop in its case. Pining over days long gone wouldn't help anybody. He shoved his laptop case into its bag. Power cord? Check. Phone charger? Check? Meds? Check. Everything that mattered.

Except for Seb.

It being Monday, Henri had the house to himself for packing. Sebastian didn't have to watch him lugging his things out to the trailer.

Afterward, he sat alone in the music room, the grandfather clock ticking off the minutes. A car rumbled up the driveway, Seb home at last. No way to leave without saying good-bye.

"I didn't know you'd still be here." Was that hope in Seb's eyes?

"What? You'd let me leave without a good-bye kiss?"

Seb's bittersweet smile did nothing to dispel the gloom. "I'd prefer it be hello."

Henri crossed the floor and wrapped his arms around the man who'd come to mean something to him over the past few weeks. "I don't want to go."

Seb's eyes appeared a bit moist. "I don't want you to go."

No. Seb couldn't possibly be as sad about their parting as Henri. An idea hit. Not a viable one, but better than nothing. "Come with me."

"Stay."

They shared a sigh. Both had careers to return to. "I'll call you."

"I bet you say that to all the boys." Sebastian's attempt at a smile fell short of sincere.

"No. You're the first." Their lips met. Henri swallowed hard to dislodge the tight ball of worry in his throat. Was this truly good-bye, or "bye for now"?

When they parted, Sebastian released him in more ways than one. "I know how it is. If you get back to LA and those pretty boys, and don't think of me again, I'll understand." He stared at the floor.

Henri wanted to deny it, but Seb wouldn't believe him. Hell, the Henri from a month ago wouldn't have either. "You might understand, but I wouldn't. I've done some pretty dumbass things in my life, but forgetting you would be downright stupid. Besides…." Henri reached down to the settee to retrieve Seb's helmet. "I'm leaving this with you so we can ride the next time I visit."

Seb paled. "No! You can't leave it here. Take it with you." His moment of panic faded. "I mean, what if it's me who visits you? Keep it with the bike and we'll always have it if we need it." Sebastian made a poor liar, but who was Henri to question? While they'd certainly enjoyed each other, they'd made no declarations or promises. And maybe Sebastian had a trail of admirers waiting. A knife twisted in Henri's gut, one he'd never admit to.

"Okay," he finally said. So this was it, then. He gave Seb one final kiss before heading out the door. Sebastian stood on the front porch, growing smaller and smaller in Henri's rearview mirror, and didn't stop waving until he faded from sight.

Before driving five miles Henri stopped at a scenic overlook and rummaged through his saddle bag for his Turtle Fur. One couldn't be too careful when making a living with their voice. The fleecy throat warmer smelled of Sebastian.

Trees, as far as the eye could see, blue sky, puffy clouds. The perfect day to ride... back to LA. No fresh air, no majestic Rockies.

No Sebastian Unger.

No way. No fucking way could he leave. Not now. Not with a dark cloud hanging over him and the best man he'd found in a long, long time wanting him there.

Henri pulled out his cell phone and called his manager. "Lucas? Seb and I are busy working on the new songs. I'm gonna need some more time." He turned the bike around.

———

"Oh God, oh God!" Henri gripped Sebastian's shoulders for leverage and rose up on his knees, only to come down and rise up again. The bedsprings squealed. Sweat dripped down Henri's face. He couldn't stop. Each downward thrust brought him closer and closer to where he wanted to be.

"I'm going to come!" Sebastian warned, gripping Henri's hips.

"I'll meet you there." Henri stroked his cock, settling down on Sebastian's thick shaft. Quivering began deep inside, growing, growing, waves crashing down.

His "Ahhh...." met and matched Sebastian's "Ohhhh...." Henri collapsed onto his lover's chest. What a safe place to rest. A breeze from the open window whispered over his sweat-slicked skin while he caught his breath. If only he could stay here forever.

"Henri?" broke through his post-sex haze.

He summoned up enough energy to answer, "Yes?"

Sebastian's tenor was a gentle purr in his ear. "Not that I'm suggesting anything, but were you planning to leave today?"

Leave? Oh, yeah. Right. Going back to a home that wasn't really home. "Yes. But not right now. I'm too comfy." Henri wriggled to get more comfortable, dragging his hair out of the way.

"How far will you make it this time?" Seb ran his hands up Henri's sides, tracing the ink patterns over his skin.

Good question. "How far did I make it yesterday?"

"Ten miles."

Hmmm... he'd made it eight the day before. "Then today I'll try for twelve." At this rate Henri would be back in LA in about five or six years.

"Since you're coming back anyway, can I ride with you? I need to pick up a few things at the store."

Sounded like a plan.

———

"HENRI? JULY's nearly half over. You need to come back. I keep postponing auditions. I can't put people off forever. Sooner or later Sebastian's gotta get back to work too." Lucas didn't sound happy.

Unease twisted Henri's insides. "How much is he charging for these few extra weeks?" And would payment put a decided kink in the relationship or whatever they'd developed?

131

"He wouldn't take a dime."

The tension in Henri's chest loosened. Seb hadn't charged for the additional time; maybe he'd enjoyed each minute as much as Henri. But the man needed the money. "Pay him anyway."

"Whatever you say. You're the boss. Now, when're you coming back?"

From his perch on the music room settee Henri watched Sebastian's turbo-charged dusting, which meant one thing: Henri couldn't put off leaving any longer, and Sebastian understood. Obligations waited for them both. "I'm leaving today, will stop for the night, and be back Wednesday."

Like a coward he waited until Sebastian drove into town for class, and then he left a single, perfect gladiola on the bedside table.

On the seat of his bike he found a rose.

THIRTEEN

"Henri, you haven't always been on the best of terms, but Giles Forrester is one of the best drummers in the business." Lucas placed one hand on each of Henri's shoulders and stooped, putting them eye to eye and effectively blocking Henri's view of Tall, Dark, and Unreliable. Henri blinked hard to remove the image of Seb bending down for a kiss. An unseen force pressed against his heart. Seb.

Now was not the time. He had work to do. "And why exactly did my mother fire him?"

"Creative differences."

"That's what they all say."

"Give the guy a chance, will ya?"

"Let him play" came out more growly than intended. Oh well. At one time Henri would have thrown up his hands and said, "Fine!" Not anymore. Time to make a stand.

He peered over Lucas's broad shoulder. "From the top —'Ticket to Nowhere.'" Henri grasped his manager's arm and turned him to watch. This train wreck needed witnesses. And if

Giles so much as sniffed once or made a single homophobic or racist comment....

Giles kept the beat, rat-a-tatting on the snare drum, adding a bit of cymbal for effect—with wooden, well-practiced precision. The guy could bang those drums in his sleep, or half wasted. He picked up the tempo, launching into the drum solo from their first hit song. With the other musicians backing him up, Giles had been adequate. Now all Henri heard was the *Bang! Bang! Bang!* of his kid sister pounding on pot lids with a spoon back in her younger days. Hell, Jenni sounded better than this.

Wait? Pot lids? A smile spread across Henri's face. Giles smiled back, probably believing he'd clinched the deal. No way in hell. From now on, Henri only stood with his back toward people who didn't carry knives.

"Giles, what happened with you and the band? And don't bullshit me."

Giles glanced to Lucas and back. Margo had trained him well in who to answer to, with another band, a lifetime ago. Here and now, Henri called the shots. After several long moments Giles answered, "I didn't get along with the new singer."

Henri snorted. "Hell, you didn't get along with me. That's no reason."

The knuckles of Giles's fist turned white. Yeah, the man had a temper, and had taken it out on his bandmates far too often. Henri aimed to build a team, a family, as much as a band. There'd be no room for spoiled brats who couldn't compromise. Weeks on a tour with hateful bigots took a toll on a man's nerves.

Henri swaggered toward the drum kit, extending the half-full plastic cup in his hand. "Play this."

Giles glanced at the cup and back to Henri's face, mouth slack with disbelief. "What?"

A sudden swelling of pride in Henri's chest assured him he'd done the right thing. "You heard me. Play this cup."

Now Giles hazarded a quick "he's still crazy, right?" inquisitive gaze at Lucas. Lucas better have Henri's back, or it wouldn't merely be a worthless piece of would-be drummer taking a hike today.

Lucas nodded. "You heard the man. If he wants you to play a cup, play the damn cup."

Giles raised a drumstick. It hovered a moment, then came crashing down. The plastic fell to the floor in pieces, showering Henri and the drummer with water. Henri didn't even flinch. Droplets clung to his lashes, showing a prism of drummers. "That will be all." Henri carefully enunciated every syllable. Again Giles eyed the manager. Wrong move. "I'm the one with the money," Henri reminded him. "Whatcha looking at him for?"

Lucas shrugged. Good. He still had a job. "We thank you for your time, but it's quite obvious Henri doesn't think you'll be a good fit for his band."

Henri didn't bother to watch the asshole leave, nor did the door slam evoke a flinch. Only when they were alone did his manager say, "I hope you know what you're doing. Where can you find a drummer on short notice?"

"Easy." A confidence unlike anything Henri ever felt settled over him. "I don't want a drummer. What we need is a percussionist." He nodded toward the shattered cup on the floor. Let the man work the puzzle out.

———

"A GARAGE?" Lucas's brows reached for his receding hairline.

"Trust me." Actually, Henri agreed the weathered garage didn't appear to hide the gold they sought. His gut told him otherwise. Either way, he'd get a visit in with someone he'd come to accept as a friend.

A side door opened and out stepped a little girl in blue jeans, pigtails, and a cutoff T.

"Hey, is Te—" The words died on Henri's tongue.

"Hey, Henri! Is this your friend?" The woman he'd seen banging on a box of Chinese takeout with chopsticks bounced up and down on the balls of her bare feet. "I can't tell you how excited I am. When I offered you a private concert, I had no idea you'd take me up on it. Come on in."

Tessa stepped aside, waving a hand toward the inside of the building. The scent of some kind of spicy incense greeted them at the entrance. At odds with the peeling exterior, inside everything seemed to have a place. A trio of weathered bucket seats that had likely come out of sports cars served as seating. "Can I get you something to drink?" Tessa crossed to a full-sized refrigerator and flung open the door to reveal bottled water, diet soda, and beer.

"Nothing for me." Lucas eyed one of the seats skeptically before grunting his way down the worn leather. He'd set his lips into a thin line. Henri couldn't wait to wipe the disbelief off his face.

"Water, please." Henri twisted the cap off the bottle Tessa handed him and took a seat next to Lucas. Tessa appeared a different person entirely in street clothes—smaller, less authoritative. Or maybe her chewing her bottom lip and rocking on her heels added to the illusion of youth. Then again, Henri hadn't explained anything in advance, not wanting to put her on edge. She might blow Lucas away and still not agree to give up her meditation-therapy gig for the exciting world of rock and roll.

"I told my friend here about your playing, and we'd like to hear you." Henri flapped his empty hand at the sheet-covered objects at the other end of the garage. "Go on. Whatever you want to play." He relaxed as much as he could without knocking his seat over.

Tessa turned and folded back a sheet, revealing a plywood table filled with bronze-colored bowls. "Anything?"

"Whatever your heart desires." He pulled out his phone and started recording.

She ducked beneath the plywood and emerged on the other side to fumble with the bowls and a bunch of sticklike objects with balls on the ends. Apparently satisfied, she took a deep breath, closed her eyes, and gently rolled a mallet along the rim of the largest bowl. With her other hand she countered with the smallest. Pure, clear notes rang out. Cold chills danced up Henri's arms. A sharp intake of breath to his left voiced Lucas's reaction. *And he ain't heard nothing yet.*

Faster and faster she shifted from one bowl to the next. She never beat, she never pounded; she encouraged the bowls to sing. And sing they did, a melody of heartbreaking beauty.

Seb would love this! But Seb was gone, who knew where, and who knew when they'd see each other again? *I'm doing this for you, Seb. You might not ever know, you might not care, but I aim to create something awesome, because you showed me how.*

The tune ended on a long note, growing ever fainter until the bowls quieted. Lucas rose to his feet, smacking his hands together. "Amazing!" He shot Henri a cutting glare that said better than words, *But what has this got to do with your band?*

Henri couldn't fight a grin. "Tessa?"

"Yes?"

"Would you mind playing the drums for us?" He operated on pure faith.

Another sheet wound up on the floor to reveal a drum kit unlike any Henri had seen before. There were the usual snares and a bass, but behind a set of Pearls another group of objects sat. One might have started life as a trash can lid—Henri couldn't be sure.

"Anything?" Tessa traded her mallets for a set of more familiar drumsticks and twirled them in her fingers.

"Anything."

"Okay. Remember, you asked for it." She answered his grin with one of her own, appearing so much like an eager teenager.

"How old is she?" Lucas side-whispered.

"Twenty-eight. I'll admit she seems a little offbeat, but trust me."

Tessa tapped softly on the snare drum, finding her rhythm. Once more she closed her eyes and breathed deeply.

"Does she always play with her eyes closed?" Lucas probably didn't even notice that he was patting his leg in time with Tessa's tempo.

"She has every time I've seen her play in person."

"And how many times is that?"

"Counting this one? Twice."

Good thing no flies buzzed around the garage. Lucas might have caught one or two with his wide-open mouth. Whatever he planned to say never came out. Tessa launched in a *doom-da-doom-doom*, rendering thoughts of anything but her music futile. Again, she never banged, never pounded. Instead, she brought the instrument to life in a way Giles never had. Holy shit was she ever good. What she lacked in experience she more than made up with style. Henri's mouth joined Lucas's in hanging open. Just when he thought the impromptu concert couldn't get any better, she spun around, tapping on the garbage can lid in a sweet calypso cadence. That part would fit right into a song Henri'd been working on.

After twenty minutes of the most stunning licks this side of the Rockies, the volume faded and died. Tessa's chest rose and fell with her breathing, and her bangs stuck darkly to her forehead. No wonder she wore her hair in pigtails, to keep it out of the way.

Henri approached, handing over his nearly empty water bottle. "Play this."

"How?"

"However you want."

Tessa took the cap off and blew into the opening, controlling the tones by squeezing the sides. With a grin, she resealed the bottle and stood to place her newfound instrument on her stool. *Rat-a-tat-a-tat,* went her drumstick on the trashcan lid, followed by a clash of cymbals and two licks on the bottle.

Henri glanced back over his shoulder at Lucas, who seemed to have lost the ability to properly close his mouth. "Told you she could play anything."

Lucas whistled and stood, affording her a one-man standing ovation. Henri joined in.

A deeper pink crept into Tessa's cheeks. "You liked it?"

"Liked it? I loved it!" Lucas approached the drum kit. "You look familiar. Did you ever play with Hocus?"

Tessa shook her head. "I haven't played with a band since college."

"What was their name? I might know them." Lucas stepped into full manager mode. Any second now he'd suggest signing her. Too bad Henri spotted her first.

"The Mighty Titans."

Lucas did a double take. "What?"

"The Mighty Titans. I played in the marching band. We ruled halftime."

"You mean, you haven't played drums professionally?"

"Well, no. Why?"

"I swear I've met you somewhere before." Lucas cocked his head to the side, as though viewing her from another angle might jar his memory.

"You might have." Henri stepped forward to wrap his arm around Tessa's shoulders. "We met in rehab."

———

"Did you get the recording I sent? What did you think?" Henri lay across his bed, phone to his ear. He hadn't hidden in his room to take a phone call since high school. Something about Seb, though, reminded him of his first forays into dating. Assuming his old "teenager on the phone" stance seemed right, somehow.

"Yes, I did. Were those Tibetan bowls there at the beginning?"

"Yes." Henri imagined Seb, sitting in the big house alone. If they both weren't busy, Henri could catch a plane and be there in a few hours. And do what? He was a student, asking a teacher's opinion. Sebastian wasn't his boyfriend.

Then why did butterflies dance in Henri's stomach? Why did he hang so much hope on Seb's approval of Tessa? Maybe because of the man's music sense. If he didn't feel Tessa was a good choice, Henri should listen. He'd deliberately sent sound only, not wanting to influence Sebastian unduly. He'd love Tessa, her passion, her fire. If he noticed, sight unseen, that was the effect Henri wanted.

"And the drums later in the recording. Same person?" Seb's voice, rich as a cup of hot cocoa, slid along Henri's spine. Was he lying across his bed too? Or was he sitting at the piano, gazing through the window at the woods? Did his heart ache as much as Henri's?

"Yeah. The woman can play anything. Put a couple of books in front of her, hand her two pencils, and she'll make music." Henri held his breath, waiting for Sebastian's approval.

"You trust her?"

Did he? "Yes, I do."

"Keep her."

One down, three to go. "I can take a day off if you're gonna be nearby. I can come up, or you can come here. Hang out, maybe. I've got some new songs I'd like you to hear." Why did Henri feel the need to show off the new songs? An opera singer's opinion shouldn't matter so much.

"I'm afraid I can't. I've got a full schedule." Seb answered a bit faster than seemed natural. Maybe, since he'd cashed the check, he had no further use for a struggling rocker. Henri's heart dropped to his stomach. Of course Sebastian didn't want any more to do with him. He'd been a paid teacher, no more. The sex had been a bonus.

"I'm sorry I'm wasting your time if you're busy." Henri started to hang up.

Seb stopped him. "I do want to see you. I'm just… busy. I have two days off next week, but my patron is hosting a party and I have to be there. He wants to show off his pet tenor." A touch of resentment flavored the words.

Henri's hackles rose. "Hey, whenever you have time, text me. If there's any way possible, I'd like to touch base with you." He dropped his voice to a whisper. "I miss you. You're the only one I can talk to who doesn't think I'm crazy."

Sebastian restored the mood with a snicker. "I don't *think* you're crazy. I *know* you are."

"That's what I like about you. I'm watched all the time, and anything I say or do gets used against me. With you I can be as crazy as I want to be, and the worst you'll do is raise the eyebrow of death at me. You also don't just tell me what I want to hear, or whatever will get your way." *You save me from myself.*

A belly laugh reverberated over the phone. "If only you'd listen." Seb's laugh ended abruptly. "Ihavetogonowbye!" Silence.

What the fuck?

FOURTEEN

"Now, Henri, I had to pull a few strings, but I managed to get Godfrey Chambers to audition." Lucas's grin suggested Henri should give a shit. "You know, formerly of The White Lions of Kent."

If he were that damned good, the Lions wouldn't have dumped his ass. Henri extended his hand. Might as well show good manners for the ten minutes it'd take to get rid of the asshole. What a pitiful handshake. "Let's see what you got." Henri wiped Godfrey's palm sweat off on his jeans and took his place beside Lucas. Godfrey reeked of tobacco smoke and appeared none too steady on his feet. He tuned up and launched into a riff. Not bad. He stopped and fired up a cigarette, letting it hang loosely in his lips while playing.

Oh hell no. Henri stalked up, grabbed the coffin nail, and flung it to the floor. He ground out the fire with the heel of his boot.

"Hey! What you do that for?" Godfrey took a swipe at Henri and missed.

"Let me ask you something." Henri stood toe to toe with one hell of a tall fucker. Didn't matter. As wasted as he appeared to be, a strong wind might blow him over. "How late were you out drinking last night?"

"Two? Three? What's that got to do with anything?"

"With a show to play at 9:00 a.m.?"

"Show? This ain't no show."

"No, it's an audition, when you'd better be your best. If this is your best, I'd hate to see you on the night we play a half-full tent at some state fair." Henri took a step forward. The guitarist took a step back. "If you don't respect yourself, don't ask me or the rest of the band to respect you. A chain is only as strong as its weakest link. The rest of us plan to get up on stage and give it our all, night after night. We deserve better than you. Now go on, get out of here."

He vaguely heard Lucas following the guy to the door, making apologies. No more half-assed shit. Plenty of musicians would give choice body parts to be a part of this band. Henri didn't need anyone only in it for the money, women, or whatever else motivated a musician besides the music in their souls. Holy shit. The music in their souls. "Lucas!"

The manager who definitely earned his money came trotting back. "Henri, what are you doing? We'll never find a lead guitarist if you keep this up!"

"I already found him."

"What? Who?"

"Back when I was on a talent show, a kid named Michael Lindley competed. Six strings, twelve, four, you name it. If it has strings, he'd tear it up."

"Michael Lindley? I've never heard of him."

"That's 'cause he didn't make it to the finals. He did join my first band for a while before my mother tossed him out." And the

143

reasons why might present more problems than simply his plain face.

———

"WHAT INSTRUMENTS do you play?" Lucas studied Michael with all the skepticism Henri had expected.

Henri turned his smug setting down to "low." Let Lucas ask questions to his heart's content. If Henri's band needed to be distinctive to get attention, he'd struck pay dirt in the originality department.

Michael Lindley was one of a kind, and quite possibly took the honor of being the lankiest guitarist on the planet. Even without his Gibson clasped before him, he hunched over, as though any minute he'd launch into a killer riff. He'd played air guitar almost constantly during the rehearsals for the talent show. Only one small problem had kept him from making finals. And come hell or high water, Henri would work out the details. The band needed uniqueness. Michael brought uniqueness in truckloads.

Michael set his guitar down with an affectionate pat, then shoved his hands into his pockets, gazing off to a point left of Lucas's shoulder. "Guitar, fiddle, dulcimer, banjo, harp." From anyone else the claim might sound boastful. Somehow Michael managed to come off humble.

"What bands have you played with?"

"Just Henri's, and only for a few weeks."

Lucas shot a wide-eyed, raised brow glare at Henri, "What the fuck?" written on his face.

Henri entered the fray. "Michael, can you play the original piece you wrote, the one that got you into the competition?"

Michael's face shaded to red. "That old thing? Nobody wants to hear something I wrote during my pimply teenaged years."

Henri fought back a snort. The guy's pimply teenaged years weren't long gone. Time to play on a musician's ego. He might be humble, but Michael's musical talents were his pride and joy. If only he didn't freeze in front of audiences. But they'd fight that battle later.

First to convince Lucas, then to convince Michael. "I loved that song, the cool transition, the slides. What do you say? A little demo?"

A muscle clenched in Michael's jaw. He darted a gaze from Lucas to Henri and back. The breath he blew out ruffled overly long bangs, revealing more of his face. If Henri needed to expand his fan base, he'd certainly win over some punk rockers with a Joey Ramone look-alike on lead guitar, while Tessa would pull in teen girls with aspirations of being in a band, and guys who preferred their women cute over sultry.

"Sure," Michael finally replied.

Henri and Lucas plunked down in two wooden seats designed for the fifth and sixth graders who unknowingly learned music from one of the finest musicians to ever live, in Henri's opinion. Michael didn't climb on the stage of the school music room. Instead he perched on a stool a few feet away, snugging the guitar up to his chest. Mother-of-pearl inlay spelled out "Sylvia." He still named his instruments, did he? His fingers flitted over the strings, faster than the eye could follow. And this was just his warm-up.

A small smile lifted the edges of his mouth, and he stared down at his Gibson, never once glancing up at his audience of two. The smile fell. The music began, dozens of notes, faster than lightning. Pleading, begging, tugging at the heart. Desperation. Longing. All from six strings.

The hairs on Henri's arms rose. Seb. He needed Seb. The comfort of the man's warmth, the security of being held. He pictured his lover, head back, eyes closed, arms thrown wide as if to embrace the music.

If this haunting melody came from Michael's pimply teenaged years, he'd win Grammies with the compositions he probably still hammered out every night and stored in a note-book. Henri'd been privileged to take a look inside the notebook. He sat in the presence of greatness. And Michael had no clue.

Now for Henri to find a way to overcome the man's one small obstacle.

———

THE *ENTER the Dragon* Bruce Lee T-shirt was Henri's first hint of Colton Ferguson marching to the beat of his own drummer—the headband came in second. The keyboardist's choice of "Kung Fu Fighting" for his audition put the icing on the cake. But damn, he gave the song his all.

"Okay, but try this." Henri handed over a music sheet for a new number he'd been working on.

Colton hit a few random chords, staring at the sheet, then launched into the melody only before heard in Henri's head. Colton paused and scratched his head. "Can I make a suggestion?"

"Sure?" Now the audition got interesting.

"Instead of…" Colton pecked out a simple measure. "…how about…." His fingers raced over the keyboard.

"Do that again." Henri added vocals to the score. Colton was right. A little tweaking went a long way. "I like it."

Colton bowed.

"He realizes he's from Topeka and not Hong Kong, right?" Lucas side-whispered.

"I don't care where he's from," Henri replied. "We've found our man for keyboards."

"Actually, Bruce was born in San Francisco, not Hong Kong," Henri's new keyboardist offered.

———

"JAKE STEADMAN, damn but I'm glad to meet you." In his teen years Henri had idolized Alternate Phantasm, Jake's former band. And Jake's mean bass playing stood out in his memory.

"You sure you want an old fart like me uglying up your band?" Jake reared back in his rocking chair, propping a pair of worn cowboy boots on the porch railing. He'd come a long way from packed auditoriums to an aging farmhouse in the middle of nowhere.

"If I didn't want you, I wouldn't have come all the way to Wyoming to track your ass down." Jake had the skills, his band had broken up, and as he'd alluded to, a whole lot of younger competition vied for any available openings. Henri wanted Jake. He needed a bass player, and a good one, with a proven track record. Jake needing the money might encourage loyalty too. But never far from Henri's thoughts were how he'd spend the extra days if he managed to put his band together early.

Henri had made up his mind. Lucas played businessman. "Come out to LA for a few rehearsals. See what you think and if you fit in."

"Oh, I'll fit in all right. Got me a chance to back up Henri Lafontaine? A man would have to be crazy to pass up such an offer." Jake's drawl "could melt ice," as Henri's late grandma used to say.

His favorite bassist had heard his music? "Really?"

"Sure. Got a teenaged daughter who plays your music from sunup to sundown." Jake winked. "But I won't hold a rebellious kid's taste in music against you. She will, however, kick my ass if I say no to her idol."

Henri left Jake and Lucas to hash out the details. He had a phone call to make.

"Seb? You wouldn't happen to be free, would you? I've got four days, and I want to spend them with you. "

Another reason to come to Casper to visit Jake in person: only a four and a half hour ride to Evergreen. Lucas didn't know it yet, but he was about to take a flight back to LA and leave Henri the rental car. Ah, nice to be the rock god calling the shots.

———

HENRI SHAVED a half hour off the GPS's estimated time of arrival, and didn't even bother to grab the bags he'd stowed in the trunk. He ran, kicking up dust in Seb's front yard, and bounded up the stairs two at a time. Seb met him at the front door, stark naked, dragged him inside the house, and slammed the door. Maybe he'd missed Henri after all.

Sebastian tugged at Henri's clothes while hauling him up the stairs. They didn't quite make it to a bed. In a tangle of arms and legs they rolled on the floor, connected at mouth and groin. Had it been only two weeks?

Henri wrapped a hand around Seb's cock. "Bed!" he commanded. Somehow they made it to the closest option—the four poster in Henri's old room. Sebastian jerked a drawer out of the bedside table. A rain of brightly colored packets showered the floor. They hadn't been there two weeks ago. A tube skittered across the hardwood floor.

"Oh no, you don't." Henri hopped off the bed and chased the escapee down. He slicked up his fingers and returned to the bed. Sebastian's cock stood out among its bed of surrounding curls. A feast for the mouth. Henri sucked the head in, sliding down the length while working his fingers against the resistance at Sebastian's opening. Seb laced his fingers in Henri's braided hair, bringing him down more fully. Oh hell yeah. He loved the man's forceful side.

The pushing turned to tugging. "Up."

Henri grabbed a packet from the floor and sheathed himself. He slid into Seb's body little by little, painting a swath with his tongue over Sebastian's chest. Damn how he'd missed this. Framed by his lover's thighs, he erased two weeks of loneliness. In, out, breathe. He twined the fingers of one hand with Sebastian's. "Stroke yourself," he ground out.

He matched his rhythm with Seb's, taking his cue to slow down or speed up. For the past two weeks, most men he'd met were too thin, too fragile, or otherwise didn't capture his interest. With Seb he let go. Seb liked rough. Seb liked lots of touching. Seb wasn't worried about mussing his hair, and he damned sure wasn't worried about damaging what a surgeon's knife had wrought.

His breath came out in gasps and moans, and he frantically tugged between their bellies. Close. So close. Henri slammed in. "Am I hurting you?"

"Oh, God, no."

Harder. Faster, Henri wrapped his arms around Seb and pushed in as far as he could. Pulse after pulse exploded from him, and still he thrust in, until spatters hit his abdomen. He slid out and connected their mouths.

Desperate kisses grew less frantic, their breathing and heart rates slowed. Only then did Henry notice the breeze blowing in from an open window, carrying the crisp scent of the great outdoors.

Damn, but it was good to be home.

———

A LAZY Sunday morning spent in bed, where they'd pretty much stayed since Henri's arrival. He'd been here three days and hadn't even taken his bag out of the car—not that he'd needed clothes.

"How's the band coming along?" Seb lay on his back, a thin sheet offering up tantalizing glimpses of his body.

Henri rolled to his side to rest his head on Seb's shoulder. "Good. I found someone for keyboards who thinks he's Bruce Lee."

"I liked Bruce Lee." Seb's energetic nod rocked his shoulder, which, in turn, rocked Henri's head. "But can he play?"

"Like nobody's business. And I found a bass player. You probably don't remember them, but he played with Alternate Phantasm back in the nineties. He crashed, burned, and now he's back. He's a fixer-upper, but he's talented."

"I've never heard Alternate Phantasm, but if he played in the nineties, isn't he a bit older than the rest of your band?" Seb. Never judging, merely offering the voice of reason.

"No one else wanted to take a chance on him because of his age and background."

"What is he? Late forties, maybe? Forty is young for an opera singer."

"For a rocker it's the kiss of death. But he's got the sound." Boy, did he ever.

"Aren't rockers supposed to be thin, young, and beautiful? Isn't skinny and hot a requirement? Unless you're one of the Stones, that is."

"What? You mean I'm not young and beautiful enough?" Actually, Seb had never once complimented Henri on his looks —only on his music. The slight soreness in his posterior said Seb at least found him useful. Many times in the past, Henri had been just a fuck, and happy for the short-term arrangement. He didn't want casual with Seb. He wasn't sure exactly what he did want, but a little genuine affection wouldn't hurt.

But no. Soon he'd leave again to go back to life in LA while Seb went off to wherever he needed to go. He'd be grateful for the time they'd had; he didn't have the right to ask for more. "I've got a problem I hope you can help me with."

A laugh rumbled through Seb's chest. "I thought I just did."

"A *musical* problem."

Henri's arm-pillow curled around him, pulling him closer to Seb's fur-covered chest. "What kind of problem?"

"I believe I've found the best lead guitarist ever to pick up an instrument." An understatement, plain and simple.

"I listened to the demo you sent. He's talented. What's the problem?"

"He's okay with small groups, and the kids he teaches, but in front of an audience, he freezes. Can't play a note. We played together for a few weeks with my first band. My mo... manager didn't think he was worth the trouble—or pretty enough."

Sebastian responded after several moments of quiet. "That is a problem. Has he been to a therapist?"

"Yes. And he's tried meds, but says they sap his creative drive. Not only does he play, he writes his own songs too."

"You signed a guitarist who can't play concerts? You could use him for a studio musician and find someone else to tour with."

Yes, Henri could. But he'd made his mind up, and he wouldn't settle for less than the best. Michael was the best. "Yeah, but I want Michael. He's incredible."

They lay in silence for a while, Henri soaking up the tranquility of being with his own personal calm and fully trusting Seb to suggest a viable solution.

"Do you attend church?" wasn't an answer Henri expected.

"Do what?"

"Come." Seb slid his arm out from under Henri's head. "If we hurry, we can make eleven o'clock services."

"We're going to pray for Michael's stage fright?" While Henri hadn't actually attended Sunday services much in his life, he'd sort of assumed that, vampire-like, he might incinerate upon breaching the door. He'd been told he was bound straight for Hell on many occasions—to his face, via letter or e-mail, phone calls, and one deranged psycho had painted the words on his naked body and offered to send Henri there personally.

If he did manage to make it past the doors, the good people inside the fancy building with the steeple might burn him at the stake after taking one look at his sleeve tats. It took a special breed to appreciate winged-gargoyle body art.

"You'll see. I do believe we'll find our answer in church."

———

Suit, suit, suit. Dress. Hat. A parade of folks passing Henri's last-pew perch dressed far finer than his blue jeans and black band shirt. He scrunched farther down, the better to hide his tats. Beside him, Seb wore pressed khakis and a button-down. "How good to see you!" a woman exclaimed, bypassing Henri to hug Seb. "Are you going to sing for us this morning?"

Seb ducked his head, his auburn ringlets contrasting with his suddenly red face. "No, ma'am. Just visiting. I'd like you to meet my friend, Henri Lafontaine."

Here it comes. The squeals of recognition, or maybe condemnation depending on what the woman had heard. Neither happened.

"Nice to have you here, Henri. Are you related to the Lafontaines in Mercer, by any chance?" The woman wandered off after a moment or two of small talk. Henri hadn't been able to go out in public unnoticed in years. Maybe the paparazzi had the same fear of being reduced to ash and didn't enter cross-bearing buildings. Yet here he sat, tattoos, long hair, and all. Hmmm... now if he held hands with Seb....

Stage curtains drew back to reveal a band, complete with a tattooed lead singer. Really? Dang! Since when had churches gotten so progressive? Instead of hymns, the band performed rock music with a religious message. Wow! Rock in church.

Once the band finished, Seb whispered, "Watch closely."

A thin man in a three-piece suit took to the stage. "Good morning," he said into a microphone. "And welcome."

"What am I supposed to watch?" Henri whispered back to Seb.

"Look at his feet."

Holy crap! Henri stared at the man now reading from a Bible. No feet! Or rather, the image faded toward the stage. "How?"

"Reverend Cole preaches at three different churches. He's physically at one. The rest are holographic projections. Pretty good likeness, isn't it?" Seb's curls framed a wide grin.

A hologram. They'd found a way for Michael to appear onstage.

Seb was a fucking genius. Oops, did Henri actually think that in church? He waited for the lightning bolt.

FIFTEEN

HENRI FACED his new band in his basement studio. He didn't have the fancy equipment necessary for professional-quality recordings, but the former owner, an eighties era producer, had left the room relatively intact. The perfect place to rehearse. First, a little business. "I'm gonna tell you up front that I'm in recovery. I don't do drugs, hell, I don't even drink anymore, and having someone fire up a joint on one of my bad days might set me back about ten thousand dollars' worth of therapy. Hookers and Cocaine gained a reputation for a drug band. That stops here. Anyone got a problem?"

Tessa chimed in first. "I'm drug tested on a regular basis. Not worth flushing four years of college down the tube. Besides, I'm on a natural high." Her leg bounced up and down. Henri wanted to tell her to knock it off, but even if she did, it wouldn't last.

Whirr, chik! She spun around in her chair.

And so it began. "Jake?" The bassist's partying reputation once rivaled Henri's own.

Whirr, chik!

Henri gritted his teeth.

"I've got six kids with four different ex-wives. I can't afford drugs, man."

Fair enough. "Colton?"

Whirr, chik!

Mental note: banish moveable chairs from the room.

"My body is a temple." The keyboardist smacked his hands together and bowed. Someone really should tell the guy he wasn't Bruce Lee.

"That leaves you, Michael."

A muscle twitched in Michael's jaw when Tessa whirled again. Ahh… it wasn't only Henri's nerves she trampled on.

"Dude, my family's from rural Alabama, the land of 'hold my beer and watch this.' We don't do drugs. Too Hollywood for us. We'd rather hang out at bars, get drunk, fight about football, puke behind bushes, and yell, 'Roll Tide!' at inappropriate moments. We do like our Crimson Tide football."

Jake asked, "What about speed?"

All eyes roved to Tessa, spinning 'round and 'round in her chair. Oh, Tessa and speed? Not pretty at all. "Anybody who gives Tessa speed is dead."

As one, they snapped, "Tessa! Stop that!"

She stopped turning. Her leg bounced. Here they went again.

"It's only fair to tell you what happened with my last band. You have a right to know." No telling what they'd heard. Time for Henri to clear the air.

"You don't have to tell us, Henri." Easy for Tessa to say. She'd already gotten a full history.

Jake, Colton, and Michael kept quiet. At least they gave him the courtesy of not asking. "After a concert a fan brought me a drink—laced with enough GHB to keep me out for days." Or kill him, if not for a handy guard with first responder training.

155

A collective groan rose from the group.

"He tried to take me back to my room, where cops found rope, duct tape, and a video camera. No telling what he planned. He's still out there, and may try again. Being around me may put you in danger." Best to let them know the truth and be prepared.

Jake spoke up first, with his deep drawl. "Dude, I've played backwoods country bars in towns no one's ever heard off. One deranged fan is nothing compared to a room full of rednecks who've had a few beers too many."

"Why can't they find the guy?" This from Michael. "Get Tessa to read your terror cards or something. Shake some crystals at you for protection."

"Hey!" Tessa shouted. "They're tarot cards, not 'terror.'"

Colton assumed some kind of weird pose. Martial arts? Or vogueing? "My body is a weapon. I will protect you."

First a temple, now a weapon? What was this guy, some sort of Kung Fu monk?

Tessa's leg bounced faster.

Next time Henri called Doc Worthington, he'd mention "a friend." There had to be a name for what ailed the woman.

"Okay." Time to move on. "Now that you know what kind of deranged lunatics might be after me, let's make some music. You've been over the selections?"

Michael's fingers flew on his guitar's fingerboard, proving he'd at least practiced the new version of "A Matter of When." "No offense, dude, but I've heard you sing. Can you actually hit the high C on 'Ice Inside'?"

Details, details. But the song wasn't the same without the high notes. "We rehearse as is. When we get there, we'll adjust as needed." And if all went according to plan, adjusting wouldn't be necessary.

"Whatever you say. You're the boss." To his guitar Michael murmured, "C'mon, Sylvia. Time to rock."

The "yes, I am the boss" didn't quite make it off Henri's tongue. "No. We're a band. This isn't about me but about all of us." Where the hell had the "all for one" speech come from? Tessa, Michael, Jake, and Colton stared back at Henri. Each of them was the best he and Lucas could find. If there was a weak link, it had to be Henri himself, with his limited vocal range and less than stellar history. In the past he'd relied on kickass lyrics to make up for the lack, which had only gotten him so far. He'd been working to improve, but had he improved enough? He focused a determined gaze on Michael. "I'll hit the fucking note. 'A Matter of When,' from the top."

Michael nodded and fingered the intro silently once before launching into a wake-the-dead solo. Ha! That'd get an audience's attention. Jake joined on the count of five, followed by Colton and Tessa. Lastly, Henri cleared his throat and joined his band in making music.

"Where have you been?
All my life spent lonely,
I know you're out there,
The one I've waited for...."

He sang toward the band, watching their timing, how they interacted. This being their first rehearsal, he expected frequent stops. Instead, Tessa caressed her drum kit, downplaying her role for the sake of the melancholy tune. No egos took over, none of the musicians attempted to dominate. They played together like a well-oiled machine, with only the odd note or two marring the perfection.

"I know I'll find you,
It's just a matter of when."

The song ended. Nothing spectacular. It wouldn't be a hit single without major work, but it would serve as a nice intermission between the edgier pieces. And it held appeal for romance-seeking fans.

The next song on the list required more skill, and featured the dreaded "C." Henri's private attempts succeeded about 50 percent of the time, but he wasn't ready to sacrifice the chorus yet, not without a fight. He needed a chocolate bar and a high shelf, and the new album needed this hard driving song to keep his heavy metal fans happy and balance out the softer tracks. "Okay, now for 'Ice Inside.'"

Michael made eye contact but didn't speak. He began playing, the others joining in. After the introduction, Henri filled his lungs per Seb's instruction and imagined reaching way up into the pantry. *I can do this.*

"Ice inside where his heart used to be,
Though he hides it well so none can see,
With a smile on his face he fools passersby
I know him well, I see the lie.
They only see what he wants them to see,
But he can never hide the truth from me."
So far, so good. The chorus approached. And the "C."
"Some may believe,
Some won't care,
Deep within he hides despair.
Lonely with his lover near,
The pain is more than he can bear."

He pulled in a deep breath and wailed, "There's ice inside, there's ice inside."

Fuck.

"Did somebody step on a cat?" Jake asked, an agonized grimace on his face.

"Dude, we can take it down a bit," Michael offered. "How about this?" He improvised the chorus in a lower key.

Henri sighed. "No, I can do this. Take five." He stalked out of the room and up the steps to his living room. "Loo, loo, loo, loo, loo, loo, loo, loo." After pulling in a few deep breaths and exhaling slowly, he tried again. "Loo, loo, loo, loo, loo, loo, loo, loo." One eye on his watch, he tried to recall all Sebastian had told him.

No one seemed to have moved out of place when he returned. "Try it again, from the top." He gave Michael a pointed look. "The original notes."

His heart sped when they reached the fateful chorus.

"There's ice inside, there's ice inside."

Holy shit! Was that sound coming from him? Henri continued to exhale, gaze locked with Michael's, which reflected Henri's wide-eyed shock. He vaguely noticed the band's silence. The note continued. Purer, sweeter, higher. Henri's voice soared, filling the room even without the microphone he'd dropped to his side. At last his lungs emptied, but the note never wavered. The perfect C ended on his command.

Jake and Colton seemed unmoved, not being privy to Henri's previous vocal limitations. Tessa and Michael stared with blank faces, jaws hanging open.

Tessa spoke first. "That was amazing!"

Michael brought reality crashing down. "But can you do it again?"

Henri's throat didn't burn as it had in the past when he'd overreached. "Only one way to find out."

On the second go-round, he never said a word to his band,

but Michael joined in, as he'd done years ago while with the band that would later be Hookers and Cocaine. His smooth tenor wrapped around Henri's deeper tones, taking the edge off, and reminding Henri of singing with Sebastian. Hookers and Cocaine had never sounded this good.

At the precise moment Henri found perfection, perfection took wing and flew on the voice of an angel. Tessa's sweet soprano wove in and out of the patchwork Michael and Henri created. On the final verse, deeper tones added to the mix, from bass guitar and bassist.

The song ended. Henri didn't. Nodding to his band, directing with his hands, together they created a sound that blew away his wildest expectations. God, he needed Seb right now.

———

"A MAKEOVER? Why the hell do we need makeovers?" Henri glared at Tessa.

Tessa glared back. Her friend backed up a few steps away from Henri's folded-arms indignation. There wasn't one damned thing wrong with Henri's appearance. Just because he'd made the worst-dressed list three years in a row didn't mean jack shit but that nosey paparazzi always seemed to catch him while taking out the trash or working on his bike.

"No offense, Henri." Tessa batted her eyes, reminding Henri of his sister, the non-made-up-to-look-forty version. "I've been to a few of your concerts, have some of your music, and check your website on a regular basis." A natural blush overpowered her cosmetics. "And let's say that, as much as I adored you and your music...."

In rehab she'd acted like she hadn't recognized him prior to his first admission. "Go on."

"Well...." She scraped her top teeth across her lower lip. "You kinda always looked... well... scruffy."

"Scruffy? I look scruffy to you?" Henri spun to face his remaining band members. Granted, it being Friday, he hadn't shaved the few scraggly whiskers on his chin, and he hadn't bothered to control his air-dried hair—it poofed out in a fluffy mass. Then there was the whole "holey T-shirt" thing, and jeans nearly worn through in the seat. Dammit, comfort came before style, in his book. "Guys, do I look *scruffy?*" He patted at his errant hair.

Colton turned away, guilt in his eyes. Jake puffed his cheeks and blew out his breath while slowly nodding. Michael, who'd known him since high school and who favored the same casual look while not teaching, declared, "Hey, you look fine to me."

"It's okay if you want to be adored by teenaged girls who want to terrify their parents by swearing they're gonna marry you someday," Tessa said. "Is that what you want, or do you want fans old enough to vote, and with enough sense not to elect candidates based on how cute they are?"

Uh-oh. Better stop before Tessa started in on politics. She made a good point, not that Henri would concede.

"Besides, you've complained about headaches. Your hair looks pretty heavy. Have you considered that maybe it's the weight causing the problem?"

She might have a point. Not to mention getting wound up in his hair in his sleep, and having to force the mass underneath his helmet. Tangles, spending precious time trying to beat curls into submission. Cutting off pieces when his hair got caught in something.

His mother forbade him to cut his hair, saying he'd ruin his reputation.

To hell with his reputation.

Would Seb like his hair shorter? "Let's see what you've got in mind. Tessa, you go first."

———

"Aww… YOU look so pur-day." Michael laughed and skipped away from Henri's swat. Damn. Somehow Tessa's friend had managed to tame the locks hundreds of stylists had backed away from in fear. Granted, his "every hair for itself" 'do had been as much a part of his image as the black leather he'd worn while performing with his old band. He ran a hand over his much-shorter hair and stroked his now-smooth chin. Would Seb like it?

"It makes those sexy eyes of yours stand out, and we can finally see your face. Your female fans will slide right out of their chairs." Tessa accepted Henri's tag and swatted Michael for him, since she stood between the two. Strange. Michael didn't duck Tessa's hand, and he wore a strange smile while rubbing the spot she'd hit.

"Um… is that a good thing?" Oh shit. Had Henri said that aloud?

The guys trotted on ahead; Tessa sidled up beside him. "The men are gonna like it too." She laughed and took off toward the rest of the band. Men in general he wasn't worried about. Only one. Though Seb would surely approve of Henri's hair tucked into a bag, on its way to Locks of Love to help a child with cancer.

They entered the mall together, Henri pulling a hat down over his head to hide. His long hair might no longer give him away, and he no longer stood out among his shorter-haired bandmates. Now they all blended in with the afternoon shoppers, with the exception of Jake, who claimed to be too old to "hang out at the mall." With teenaged daughters, he probably spent enough time there without being dragged back by Henri and the crew.

Damn, but he felt so much lighter, and the beginnings of a

headache faded the moments his hair fell to the floor. Tessa might have been on to something.

"Over here," Tessa called, pressing her nose to the glass of a department store window. Inside the shop dwelled Goth Heaven.

"Not my taste." No way was Henri struggling into skinny jeans to try to move onstage.

"Who said anything about you?" She wormed her way between Henri and the window to get through the door. Henri rolled his eyes and followed her inside. Best to keep her close. She had a tendency to wander off.

Twenty minutes later they emerged with a black lace hat and fingerless gloves. "Tessa, repeat after me: 'I am not Sheila E.'"

"I'm not!" Her indignation gave way to a grin. Holy hell. She was gonna get carded at every club they played. "I'm Tessa E.!" She marched over to where the remaining band members waited on a bench.

"Oh my, God! I know you!" a teen girl squealed. Fuck no! Henri wanted to shop in peace. The fan charged right for…. Michael. "You're Michael Lindley, aren't you? Tell me, what's Henri Lafontaine really like? He's dreamy!"

Dreamy? Dreamy! Henri was *not* dreamy! That was so "boy band."

Tessa flashed an "I told you so" smile.

What to do when a fan squealed and bounced two feet away, harassing a bandmate? Why, throw the bandmate to the wolves. Henri spun on his heel and made a quick escape.

After downing a hot dog and soda in the food court, he ventured into the main part of the mall again. He found Tessa at a perfume counter, bottle in hand. "Which do you like best, Acqua di Gio—" She sprayed a card and held it under his nose. "—or Burberry?" She repeated the process with the other fragrance.

"Both are nice, but aren't they a bit masculine for you?" If rhyme or reason existed in her fashion sense, Henri hadn't yet spotted a pattern.

"It's for you, silly! I got you cleaned up, now to make you smell nice."

Henri sniffed a few bottles. What did Sebastian wear?

"Well?" Tessa waited, hand on her hip.

"Let me think about it." He shot toward the back of the store to text Seb in private. *Buying cologne, which u like? Acqua di Gio or Burberry?* Answer, answer, answer, answer!

His phone pinged almost immediately. *Anything but Burberry.*

"Acqua di Gio it is!" Tessa would be proud.

Henri glanced around to make sure of no witnesses, ripped off his hat, and took a few quick pictures of himself with his phone. The best one he sent via text and hoped Seb wouldn't laugh. His phone chimed a moment later with a reply. *You clean up nice.*

Hey! He recalled the first time he'd met Sebastian, the "clean up before dinner" comment. Did he really used to look scruffy?

Maybe.

———

THE STUDIO wasn't the most state of the art Henri'd ever been in, but it wasn't the worst. At least he wasn't starting at rock bottom again. Besides, if he and his newly acquired group couldn't provide the goods, no amount of equipment would turn them into Grammy winners.

Lucas observed from the sound booth. A burly technician sat beside him. Henri addressed them both. "What we're trying to create is a studio jam session effect. Nothing too structured." Not for 'Ice Inside.' If they even came close to their practice session, he'd be a happy man.

One by one his band arrived. What the hell?

So much for their afternoon with a stylist.

Colton's attire suggested he'd been to a dojo for training, Jake's jeans and T-shirt had survived at least four different presidents, Michael appeared ready to mow the lawn—in slept-in clothes—and Tessa....

"What are you wearing?" A filmy, gauzy creation floated around her slender frame. She stood out as a rose among thorns.

"I spent the morning at the Ren Faire and got back a little late. Sorry. This is my fairy costume."

"You're going to play in that?"

"At least I left the wings in my car." A small favor.

Okay. Whatever. They planned to record, not film. "Let's do this."

Lightning struck twice, or rather, the magic of their practice crackled within the room. Gorgeous. Absolutely gorgeous.

Kids at Christmas didn't grin as broadly as Lucas when he emerged from the control booth. "Damn, boy! Whatever's gotten into you, I like it."

Now probably wasn't the time to mention Seb's name. "What? You doubted me?"

Lucas slapped Henri on the back. "Not for a minute." His smile fell. "It's hard to pitch an album if the band doesn't have a name."

Henri took in his band: lanky, T-shirted Michael leaning down to talk to a living, breathing, fairy maiden, while blast-from-the-past Jake stared over a white-clad shoulder at something Colton pecked out on the keyboard. Henri was crazy as hell if he thought this would work. Too bad Crazy as Hell was already taken as a band name. Alternate Reality?

Maybe he should leave the decision making to someone else. "Tessa, if you had to label us with one word, what would it be?"

She tilted her head to the side, favoring each band member

with a lopsided smile. "Either 'mismatched' or 'delusional.' Take your pick."

Mismatched? Delusional? Henri rolled the words around inside his head and broke out in a grin. Oh hell yeah. "How about both? We're Mismatched Delusions."

SIXTEEN

"Okay, Tina, sweetheart, why don't you climb up on the back seat of the bike?" The photographer flipped a hand at her: *Up! Up!*

"Her name is Tessa," Henri growled. He glowered at Lucas, sending the mental message, *Where the hell did you find this asshat?*

Lucas replied with a raised brow, a reminder of Sebastian and his animated expressions. "Trust me. This guy rocks cover art."

Henri steadied his Harley for Tessa to crawl up on the seat. The last person to sit there had been Seb. Goose bumps adorned Tessa's arms. She must be freezing. If she'd been Henri's sister, he'd insist she go put more clothes on. The leather miniskirt and bustier didn't leave much to the imagination.

"Now, you." The photographer gestured to Henri. "Stand in front of her, and grab the edge of the seat."

"Here?" Henri placed his hand dead center, where his ass normally perched.

"No, further up."

He slipped his palm north a few inches. "Here?"

"Higher."

Henri ran out of driver's butt real estate and moved up to the passenger seat. "Here?"

"Higher."

He glanced up at a wide-eyed Tessa. "If you're asking me to put my hand between her legs, I will not disrespect my drummer, or any other woman. She's a serious musician, same as the rest of us, and I'll treat her no differently." Asshole. He sure as hell wouldn't ask Henri to appear to fondle Michael, Jake, or Colton.

Behind him Jake whispered to Michael, "I'm not a serious musician. Are you a serious musician?"

Henri barked, "Jake, you aren't helping."

The photographer on the brink of losing a job didn't know when to shut up. "Sex sells. Now, Tina, lean over. Show me some cleavage."

"Lucas?" Henri glared at their manager, who shifted to focus one mean case of gimlet eye on the photographer. Time to cut their losses. If they got crappy cover art, at least it wouldn't be exploitative.

"Yes?" Lucas gave his approval with a nod.

"Show this guy the way out. And get someone we can work with."

"I'll get right on it."

Henri turned to his band. Michael shrugged out of a black leather jacket. "Man, that thing's too damned hot."

Jake attempted to scratch his leg through his leather pants. "Anybody got a ruler… or something?"

Tessa's biker girl from Hell garb wore her instead of the other way around—what little bit there was. Fuck. They'd been made up to look like Hookers and Cocaine. Hell the fuck no.

"Remember how you showed up for our recording session?" Time to take control.

Colton replied first. "Yeah, I came straight from the dojo and didn't change, and fairy princess over there showed up glittery." He hiked a thumb at Tessa.

"Hey!" Tessa tried to glare but her too-big hat fell down over her eyes.

Being eaten by her own clothes wasn't a good look for her. Or the rest of the band. "Go home and dress exactly as you did before. And Tessa? Feel free to bring your wings."

———

"I can't tell you how thrilled I am to be here. I'm a big fan, Mr. Lafontaine. A big fan. Now, I want you to stand naturally, don't over pose, but be comfortable. Tessa, this would work better if you climbed on the back seat."

Uh-oh, not again. Tessa clutched Henri's arm for support. Michael arranged a pair of gossamer blue wings behind her.

"Oh, yes! Perfect! Now Michael, over there. Stand behind the bike. Tessa, lean back towards him a bit, watch the wing. Raise your chin. Jake, over there." The photographer pointed. "Now, Colton, crouch down in front. Adjust your belt. Perfect!" The guy flipped his fingers. "Henri, turn a touch to the right, please. Yeah, that's it. I want to get the full pattern of your tattoos." This photographer at least had taken the time to learn his clients' names.

Click, click, click went the camera. The photographer adjusted lights, moved the band members around, and took a few more shots. Singly and in groups, Henri, Tessa, Michael, Jake, and Colton posed for the better part of the afternoon, to a chorus of "Nice!", "Awesome!", and "Oh yes, perfect!"

At last the guys broke for dinner and to review digital proofs.

Of the many poses, the first best captured the spirit of the band. Tessa had draped an arm over Henri's shoulder, not like a woman clinging to a man for support but like an equal, a friend, a buddy. And she flat rocked as a fairy.

Each and every band member appeared exactly as Henri imagined them in his mind: Michael, Mr. Average Boy Next Door; Jake, aging rock star who still had the moves; Colton, the living tribute to Bruce Lee; Tessa, ethereal, unconventional, a free spirit; himself, caught somewhere in between, wearing his bike chaps and a band T-shirt.

No one member stood out any more than the others. They were an ensemble cast. A band.

They were *Mismatched Delusions*.

And they were gonna kick some rock and roll ass.

———

"Henri, a word please?" Lucas lounged in the hallway, leaning against a wall. Snippets of conversation came from the hotel's conference room down the hall. A cameraman hurried past, gear hoisted onto his shoulder.

"You go ahead, guys, I'll be right there," Henri told the band, nodding in the direction of the voices. "What's up, Lucas?"

"Two things. First, I want them to go ahead so you can make a grand entrance. Secondly, I want to give you a heads-up. Give them thirty minutes. Answer the reporters' questions, evade what you want to, but at the end, call on the woman in the purple sweater. We'll leave these newshounds with something to chew on." Lucas hiked up one side of his mouth in his conniving manager grin. Thank God he was on Henri's side.

Henri paused in the doorway, studying what lay ahead. Damn, but he needed a joint right now. Or one of his emergency pills. Or better yet, Sebastian Unger holding his hand. *Face your issues, you wuss.* He filled his lungs and leaked out the air in a controlled exhalation. Then he nodded to Lucas and followed his band into the conference room. A long table sat before several rows of reporter-filled chairs, his band already seated at the table. One empty chair remained. He blew out his breath and joined his crew.

Flashes announced the moment's preservation on camera. A few people murmured when he sat down, and he fought a grin. He'd changed a hell of a lot in the last few months—for the better. He'd worn a sleeveless shirt to let his tats show, but his bandmates didn't have to pull back their chairs to make room for his hair.

"Good afternoon. I'd like to thank you for coming." For the first time Henri got to address the press directly. Normally his mother would have taken control. Not this time, and never again. "I'd like to introduce you to a few people I've been hanging out with."

A few giggles sounded from the audience.

"To my right here is Tessa Eklund, the finest percussionist in the business, and beside her is Michael Lindley. You might remember him—we started out together years ago. He plays lead guitar, among a million other instruments.

"To my left is Jake Steadman, a man with a lot of…" He let the sentence hang before adding, "experience." Several journalists chuckled. "Lastly, a man who can flat tear up the keyboards, Mr. Colton Ferguson."

Hands shot in the air. Without being called upon, a man in the front row shouted, "Mr. Lafontaine, why did you leave Hookers and Cocaine?"

"I learned the error of my ways?" Snickers sounded from the back of the room. Henri invoked his bland face. Maybe he should have gone to acting lessons with Sebastian. "Why would any *sane* human being leave a successful band? Is that what you're asking?" Let them chew on his words awhile. "Creative differences. Most of the band liked our direction, while I wanted to try something new. That's why I'm now working with the fine folks here with me today. Each has something unique to bring to the table."

"Is it true you had a falling out with the band?" Mr. Rude-and-won't-wait-my-turn asked.

Fucking vulture. "They're my brothers. They'll always be my brothers even though we've parted ways." And he wasn't wasting any time or money on a slander suit by saying what he really thought of the assholes.

"Will you be playing any of your old songs on tour?"

Would someone please shut this fuckwad up? Why the hell was he dwelling on the past, when this was a Mismatched Delusions *press conference?* "What's the use of making changes if I intend to do the same ole, same ole?"

Someone groaned.

Henri winked. "I'd reserve judgment if I were you."

A woman asked, "You've certainly changed your appearance recently. I, for one, like what you've done. Is there a reason for the sudden turnaround?"

"Do you mean like the love of a good—" He couldn't resist teasing. He could almost see the news-hungry predators' ears flapping. He finished with "—cop?"

Fits of laughter erupted from the gathered journalists. Some of them hadn't known him during "The Great Cop Incident," but the most embarrassing news story ever likely hadn't been missed by any of them, thanks to YouTube footage. "Now if you don't mind, I'm getting a bit tired. How about a question for Tessa?"

Henri sat back and let his bandmates have their moment, while carefully deflecting questions from Michael. Poor guy appeared ready to bolt and clung tightly to Tessa's white-knuckled hand. Henri checked his watch. About thirty minutes. Time to wrap up. He scanned the room for the woman in purple. There she was. Oh, wait. Or was she over there?

Frantically he searched for Lucas, who held up his hand and wriggled his fingers. What the hell? Henri studied the two women again. One sported three-inch, purple claws to match her outfit. Oh, those were fucking scary.

"One more question," Henri shouted to be heard. "The lady in the back."

"Henri, is it true your supposed breakdown resulted from having been drugged by a fan, and you took a hiatus to recover from your ordeal?"

The crowded room quieted fast.

Henri exaggerated a frown and put-upon sigh. He lowered his eyes. Damn, what dirty carpet. *Make them feel it,* he heard in Seb's voice. "I'm sorry, ma'am. Due to an ongoing investigation, I'm not at liberty to answer your question."

Take that, tabloids!

But… the crazed fan might still be out there, and would now know of Henri's return.

———

THE NEXT night Henri sat in his living room, watching the press conference on the big screen. He'd texted Seb a few times, but no answer yet. More than likely he was still singing his heart out for the good folks of Peoria.

Tessa was right. The white sleeveless T-shirt and simple blue jeans, minus facial scruff and with a touch of eyeliner, gave Henri a more professional appearance.

Plus, he nearly didn't recognize himself without his hair.
Good.
The questions came to a close. Henri on-screen dropped his

bombshell; Henri in his living room munched popcorn while the news anchors puzzled out his meaning. Oh, yeah. They'd been the first in line to kick Henri when he was down, adding fuel to the "drug" fire. Let them eat those words.

His phone buzzed and he snatched it up. Maybe he'd get to talk to Sebastian tonight. Instead he found a text message from Margo: *Is it true? Were you really drugged?*

He tapped a reply on the keypad. *What do you care?*

I'm your mother!

Then act like it! Henri silenced his phone and tossed it to the side. Hopefully, she'd spend the next few hours recalling what she'd said and done after the incident. Especially the not-hugging him part.

SEVENTEEN

"ANSWER THE phone!" Henri checked his watch: 10:00 p.m. No telling where Sebastian might be. This news couldn't wait.

His call went to voice mail. "I e-mailed you a recording of today's session. You won't believe this, but I hit high C consistently now." How Henri would love to speak to Sebastian directly and share today's triumph. Sebastian would smile, say, "Told you so," and then he'd reward Henri with a kiss.

"We're starting off small, trying out the new songs in a club next week in Fresno. I... I'd like if you were there. I understand if you can't be, but I owe you more than I can ever repay. Especially the high note."

He hung up, today's achievement somewhat dampened by the inability to properly share with the one person whose approval he still sought. Maybe he should give the band the day off for good behavior and pay a little visit to the opera world. If he could enter a church, he could enter an opera house.

———

HENRI TUGGED at his collar. No use. The damned suit seemed made for discomfort. He passed by a mirror. Seb was right. He did clean up nicely. Now if only he cleaned up well enough to impress Seb. If not, the two dozen gladiolas should help. Or the late reservation in a private dining room at Akron, Ohio's swankiest restaurant.

Dressed to the nines and with his trademark locks missing, no one seemed to recognize Henri. Of course, if they recognized him, it might be for the wrong reasons. He still had a ways to go to undo his bad-boy reputation, if he ever managed such a feat.

Outside the opera house the billboard displayed "Othello." Maybe Henri should have Googled, found out more. Then again, Sebastian sang the role of someone named Cassio. What else did he need to know? He'd sit through the performance, make sure to show his appreciation, then whisk Cassio away for a private evening. Simple.

He relaxed back into his seat overlooking the stage and tuned out the murmurs around him. At last the lights when down and the stage lit up. The sets, the costumes, the orchestra—nothing else mattered when Sebastian took the stage. As before, in the theater, when he raised his voice, the room filled with sound. Cold chills cha-cha'd up Henri's spine. He chanced a glance around him at the transfixed audience. He wanted this enthralling magic for himself and his band. The chanting, the wolf whistles, the fanatical idol worship were one thing, but to be able to captivate the crowd, elicit a collective gasp or titters that echoed throughout the room…. the ability to play a group of people like a piano was a gift. A gift Henri envied.

After the performers took their final bow and the applause died, Henri made his way backstage, having greased a few palms to gain entry.

He tapped lightly on the dressing room door. "Come in," a familiar voice called.

Henri opened the door and slipped inside, cradling the box of gladiolas under his arm.

"You're early. I told you to give me twenty minutes." Sebastian didn't sound happy. He sat with his back to the door, scrubbing at his face with a cotton ball.

"You were awesome." Henri sat the box on the vanity and wrapped his arms around his lover.

Seb whipped around so quickly he nearly fell off his stool. "You!" Not exactly the welcome Henri envisioned. "You can't be here! You have to go. He can't find you here!" The pallor of his skin couldn't be explained by makeup alone.

"If who finds you here?" came from behind Henri.

Seb cringed and blanched even further, begging *please, please, please* with his eyes. Please what?

In the doorway stood a well-dressed man, a bit of gray showing at his temples. "Who is this, Sebastian? And what is he doing here?"

Henri stepped back. Who was this guy, and why did he act like he owned Seb? "I'm Henri Lafontaine. And you are?" Henri didn't offer his hand.

Seb answered for the man. "Henri, this is Charles. My patron. Charles, this is Henri. A singer I've been working with." *A singer.* Not "my lover." Hell, not even "a friend."

Charles raked his gaze over Henri and cast a narrow-eyed glare at the flower box. "I see. Well, Mr. Lafontaine, I hope you enjoyed the performance, but *fans* aren't allowed backstage. I'll call security to escort you out." Seb flinched when Charles dropped a hand to his shoulder so hard it smacked.

Granted, Henri had only known Sebastian a short while, but the cowering seemed out of character for a man who carried himself with such confidence onstage.

"No, I'll go. I came to watch the show and tell Sebastian thanks for his help. He's made a tremendous difference." *Look at me!* he silently ordered Sebastian. Sebastian stared at the floor, as drawn in on himself as a man of his size could be.

"Hurry, Sebastian, I don't like to be kept waiting." Charles's fingers on the back of Sebastian's neck squeezed too tightly. Asshole.

Maybe Henri should call security.

"Henri, thanks for coming. I'll see you at our next lesson. Now, if you'll excuse me, Charles is hosting a private party tonight. I need to get ready." The hand on Sebastian's neck might as well have belonged to a ventriloquist—the words weren't Seb's.

Leaving the room took all of Henri's willpower. As he passed by, Charles's scent tickled a memory.

He leaned against the wall outside, straining for bits of conversation from within the room. Charles spoke too softly for him to hear, but the occasional hissed threat didn't bode well for Sebastian.

"Oh my. Look what I found!" A man in a dressing robe strode down the hall and stopped in front of Henri, fluttering his lashes. "I call dibs!"

Not now. Not fucking now. "Who are you?"

"Me? Darling, didn't you watch the performance? I'm the guy so far in the back you needed opera glasses to see me. However, I'm not above a private performance. Say, at your place?"

Henri was not in the mood for flirting. Wait. Private performance. Maybe this guy had information. "What have you heard about Sebastian Unger?"

"He landed my dream role, dammit."

"What about his patron, Charles?"

The guy grinned, more sharkish than friendly. "His *patron* is loaded, for one thing. And between you and me, I think he's a little more than merely a patron."

Oh hell no! This guy was not going to drag anything to do

with Sebastian through the mud. "What are you talking about? Lots of opera singers have patrons, don't they?"

"Oh, we do, but not many have a patron like Charles. He's possessive. Keeps Sebby-poo on a tight leash."

My fist and this guy's face should meet. Henri fought back a growl when the guy dropped a silk-coated arm around his shoulders and whispered into his ear. "While the rest of us attend the after party, Charles insists on taking Sebastian away to a *private affair.* The people who hold season passes to the opera house pay good money to mingle with the stars. Let me tell you, good ole Charles's selfishness isn't winning Sebastian any fans."

"What are you talking about? Wouldn't these same people attend Charles's party?"

The guy laughed, a raucous, evil sound. "You haven't been around much, have you? The *private party* might be only for Charles and Seb. Not all patrons are like that, but some definitely are."

Rose to the Heart, a dagger of love.... Seb, how could you? Henri closed his eyes and sagged against the wall. His unwelcome witness chattered on, words falling on deaf ears. Seb. The one thing in Henri's life he'd been able to count on. No, they'd never said the words, they'd never even discussed being exclusive. In fact, Sebastian had even said he understood if Henri found others upon his return to LA. It didn't lessen the pain. Seb, his Seb, wasn't his.

His heart a lead weight in his chest, Henri stumbled down the hall toward the exit. The elusive scent memory clicked into place. Burberry. Charles the dickwad reeked of Burberry.

EIGHTEEN

MY MUSIC. I still have my music. "Okay, guys. From the top again."

Groans sounded around him. "We've already done it six times." The whine came from Colton's direction.

"And we'll keep on going until we get it right. We've only got one more practice until our debut." "A Matter of When" rocked in Seb's music room. Why couldn't Henri reproduce the effect here? *Maybe because every time you sing you hesitate, waiting for the Italian echo?*

"This old-timer needs a nap." Jake yawned.

"That's enough for now," a disembodied voice announced over the speakers. Lucas waved from his vantage point in the unused control booth. "Henri, I need to talk to you."

Yeah. Lucas, the man who'd introduced him to Seb to begin with. The bastard had a lot to answer for.

"See you later." Tessa led the charge out of the room, followed closely by Colton and Jake. Michael took time to pack up Sylvia before joining the other traitors in their mad dash for freedom. The man might be a little too attached to his guitar, explaining why he hadn't snagged a recent girlfriend. Jake didn't have issues getting dates—the fresh marks on his neck said so.

Lucas stepped into the room, lightly slapping a rolled-up magazine against his palm. Another tabloid, no doubt. Spewing whatever venom sold copies. "When was the last time you talked to Sebastian?"

"About a week ago. Why?" And no, he wasn't disclosing the circumstances. Lucas owed him an apology about the "don't hurt him" thing. It's Seb he should have talked to.

"This." Lucas unrolled the magazine and opened to the last page. "Othello" topped the first column.

Henri perused the article, hunting Sebastian's name, but found no mention. "Why isn't he listed? Wasn't he supposed to play at every venue?" No one had actually explained how opera touring companies operated; Henri assumed a role to be like a band member. You occasionally shared the spotlight with someone else but never gave your place away.

"He's not mentioned because he dropped out. After a certain *rock star* made an appearance backstage." Gruffness reared its ugly head into full blown rage. "Exactly what were you doing in Akron?"

"Jeez, dude, chill! I wanted to hear him sing. It's a free country. So what if I wanted to take a friend to dinner?"

"But he's not just a friend, now, is he?" The low, simmering growl had Henri ready to shout for help. Lucas seemed ready to blow a gasket, and for the life of him, Henri couldn't figure out why.

"You fucked him." It wasn't a question.

And none of Lucas's damned business. "Sebastian and I are both grown men. What we choose to do with our own time isn't your concern." Henri edged toward the door.

"Listen...." Lucas moved so fast he closed the distance one

minute and had Henri pinned to the wall the next. "I sent you to him hoping you'd help each other out, but not *that* way. He'd teach you how to make the most use of your God-given talents, you'd teach him to stand up for himself and give him the means to break free of that vulture. If I'd known you were gay, I'd never have sent you to him."

"What are you talking about?"

"Don't you get it? He's not like you. He can't sleep with someone and walk away the next morning. You? You're free to do anything you want. Even squandering money like you've done the past five years, you lack for nothing. Homes, cars, men, women. And it comes easy to you." Lucas dragged a hand through his sparse hair. "You take everything for granted and earn more in a year than Sebastian can in ten. And yet every waking moment he devotes to his craft."

This wasn't news. Sebastian had said similar things. "And I bought a ticket to hear him perform. How am I hurting him?"

Lucas snatched the magazine from Henri's fingers and hurled it to the floor. "In opera, it takes money to make money. The guy only makes about $55,000 a year. Do you have any idea how much he pays for acting and dance lessons? How much it costs to travel to auditions? Do you?"

"It's not like he's hurting," Henri countered. "He's got a huge house—"

"And not one damned thing to call his own." Lucas blew out his breath in a huff. "His mother was much like Seb—spending every dime to make the big time, only worse—she liked to pretend she'd already arrived. She left a world of debt behind when she died. Debt a struggling tenor couldn't pay."

"Why didn't he sell the house?" A question Sebastian had nearly ripped him a new asshole for asking.

"He did, to Charles, his patron. After Annette's death I

offered to help him, with what little I could. I hadn't seen him since he was small. Annette and I weren't on speaking terms for a while." The anger seemed to drain from Lucas. "I went to visit her in the hospital—I refused to take no for an answer. She told me everything. How Seb's new patron promised to take care of him. She put a lot of stock in a man she hardly knew."

A tangled web of lies hung in the air, things said before not matching Lucas's current speech. "You said you were a family friend and had been watching over Seb his whole life."

Lucas paced to the far side of the room to contemplate Tessa's drum set. "I have. From a distance. That's the way Annette wanted things. And I always gave her what she wanted. Right now I'd like to go back in time, though, and make a few changes."

He glanced back over his shoulder. There was pain in his eyes, and pleading, when he focused on Henri. "Regardless of how she went about it, she truly did want only the best for her son. I don't think she meant for him to wind up in involuntary servitude to a man as manipulative as Charles. He promises the moon and takes all of it away for minor infractions to rules no human can live by."

"I don't follow you. He and Sebastian are lovers." The bitterness still burned. When Henri closed his eyes visions of Charles and Sebastian filled his mind.

Lucas snorted. "Not lovers. More like owner and property. With his talent, Sebastian should be singing at the Met. While Charles enjoys basking in Seb's glow, he's not about to let his pet get big enough to break away. That's where you came in. I was hoping you'd help me save him. You weren't supposed to use him too."

"Wait a damned minute! I didn't use him. Whatever he and I did was consensual, I can assure you. I'd never do anything to hurt him." Lucas couldn't be as surprised as Henri by the claim, or by the truth in the words. But wait! "Owner and property?" The frantic cleaning, the too-tidy house, the "my patron this" and "my patron that." Seb wasn't trying to impress the man or show respect, and his cleanliness wasn't a nervous habit. He'd been terrified.

If only Henri had noticed when he'd had the chance to do something. Even now, as the knee-jerk hurt at Seb simmered for being with another man, first and foremost Henri wanted to ensure Seb's safety.

"Annette died before Seb turned seventeen. I filed a custody suit and got laughed out of court for my efforts. No one would give a teenager to me when I had a record of being in and out of rehab and a few minor arrests for drunk and disorderly."

Some of the web came unwoven. "Why did you want custody when you hadn't even seen him in years?" Ice water poured through Henri's veins. Oh shit. He'd seen the similarities and hadn't put two and two together. Until now.

"Why wouldn't a father want to care for his son?"

———

A CONVERSATION of this magnitude required coffee, privacy, and doughnuts—in that order. Henri started the coffeepot and rummaged through his cabinets for junk food. Not fresh doughnuts, but a pack of nearly expired chocolate sandwich cookies might offer enough comfort to get through an enlightening talk.

Only when they'd settled down to the kitchen table did Henri say more than "Sugar? Cream?"

"Okay, now back to business. How can you be Seb's father? What about...?"

Lucas stared into his coffee cup. "Tell me, Henri, what would you do if you were a rising starlet, fighting tooth and nail to start a career, and discovered you were pregnant... and unmarried."

"Couldn't she have married the father?"

Lucas raised watery eyes. "And ruin her career by tying herself to a man with no money? No. As much as I loved the woman, I'm the first to admit her drama extended past the stage. A certain tenor of some renown had escorted her out a time or two." Lucas gave a humorless smile. "He enjoyed having pretty young women on his arm. He also loved racing. When he crashed in France he made headlines. Leaving behind a bereft and pregnant *fiancée*"—Lucas added air quotes—"earned Annette pity, not scorn, and catapulted her into the public's eye.

"That's why we had our falling out. We'd met at an after party. I was only there because a business partner gave me tickets. I pitched a musical idea and she was all ears. We started seeing each other, quietly, of course. To be honest, I was thrilled when she told me she was pregnant, and even pawned a few things to get her a ring." Lucas examined his cup as though the answers to his problems lay at the bottom. "She said Sebastian wasn't mine. I suspected differently, but when he began to draw notice as a tenor, the opera world touted him as a chip off the old block. Not that I could have given him much in the way of the life."

"What would Sebastian Senior's family do if they found out?"

"He didn't have much family, and Annette didn't inherit. She took the man's name for her son. Nothing else."

It wasn't right to think ill of the dead, but Henri didn't like Sebastian's mother much. "And she confessed all on her death bed."

Lucas nodded. "I can't figure out if I should praise her for raising him alone to be such a fine young man, or bring her back and kill her myself for denying me my son."

"I'd give everything I have to be able to sit down at dinner with

my parents, or call them, share my good days, get their advice," Sebastian had said.

"Have you told him?"

"Are you mad? Do you have any idea what kind of damage coming forward now would do to his career? No, I watched from the sidelines and put my faith in others. But I pulled myself out of a bottle, stood on my own feet again, and tried to be someone he might one day look up to, if he didn't stare too closely at the tarnish around the edges." Lucas raised his head high enough to give Henri a sidewise glare. "Which brings us back to where we were. I have no idea where my son is, but he isn't onstage where he belongs, and he disappeared the day after you paid a little visit. I ask you again, when was the last time you saw Sebastian, and what did you do to make him run away?"

Oh shit. "I brought him flowers. And had made dinner reservations. I'd hoped to make a night of it."

"Charles found out."

"Yes."

"I've never liked the man, how he manipulates everyone around him, using money to buy people. There's a special place in Hell for men like him."

A special place in Hell. And yet Sebastian attended the church of the hologram. Was he hoping to find Heaven there? What a mess. Henri kinda preferred the tangled web to the unraveled ends. Charles had made his shit list, he wanted to smack Lucas around a time or two for being a pushover, and he definitely wanted a talk with Sebastian's dearly departed mama. But the one he most longed to see was the innocent victim in a lot of schemes. "Call the band. Tonight's practice is cancelled. I'm going to find Seb."

"Henri, the debut is tomorrow. You can't afford to miss practice today, and you have to be on a bus at 10:00 a.m." If Lucas squeezed his cup any harder, it'd shatter. "He's my son. I'm going."

It might take a while for Henri to get used to this man being Seb's father. "Now's not the time. He needs a friend, not a.... Look, I'm the one who showed up unannounced, I'm the one—"

"—he slept with."

"I didn't say that."

"But it's true." The glint in Lucas's eyes hinted at violence.

"I'm heading for the airport. Have a plane waiting for me and a rental car in Denver." Henri laid a hand on his manager's shoulder, softening his words. "I'm not going to hurt him. I just need some answers." *And I need to know he's okay.*

———

HENRI RANG the doorbell, tugged his jacket tighter around himself, and settled on the front porch to wait. Damn, it was getting cold. Seemed like yesterday he'd been lying in Seb's bed, enjoying a cool summer breeze. Now, late in October, the flowers in the flower beds were a withered memory. No matter how cold, he wasn't leaving until he spoke to Sebastian. What was he angrier about? Not seeing the truth sooner, or not trying harder to take Seb with him? Or with Lucas for not recognizing his own child, despite what the mother said? And mostly with Charles, for being an arrogant asshole manipulator. Henri eyed a loose shutter. One good punch would knock it down. But he'd get sore knuckles and a pissed-off Seb. He wrapped his arms around himself to ward off temptation. Damn, but he needed... something.

After the fifth time Henri jabbed the doorbell, the door opened a crack. *Sebastian! Hallelujah!*

"How long, Seb?" Molten lava rumbled up from Henri's stomach, bile burning the back of his throat.

A three-inch glimpse of Seb's face showed in the narrowly opened door. Three inches of green, blue, and yellow. Oh fuck.

"How long for what? How long has he been fucking me?" Seb threw the door open wide, showing the full range of his injuries. Bruises circled one eye and the vicious welts along one arm appeared to have been made by a belt. "Or how long has he been hurting me?"

NINETEEN

"Why didn't you tell me?" They sat in the music room—Seb at the piano, Henri in a nearby chair. Oh how he'd come to love the time they'd spent in this room. Not now.

"Why should I have told you? This isn't your problem." Seb idly stroked the piano keys, avoiding Henri's scrutiny.

"How about because I'm your lover?"

"Are you?" Sebastian met Henri's gaze and quickly glanced away again. "I thought you were a spoiled rock star who needed guidance. Sex was a bonus."

Anger rolled back through Henri. "I've about had enough of your insults. Yeah, I'm a rock singer. No, I didn't have years of training. No, I didn't pay my dues your way. No, I don't take care of my voice. But I'm sick and tired of you condemning me for being a bad person without knowing me first. Yes, I screwed up in the past, but have I ever, *ever* mistreated you?"

"No." Seb didn't look up. "Not directly."

What? "How have I hurt you indirectly?"

"Every time you leave. I knew you wanted me because I was

the only one available. And while you're here, I can dream. Whenever you leave, reality returns. Each time you leave and come back confuses me more. I'm nothing to you. Could never be anything to you."

"You're wrong." Henri crossed the floor and stooped down by the piano bench. He cradled Seb's face gently in his palms to avoid his bruises, and lifted. "You mean more to me than you realize. At first I thought it was the music. But now it's more." He shifted one hand down to Seb's chest. The *thumpa-thumpa* of the man's heartbeat thrummed against his skin. His Seb, so warm, so alive. "You don't have to put up with Charles. Leave. With me." He hadn't intended to make the offer, but now couldn't do otherwise.

"And do what?"

Henri only meant to lighten the mood. "Let me be your patron." He found himself on the floor while six-plus feet of pure fury stalked away.

Sebastian threw his hands into the air. "Ah, you'd be my pimp now, huh? And I'd still be the kept man. Tell me, would you at least make promises you plan to keep, or like Charles, will you offer me the world on a platter, only to snatch it back?"

Henri bolted to his feet. "Look at you! You're one hell of a tenor. You don't need him. You can go anywhere and sing."

"Can I? Do you have any idea how many in the opera world have their hands in his pockets? A word in the wrong ear and I can come crashing down. All my hopes, all my dreams, crushed on one man's whims. My own mother appointed him my guardian, and for years he's guided my career. If I dared to tell the truth, no one would believe me. Either way, his word or mine, I'm ruined.

"I'm trapped. If I had any sense I'd kick you out, not risk him finding out you were here."

"Why do you let him act like he owns you?"

"Because he does!" Sebastian stared out the window. Heavy snowflakes began to fall. "This house, my car. My lessons. All paid for by him. He makes sure I have to use enough of my pay to keep me broke and dependent. And he constantly reminds me that one wrong move and he'll throw me out. Tenors are a dime a dozen." He didn't yell. He never raised his voice. Too easy to damage vocal chords.

"How long has this been going on?" Henri regretted the question the moment the words left his mouth. Did he honestly want an answer? He might have to give up his lucrative singing career to make license plates in prison if his "he needed killing" defense failed in court.

Sebastian whispered low. Henri strained to hear. "Since I was sixteen. About a week after my mother died. But this is the first time he let his temper get the best of him to the point I couldn't hide the marks."

Oh dear God, no. Henri closed his eyes for a moment, shutting his hand into a fist. Sixteen. Younger than Jenni. Younger than Henri when he'd made his first record deal. And no telling how old asshole Charles had been. At least thirty years older. An unreleased song languished on Henri's mental hard drive: "He Needed Killing." Mama Unger, or whatever her last name was, might not have known at the time, but she'd left her son in the worst possible hands. And Lucas should have fought harder for his son. Henri couldn't change the past, but the future remained open. "Why did you sleep with me?" *Give me something to work with here.*

In a more authoritative tone, Sebastian replied, "Because I wanted to." He scrunched his eyes closed. "Selfish of me, I know, but just once I wanted to know what it felt like to be with someone I chose of my own free will."

If letting Henri past his guard, even a little, was intended to be selfish, Henri would never fault the man. They'd shared something precious—at least to Henri. "I have money. Let me help you."

Folding his arms across his chest announced Seb's decision loud and clear even without words. "I'm not letting you spend your money on me." He focused on Henri, a stubborn glint in his eyes.

"Why not? If I don't spend it on my friends, I'll only blow it on hookers and cocaine."

Sebastian's mouth fell open. "Wha...."

Henri tried to force a grin that said, *I'm joking—maybe.* "How do you think my old band got its name?" The joke had grown old a long time ago. People weren't supposed to believe the hype.

Sebastian dropped down onto the settee, face buried in his hands.

Oh crap. Open mouth, insert foot. "Sorry, Seb. Bad joke. But really, let me help you?"

"This isn't your fight. I can't allow you to rescue me. I have to get out on my own."

"But you're going to get out?"

"Yes."

Henri gently tugged Sebastian's finger and pulled his hand away from his face, revealing the evidence of Charles's mistreatment. He lightly caressed an angry purple welt on Seb's cheek. "No offense, but you're not the first person I've known who put up with shit 'cause they were afraid to walk away. I'm your friend. Friends get to help. "

"Noted." Seb trained his vision on something beyond the window, a shimmer in his eyes. Stubborn oaf.

"Seb, I have to be back in LA tomorrow morning."

Seb's only acknowledgement was a sigh.

"I don't want to leave without you."

"You know I can't go. I have my life, my career to think

about." His words came out flat, so unlike Sebastian's normal melodic tones.

No. He wasn't going to evade. Henri maneuvered his way into Seb's line of sight. "Then leave him. Pack a bag and get the hell away from him." He raised his hand, intending to indicate the man's injuries. Sebastian flinched. If Charles were here right now, he'd rip the bastard's fucking head off for daring to lay a hand on someone else... or daring to make another person a virtual slave.

"I've heard you sing," Henri continued. "You don't need him. You're a star in your own right. And I'm not leaving Evergreen until I see you checked into a hotel. Someplace he can't find you."

Sebastian nodded. "But this house...."

"Is only a house. No matter how much it means to you, it's not worth your soul." Of all the places Henri had lived, Seb's old cabin had come closest to being home. If he could, he'd give all he had to buy the place, give it to Sebastian outright. But Sebastian would never allow such a gift.

"I don't even have a way to go. He owns my car."

"I have a rental. All it takes is one call to the rental company to add you. C'mon."

With wooden motions Sebastian packed two suitcases and rounded up his toiletries. The sun began to set as Henri loaded the luggage into the car.

"Wait!" Sebastian ran back to the house.

Oh no! What now? Henri found him in the room where Henri had slept. "Help me!" he cried, rattling the picture frame above the headboard.

His grandmother's painting. Together they lifted the heavy framed canvas from the wall, carried the artwork outside, and tucked it precariously into the back seat. As they pulled away, tears streamed down Sebastian's bruised face.

———

"ARE YOU sure you'll be all right? I'd rather you come back with me."

If he had more time, Henri would have loved to stay a few days at the hotel they chose outside of Denver, but he'd already been gone longer than he should have.

Sebastian stared blankly at his grandmother's painting. "Go. Do what you have to. I know people here at the Central City Opera, and though it's too late for starring roles, Opera Colorado might need understudies. They may not have the kinds of crowds I'm used to, but they've been after me for years. I'll be fine." He gave Henri the world's most insincere smile. But he followed the lie with a kiss. "Go on. Don't forget—I want to be in the front row when you make your comeback."

"And I want you there. Lucas knows to let you in no matter where we are." Henri placed his rental's keys in Seb's hand. "Stay here as long as you need to. I'll catch a cab to the airport."

"I could drive you."

Henri glanced out the window at darkness. In twelve hours he needed to be boarding a bus with his band. "No. Call room service. Have a nice meal and a hot bath. That always works for me." Damn, damn, damn, damn, damn. Why did Henri have to leave?

"It's not just you, you know." His mother's voice echoed in his brain. *"Think of the band, the vendors, everyone who depends on you."*

"I am thinking. Of Seb!" he snapped back in his head.

As if reading his mind, Sebastian said, "I'd really like to be alone for a while, if that's okay with you." Another kiss softened the blow.

"Call me if you need anything. And I'll try to get away next week, come see you."

"You do that."

———————

LET HIM sleep! Henri stared at the clock. Was 9:00 a.m. too early to call? Poor Sebastian needed his rest. He gave up fighting and dialed at 9:05. The call went straight to voice mail. A nagging feeling wriggled in his gut. He called the hotel. "Sebastian Unger's room, please."

"I'm sorry, sir. Mr. Unger checked out last night."

He what? With numb fingers Henri dug a business card out of his wallet and dialed the rental car company.

"Yes, sir. The car was returned before midnight."

The phone slipped from Henri's fingers. He followed it to the floor. Why couldn't he fucking breathe? *I never should have left. I should have said to hell with the band. Seb could be with me now, instead of God knows where.*

An image came to mind: Sebastian staring at the painting of a sunny meadow, with rain in his eyes.

———————

"WILL THEY fucking get back?" Henri paced the length of what passed for a dressing room, spun on his boot heel and paced some more. How fucking long could it possibly take to eat a pizza and run by a salon for Tessa to get her hair done?

"We've got plenty of time." Lucas sat draped across an upholstered chair, which had seen much better days. He squirmed and checked his watch, the liar.

This wasn't the most glamorous venue, but Henri had to start somewhere. Restart. Whatever. He'd checked his cell phone a thousand times, heart thudding each time a chime announced a new text message. Nothing from Seb.

He smoothed a hand down his vintage T-shirt to dry his sweaty palms. Why was it so damned hot in here, and where was his band?

"We're here!" Tessa's hair beat her into the room.

"What the fuck is that?" Henri pointed at the poof above her head.

"I told you I'm a fan of Sheila E. I'm appealing to her fellow fans." Light makeup formed a band across her face, starting at one temple and ending at the other. She stared out from a ribbon of pink and twirled her drumsticks in her always-in-motion hands.

Colton wore eyeliner. He'd also drawn some kind of runes on himself with black body paint. "For luck."

Henri didn't mind the liner—he wore some himself. The runes, however, were badly drawn. Jake wore a T-shirt with the sleeves cut out, and Michael appeared ready for his middle-school class in a button-down and brown pants. What the hell? "Okay, people. Listen up. Before our next gig, we need to work on our style." He was all for "do your own thing" but could they do it more fashionably?

As they headed out the door to the stage, Michael hung back. "What about my problem?"

"Got you covered. There's a storage area right off the stage. There wasn't enough room to hook up a projector, so you'll have to play offstage. We have you plugged into the amps." With a flourish of his hand, Henri declared, "Your office awaits."

Tessa tugged on Michael's arm to get his attention. "I think meditation would help. If you ever wanted me to...."

Henri tuned them out and stepped out onto the stage, heart pounding a mile a minute. In the semidarkness, the audience members all looked the same. They could be anyone. Sebastian. His sister. Or a deranged fan. Whoops and whistles met his arrival.

Tessa clashed her cymbals, Jake struck a chord, and Colton made his presence known on the keyboards. Now, if only the closet provided enough seclusion to get Michael over his stage fright. A moment later Sylvia cried out in triumph. Whew. He could play.

They opened with "Nightmare," a song designed to catch the feel of Henri's former band. Halfhearted applause followed. Okay. That was awkward. He peered out into the poorly lit club. Was Seb out there? Rooting him on?

They played through a few more songs, before launching into "Ice Inside."

The opening chords got the crowd to their feet. Finally! Signs of life.

The moment of truth arrived. Henri sucked in a deep breath and… out came the elusive C. Hollers and squeals filled the air before the note died.

A grin stretched Henri's cheeks when his band joined the revelry. To no one in particular he whispered, "I'm back."

If only Seb were here to share the moment.

———

FIVE NIGHTS of back-to-back shows. Five nights of lying awake at night worried about Sebastian. If Henri didn't get some peace of mind soon, the coke rumors would start swirling again. He stumbled off the bus, shielding his eyes from the sun's too-bright glare. Where were they, anyway? Anaheim? Again? Why the fuck did he always wind up in Anaheim?

Sweet relief wrapped around him when they stepped into their evening's venue. A poster of the band huddled around his Harley hung on the door. He smiled. His band. And suddenly he found himself swept back ten years, to the first time he'd seen a

Hookers and Cocaine poster. How proud he'd been. If only he'd known.

"On stage in one hour," Lucas announced, breaking into Henri's thoughts and leading him to the dressing room. The rest of the guys fell in step behind. Where the hell was Tessa?

Henri stopped short in the hallway. "Who is this?" The blue-Mohawked guy lounging in the doorway sent the weirdness factor into the stratosphere. And a rock band featuring everything from Tibetan bowls to a hammered dulcimer had already set the weirdness bar pretty high.

"This is Steve. Steve, meet the band." Tessa peered out from around the tall, dark, and heavily made-up man. "He's a stylist."

"But we've been through this already. The leather look didn't work, so we tried our own thing." Henri was through with a manager, or anyone else, telling him how to dress. And hell if she'd get him to change his hair again. "What's wrong with my Ramones T-shirt?" Oh, wait. After their first night, he had wanted a stylist, hadn't he? Funny how the later shows and worrying about Seb made fashion slip his mind.

"Nothing. It'll win over the punk fans. He's not here to change any of us. He's only going to help us market what we have." Tessa skipped across the floor to lay a hand on Henri's arm. "Trust me."

Well, yeah, based on their first show, they probably could use some help with style. At least Henri could get his warm-ups in while waiting his turn.

One hour and a lot of hairspray later, Henri had to admit the band looked better. Tessa once more wore a stripe of pink war-paint across her face, accentuated with a glittery rhinestone at the edge of her mouth. Her hair stood on end, teased into plumage that Steve sprayed with glitter. Black lined her eyes, making the green even more vivid.

"Can you play in that thing?" Henri eyed the magenta puffy dress she wore.

"It's more comfortable than it looks."

Good, 'cause it looked excruciating.

Jake sported a retro ambiance, a la Keith Richards from the Stones, who he sort of resembled. Well, a younger version of Keith Richards, anyway. Colton wore black: T-shirt, jeans, and fingerless gloves. Applied with Steve's sure hand, the runes were more interesting than weird.

A little bit of squirming got Henri into low-cut black skinny jeans—a black leather vest obscured part of his T-shirt. *Ah, hell. I'm a sellout. I'm wearing skinny jeans.*

"Here." Steve pulled out a cross necklace.

Henri bent to have the chain slipped over his head. Steve threaded the chain through Henri's belt loop, letting the pendant hang down. If he moved right, it'd hang between his legs. Oh. Naughty.

"Wear that to every show, and in a month, it'll be the next big thing," Steve assured him. A touch of liner and mascara later, and the stylist pronounced them ready.

Now to test the new look. And no fairy wings, thank God.

A bigger venue this time: a small club. Anaheim. Where he'd met stalker boy. The band waited backstage, soaking up thunderous applause when an announcer called their names. Whether the fans cheered for real or were influenced by a certain manager was left to question. Henri wouldn't put it past Lucas to hire folks to whip the crowd into a frenzy.

This time, an opaque sheet would hide Michael from view. Or rather, he couldn't see the audience, but backlit, they'd see his silhouette. With Michael's wild gyrations while playing, they'd get an eyeful.

The crowd chanted, "Henri!" Time for an image change. He wasn't a solo act and had no intention of using his band as a backdrop. They were Mismatched Delusions. Five people coming together to be awesome. Michael waited behind his screen, nervously caressing Sylvia's fingerboard. A spotlight illuminated him, and he worked his magic on the guitar, keeping the crowd occupied while Colton and Tessa darted onstage.

"Young'uns," Jake declared before sauntering out at a leisurely pace. Mr. Been There, Done It All simply couldn't appreciate the excitement of a concert. Henri followed the others onstage.

The lights came up, the cheers grew deafening, and the band launched into their first song. Damn, he'd missed this.

He stood in the spotlight, folks he trusted at his back, and Lucas smiling at him from the wings. How had he lived without the adoration? Was this how Seb felt onstage? Was this why he put up with a manipulative asshole of a patron? Wait. Except for the sex and beating, Henri had pretty much done the same thing. It had started slowly, someone he trusted pushing for more and more, until his life wasn't his own. And his mother once threatened his career as that bastard Charles had Sebastian's.

Why? Because Henri was her bread and butter. He hadn't needed her anymore, so she'd had to convince him he did. And Sebastian sure as hell didn't need Charles.

Even if he never again held Sebastian in his arms, even if Sebastian never loved him, Henri would free the man or die trying. Though he belted out "Ice Inside," in his head the words to a new song formed: "Die Trying."

The audience cheered and screamed. Thongs, joints, and a few hotel keys hit the stage. The euphoria ended too soon.

"Oh my God, that was the best thing evah!" Tessa tapped out a beat on Michael's back all the way back to their dressing room. Colton's wide grin had to hurt his cheeks. Jake tried to play it cool, but Henri caught him smiling whenever he thought no one was looking.

Lucas slapped Michael on the back. "Rumors are flying, speculating who the mystery guitarist is. You've been compared to guitar legends!"

Their shared elation died the moment they opened the dressing room door. A bouquet of dead roses sat on a dresser, with a note that read "Miss me?"

Oh fuck. Dead roses. A line from "Rose Through the Heart."

———

"LUCAS?" HENRI sat in the back of the tour bus, away from the prying ears of his bandmates.

"Yes."

God, how he hated admitting defeat, but out there lurked a foe he didn't understand and couldn't pin down. "Remember the cop I kissed?"

"Yes."

"He could have sold me out, but he didn't. And Detective Shepard spoke highly of him." If he had to resort to a bodyguard, he'd find someone he trusted, who'd already witnessed him at his worst and hadn't run screaming.

"What do you have in mind?"

"Find out how much he makes, offer him double. Tell him the job has shitty hours, he'll be on the road a lot, and seedy bars come with the territory. As a perk, though, his sister gets free tickets to local concerts. Oh, and contact the security guard who called 911."

"What's the job?"

"I need security for me and the band. I laughed off the roses, but I'm—I'm scared. No telling what this guy might do." Or what he'd intended the first time he'd had Henri in his sights.

Officer Arnulfo Reyes joined the band. Henri nearly kissed

him. Again. The security guard couldn't travel, due to school. Henri paid his tuition.

In Des Moines they played a big enough hall to experiment with video. Now to see if Henri's investment in hologram projectors paid off. Michael appeared onstage with them, though in actuality, he stood backstage, in headphones.

A cry rang out from the audience. The fans up close pointed to the stage. There was Michael, fuzzing around the edges, disappearing and reappearing. Holy crap. Someone get the projector fixed now!

Henri and the band played on. Damn. Their ruse was up. A few years ago a duo had gotten caught lip-synching, a scandal to end their careers. Michael hadn't exactly done anything wrong, he simply... wasn't actually there.

The next morning the papers read "'Starman' Makes a Hit in Des Moines." A full-color picture showed Michael's fade out from the night before. Damn. That image might look good on an album cover.

Okay, in the plus column, a Michael Lindley fan club started on the Internet for "Starman." Also a plus: no sign of Batshit Stalker. In the negative column, Seb hadn't returned Henri's calls.

TWENTY

DAMN BUT the neighborhood hadn't changed much. Shards of ice formed in Henri's belly when he pulled his car into his parents' driveway. He'd never thought of this stucco monster as home, with its professional landscaping and chilly stainless steel kitchen. Home had been a three-bedroom duplex in a rundown neighborhood, which Margo couldn't leave fast enough once fortune started smiling on them, as she'd put it. No, not fortune, but Henri working his ass off.

He needed drugs in the worst way. If he made it through today without help, he'd have set the bar pretty damned high. "Wait here. If I'm not back in a half hour, come in and get me."

"Sure you don't want me to come in with you?" Arnulfo glanced at the house and back at Henri.

Actually, Henri wouldn't mind backup. But for a showdown of this magnitude, the gunslinger must go alone. Only, what role did Henri play? The good guy or the bad guy? But if things turned to shit, he didn't want witnesses. "I'll be fine." Liar.

Even dragging his heels he made it to the front door before

he was ready, and took several deep breaths before pressing the doorbell. From inside the house the door chime played the opening strains of "A Matter of When." How fucking depressing.

Henri gazed back toward his car. If he ran, he could be safely inside and down the street before anyone noticed he was here. Arnulfo gave him a friendly wave. Oh, right. A witness.

"Hen…. Henri?" Margo stepped back from the door, her face paler than Henri had seen it in a long time. The woman who'd said plenty during their last face-to-face didn't seem prone to talking now.

"Are you gonna let me in?" *Say no. Give me an excuse to leave and never come back.*

"Um… oh!" The woman he'd once called "Mom" stared at him as though he'd suddenly materialized from thin air. She gestured down the hall.

Henri spared a glance toward the car and his waiting escort. Margo peeked around the door, following his line of sight. "Tell your friend to come in." For a moment, for one split second of a fraction of a heartbeat, she sounded like she had back when she'd been "Mom," he'd been "Henry," and he'd trudged through the front door to hugs, kisses, and questions about his day.

The fame, the wealth—sometimes he'd give it all for a few moments back in those simpler days. But then he wouldn't have met Sebastian. His chest tightened. He couldn't think about Sebastian now. One step at a time, on the road back to where he belonged.

Hey! That was pretty good! He needed to write those lyrics down. "He's not a friend, he's my security. He stays where he is." Would Sebastian be proud of Henri for taking this first step toward peace with his family?

It shouldn't have been possible, but her face paled further and she slammed the door shut the moment Henri stepped through.

Murmuring voices pointed him toward the family room. Good. The rest of the family was home. *This show is one night only, folks.* His father and sister shut up the moment he set foot in the room. So much for a hero's open-armed welcome. Well, he'd come here to make some changes, might as well clear the air in the process.

Jenni gave him startled eyes and jumped up. A cutting glance from Margo returned her to her seat on the couch.

His dad lounged in the recliner, as he'd done throughout most of Henri's childhood—the illusion of the breadwinner relaxing after a hard day at work. Only,

Henri's dad hadn't often held a steady job and had never in Henri's life been the breadwinner. Not even close. He almost felt sorry for his mom. Almost, but not quite. Yes, she'd done what she'd had to to get her kids raised. Yes, she'd worked her ass off and managed to make ends meet. No, she didn't have to let her heart shrivel into a dried-up prune in the process. And she didn't have to start treating her kids as a means to an end.

But why did Henri have to be the spitting image of his dad? Jenni looked like Mom, with dark blonde hair and light brown eyes, even if her tresses did defy gravity and fluff out like Henri's had until recently. She'd also been blessed with honey-gold skin, several shades lighter than Henri's but still exotic, and a few extra inches in height. Yeah, he could understand why she'd be in demand by fashion designers. Jenni hugged a throw pillow to her chest, darting glances from Henri to Margo, and then to Dad.

Henri's blood boiled. They controlled her much as they controlled him. She'd be eighteen in a few months. Then he'd see to it she made her own decisions.

"No, no, don't get up." He glared at his father. "It's just the prodigal returned home." And bringing vengeance. "I'm not here because you deserve an exclusive. You, the ones who should have been there for me, deserted me when I needed you the most."

"But…," Margo began.

Henri cut her off. "Start talking—" If looks could kill, Henri would now be the relative of two melted piles of goo. "—and I'll walk out the door and never look back." Damn, how he hated having to blackmail them for a few minutes of their undivided attention. But if threats got them to listen, so be it.

The only sound came from the big-screen TV. Henri grabbed the remote and clicked it off. "First off, my 'episode' as you put it in the media, was not me strung out on drugs.

"Yes, I'd taken my pills that night, like I did before every show, and another for the party." Margo slid down on the couch next to Jenni. Henri paced, ignoring the burning in his throat. Dammit! They should have been there for him. It'd be easy to leave. Sebastian appeared in his mind. *I'd love to have a family. Any family.* Henri stayed.

"And I foolishly accepted the drink a fan kept forcing on me, mostly to get him to shut up and leave me alone. When the drink hit me he tried to take me to my room, acting concerned. I went up with a member of the security team instead. He's the one who spotted trouble and called an ambulance." They didn't need to know how Henri begged the man to hold him. How in that moment, he hadn't cared if he lived or died. He hadn't attempted suicide, but he hadn't wanted to live much either.

His parents sat motionless as statues. Shock? Or did they truly not give a shit if Henri lived or died? "When the cops searched my room they found a video camera, rope, and duct tape. Whatever the asshole at the party had planned for me, it wasn't going to be pretty." Normally, he wouldn't talk harshly in front of his sister, but he'd never lie to her. And if she was slated to live her life in the public eye, she needed to know the types she'd be up against. The good, the bad, and the hopelessly insane psychopaths.

"Are you—?" Margo blurted.

"Not another word. I've got the floor. After I say what I have to, you can have your turn."

She nodded, emitting a tiny squeak.

"He hasn't been caught yet. I left town to get away, regroup, and write some music without having to look over my shoulder every five minutes. I'm back now, and batshit crazy stalker or no, I'm taking my life back.

"Jenni." His sister went wide-eyed again, seeking out their mother. Mom wasn't going to interfere now. This was Henri's finest hour. "I got the impression you'd wanted to be a doctor. I don't mind being wrong, and I'll support you in whatever career you decide." He glared at Margo. "It's got to be your decision. But don't be in such a hurry to grow up, and don't put your faith in beauty and fame. When those go, there'll be nothing left."

"Henri, I'm—"

Henri wasn't done yet. "You're young, and for the time being you have to live here and follow their rules." He hiked a thumb toward their parents. "I'll admit I haven't been the best role model for you, and I'm sorry. But I'm getting my act together. Finish school. Graduate. Then if you want to, you can come stay with me while you go to college or figure out what you want to do with your life. Just… don't let anyone else decide for you."

"I…. I won't." She sat up a bit straighter.

He fixed his dad with a glare. Words twenty years in the making bubbled out of his mouth. "For years, you've let your wife and son support you, and haven't lifted a finger to help."

"But—"

Henri held up a staying hand. "My turn to talk, remember? You have a bad back. Yeah, you've told me often enough over the years. Guess what? You're going to a specialist. I've made arrangements. But you'll either support yourself, or get Mom to. I'm done." Damn, but Henri should have delivered this speech years ago.

"Last but not least." Henri turned to face the woman who'd guided his career, and much else of his life. "I guess I should thank you. If you hadn't turned your back on me, I'd never have picked myself up and started making my own decisions. I'm writing new songs now, better ones. Where once I might have been good, now I'm heading toward. great. And I owe it all to you."

A pleased smile crossed her face. He wiped it away. "After I'd been drugged and wriggled out of some lunatic's plans to do God only knows what to me, I asked you for one simple thing. Do you remember what?"

Deer caught in headlights didn't appear as frightened as she. "I didn't ask you for money. I didn't ask you for one damned thing you couldn't easily give. You could give it, but you wouldn't. I asked for a hug. And maybe for a little understanding.

"Because you couldn't be bothered, I found someone who could. Not to gain from me, not to use me, but simply because I needed it." What he wouldn't give right now to have Seb standing beside him. "It's because of my anchor that I'm here. Don't think for a minute I won't turn back around and leave. I can. And I will. The choice is yours." He leaned over the back of an empty chair, bracing against the headrest to hide his trembling. No way would he confess the emotional toll this visit took. He glanced at his watch. Twenty minutes. Ten more and security would come to the door to check on him. Nothing like having a backup plan. "Here's the part where you get to talk."

"I'm sorry. I didn't know what was happening at the party. You have to admit you have a reputation for…." Margo, always ready to spin a deal.

"Don't apologize and then try to make me feel guilty. Yes, I've taken some stupid chances. My irresponsible behavior is behind me. I found a reason to do better."

"The band wants you back."

"Say what?" Okay, she'd definitely surprised him. "Why?"

The truck-driver snort belied her dainty appearance. "Have you been to the website lately? Traffic is way down, ticket sales are down. There're even rumors that I fired you, and a petition to get you back."

"You did fire me. Sort of."

"In the heat of the moment I might have said something...."

"You told me if I embarrassed you one more time, you'd wipe your hands of me. I did, you did, the rest is history." The humiliation and rejection weren't supposed to burn after all this time. Bile rose in Henri's throat, the ghost of the horrifying day etching her wooden, halfhearted hugs into his heart. Utterly and completely alone. What the hell had he done in his life to deserve abandonment? Was this how Seb felt? After he finished his business here, Henri ought to hunt down Lucas and kick his ass until he confessed everything to Sebastian. Sebastian wanted a family. He deserved a family.

Now for Henri to lay his cards on the table, much like the family's skeleton-in-the-closet-card-shark. "I'll tell you what I'll do. I won't rejoin the band. Ever. What I said in the interview was true. I've grown past them. I'm ready to go in a new direction, expand my horizons. However, I heard you need an opening act. As a gesture of truce, Mismatched Delusions will open for you until you find someone else. Six shows at the max."

The relief on his mother's face was short-lived.

"They'd better step up their game, too, if they want to keep up with me. My new manager will be in touch for the necessary evil paperwork. Now, one final thing before I go." He slowly inhaled, taking a deep breath without appearing to. He'd never show his folks how riled he'd gotten. This next confession would either set the course for future dialogue, or he'd soon find himself as alone as Sebastian.

209

"What's that?" Margo demanded. *Ah, be careful what you wish for.*

"I'm in love with a man. Get over it."

Three mouths hung open. *Oh, Sebastian, wherever you are, you'd be fucking proud of me.*

Jenni broke free of whatever magnetic field had held her to the couch. Henri stumbled, barely keeping himself upright from her hug. For such a wisp of a girl, she tackled like a linebacker. Margo could learn a thing or two about hugging from Jenni.

"Oh, Henny," she murmured, using her childhood nickname for him, "I missed you."

After a moment he wrapped his arms around her, face pressed to a mass of unruly curls. "I miss you too. One day soon, I promise, you can come stay with me if you want. Okay?"

She gazed down at him with watery eyes and sniffled. "Okay."

Henri found a genuine smile on his face. "I love you, pipsqueak."

"Love you too. And Henny?"

"Yes?"

She whispered, "Are you really in love with a guy or did you say that to piss Mom off?"

He met her gaze with his own. "I meant it."

"Good. You should be happy."

TWENTY-ONE

WEEKS WITHOUT word might drive a man insane, but no telling what Charles might do to Seb if Henri showed up while he was there. Why the hell had Seb gone back? If he'd gone back. Why the hell didn't he at least call? Oh yeah, that whole "gotta save myself" thing. Martyrdom was highly overrated. Like patience.

Henri rented an inconspicuous economy car and paid a visit to the house he'd fallen in love with last summer. Christmas would soon be here. With six inches of new-fallen snow, the place would look awesome decked out in garland, a Christmas tree in the foyer.

And Seb, smiling, greeting Henri at the front door. Maybe in another lifetime.

Henri arrived midday and nearly turned around when he spotted other cars in the driveway, until he noticed a "Barclay Realty" sign on the door of one. Not good. The second vehicle, a late model Ford, didn't appear to be the kind of car a man who flashed his money around would drive. After ten minutes the front door opened. Two women and a man stepped out. Henri unrolled his window far enough the eavesdrop on their conversation.

"Oh, it's perfect! And those antiques! I know a shop that'll pay top dollar." The man and one woman bustled into their car.

Selling the house with Sebastian's heirlooms inside? Oh fuck no! Charles had made good on his threats, but where the hell was Sebastian?

The remaining woman turned the collar of her coat up against the chill and picked her way through snow to Henri. He stepped out to meet her. "This house is for sale?"

She pulled back bright red lips into a predatory smile. "With the furnishings. You'd make a lot of money selling those off."

"Why would I sell them off? Why not keep them in the house?"

The woman's perfectly groomed eyebrows shot up to her cherry-red hair. "You'd keep the house?"

"What else would I do with a house if I bought it?"

"Do you have any idea how much this land is worth to a developer? The couple who just left plan to build a resort here."

Tear down Sebastian's house? The house his family had lived in for generations?

Over Henri's dead body.

Henri dialed his manager's number. Lucas had better damned answer.

He answered on the first ring. "What's up, Henri?"

"We have a problem. There's a house for sale in Evergreen, Colorado." He paused long enough for Lucas to gasp. "A buyer wants to tear the house down and build a development. We're not gonna let that happen, are we?"

If the bastard wouldn't pull strings for himself, maybe he would for his son and his dead lover. "Nope," Lucas answered. Oh yeah. Henri loved the pit-bull growl—as long as Lucas directed it at someone else.

"Do whatever it takes, but this house will have Sebastian Unger's name on the deed. Got it?"

"Got it."

Henri nodded at the Realtor. "Your phone number?" She dug in her purse and handed him a business card. "Call this nice realty lady and do what you have to." Henri recited the number from the card.

He waited until her phone rang and she'd submerged herself neck-deep in negotiations, then walked away from the woman's excited chatter. Time for some changes. If only he could convince Seb to accept the house. Oh hell. How could he do that if he couldn't even find the man?

―――――

ANAHEIM. A-FUCKING-GAIN. The city of Henri's nightmares. If only he wasn't on tour and had time to focus more effort on finding Sebastian—without having to watch his back for crazy stalkers.

"A man called asking for you," Arnulfo said after speaking with the hotel manager. "They didn't confirm you had a reservation here."

"Did they get a name?" Not that he remembered much about someone he'd only met briefly, in a darkened club, months ago. Stalker Boy hadn't even given his name.

"Seb was all he said."

Oh, thank God. "Arnulfo, Sebastian Unger is a very, very dear friend. I should have told you sooner, but if he ever shows up at a concert, bring him down front, and no matter where I'm staying, he gets full access to my room. Understand?"

Arnulfo cocked a brow and gave Henri his best cop look over the top of the mirrored shades he never seemed to be without. "Is it wise to let someone into your room while you're not there?"

"This isn't just anyone. This is my best friend." Even if it had taken way too much time for Henri to figure that out.

He marched out of the hotel to a waiting limo, ready to tell the band to go out without him. He'd stay here and wait for Seb to come back. They'd worked hard, they'd earned a bit of excitement. A cab sat across the street, idling. The moment Henri's foot hit the curb, the cab door swung open. He jumped and Arnulfo stepped ahead of him. In the dimly lit interior sat Sebastian, a little worse for the wear. Sebastian. Henri's heart caught in his throat. "Tell the others to go on," he said. "I have something I have to do."

"Are you sure? I should stay with you." Ah, Arnulfo the bodyguard was worth every penny they paid him—all six feet of him.

"I'll be fine. I promise not to leave the hotel. Now, go, before I kiss you again."

Arnulfo cracked a smile, swiveled his head from the cab and Henri, and wandered away.

Henri waited until the limo pulled off to approach. Had Sebastian come to say hello or good-bye? With each footstep Henri's heart beat harder and harder, threatening to explode in his chest. He cleared his throat. "Sebastian."

"Henri." Pure misery shone from the man's eyes. He'd lost weight. Not enough to label him skinny, but for a man terrified of changing his vocal tone, he'd sure dropped a few pounds.

Without a word Henri slipped a hundred dollar bill out of his billfold and handed it to the cab driver. "This cover the fare?"

The man stared at the bill a moment and grinned. "It will."

"C'mon, Seb. Let's get you inside." Seb didn't resist when Henri gripped his arm and helped him from the car. "Do you have a bag?"

"I can't stay."

Arm around Seb's waist, Henri led the way into the hotel.

Damn, he should have kept Arnulfo around to ward off camera-bearing tourists. Too late now. Anyone staring directly quickly turned away. Once they'd reached the brightly lit lobby, Henri discovered why.

Sebastian's eyes were nearly swollen shut.

———

"Bruises, cuts, and cracked ribs," the doctor pronounced. Seb lay sleeping in Henri's bed. Outside the door Arnulfo stood guard, though technically his shift had ended an hour ago.

"Thank you, Doctor."

"Someone worked him over. I assume he'll press charges?"

"I'm not sure." The doctor not asking if they were *the* Henri Lafontaine or *the* Sebastian Unger didn't mean he hadn't recognized them, or that he couldn't guess how such charges might affect their lives and careers. Would Sebastian finally break free from his abuser? Damn, what a beating. If Sebastian didn't need Henri here, he'd hunt down the bastard responsible and give him a taste of his own medicine. It wasn't just singing Henri'd done in clubs. He'd encountered, and won, his fair share of barroom brawls back in the day.

Or maybe he'd ask Arnulfo to pay a courtesy call, a la a B-movie mobster.

Henri showed the doctor out, sent Arnulfo home, and sat beside the bed, a cup of tea in hand.

"Henri?" Poor Sebastian's voice came out barely a whisper.

"Yes, Seb." Henri put the cup down and eased onto the bed. He forced himself to look at Seb's poor ruined face. "Is this because of me? I'm sorry I showed up unannounced. I had no idea about Charles."

"Yes and no. He didn't take to kindly to me leaving. After

you left, I…. I got scared. I went to stay with friends. Charles found me."

Henri lay down beside Sebastian, not close enough to touch, but close enough to hear his husky words.

"I told him no more. He was my patron, and I'd sing at his parties, but nothing else. He didn't own me, and he sure wasn't entitled to my body." Sebastian laugh held no humor. "He… didn't take the news too well. He put the house, and everything in it, up for sale to force my hand. It didn't work. No house is worth my soul."

A tear leaked from the corner of Seb's eye. Henri wiped it away. "Can you buy him out?" Better to let Sebastian think he'd saved himself than to hint of Henri's intervention.

"One of the problems with being a rich man's plaything is you never develop a credit rating. I tried. Believe me, I tried. No one will give me a loan."

Sebastian showed no sign of closing the gap between them. Henri needed to feel him. He wrapped an arm loosely around Seb's chest and pressed a kiss to his forehead. "I'll help in any way you'll let me."

"All I want is for you to hold me, tell me things will get better."

"They will. Especially if you let me help."

"My company dropped me."

Oh shit.

"Charles took the car and credit cards."

Henri wanted to say, *I'll get you new ones.* Seb wouldn't accept a handout. "Stay with me."

"I can't."

"Why not?"

"I've let someone else call the shots in my life for too long. I need to stand on my own two feet, make my own destiny."

"But your pat.... Charles... is acting against you. Let me level the playing field. C'mon, Seb. Please."

"Sorry, Henri, but I can't."

Stubborn ass. "I have three houses." Soon to be four. "I'm not using any of them right now, and Charles sure as hell doesn't know where they are. Why don't you stay at one of them until you work out what to do next?"

Sebastian's silence answered for him.

"Are you going to press charges against Charles?" Why the fuck wouldn't he fight back?

Seb snorted. "Who'd believe me?"

"It might not be just you, you know. What if he treats his family the same way?" Killing was too good for the man. If Henri ever caught him. "Twenty Years to Life." Oh yeah, he'd act out one of his own songs about a guy who went on a rampage against his brother's killers.

"He doesn't. His wife is too highly placed, and too visible. Besides, I met her once. She'd kill him if he dared lay a hand on her or the kids." Seb trembled as he spoke.

Henri held him tighter. "What now?"

"Now I want to spend a night with you, if you'll let me. You don't have to say anything. In the morning I'll go and attempt to win back my life."

"Seb?"

"Yes?"

"If you won't ask anything of me, can I ask a favor of you?"

"Sure."

"Four favors, actually. First: call me whenever you can, let me know you're okay."

Silence.

"Second, we're opening for Hookers and Cocaine in a month. I want you in the audience."

"I'll do what I can, but I can't promise where I'll be. What are the other two?"

With a brush of his lips against Sebastian's forehead, Henri murmured, "Get away from him. He's poison. I know how his kind works. He'll say things, do things, to twist your mind. Get away from him."

"That's only three favors."

"And you haven't given me an answer."

Seb huffed out a sigh. "I'll avoid him as much as I can, but as I mentioned earlier, he's got a lot of pull."

"Then here's the fourth thing." Henri reached into his back pocket, pulled out his wallet, and extracted a card. "If you won't take my help, then please call Dr. Worthington. She's really helped me. She can help you, too, to sort through all the shit. Please?"

Sebastian studied the card and placed it on the nightstand. "Yes, I will."

Henri held Sebastian until gentle rumbles announced his sleeping, then he got up to gaze out over the city. What good were fame and success without anyone to share them with— without *Seb* to share them with?

And here was poor Seb, with no one to call his own, too proud to take the offered hand. Henri stepped out of the bedroom and closed the door. He had phone calls to make. No way in hell would he let Seb out of his sights again. Sooner or later, he'd convince the man to let him help.

"Do you have any idea what time it is?" Lucas growled. At least he answered the phone, though he sounded groggy. He still had a job.

"Your son was beaten black and blue. He's in my bed."

"What the fuck? I swore if you ever hurt him...."

"Save your threats for his fucking patron. Now, you have two choices here: you can tell Sebastian you're his father and try to have a relationship with him, or I'll tell him and he'll hate you for not coming forward." *Walk through fire for love.* They'd only been words strung together when Henri penned that song, meant to appeal to his teen and twentysomething fans who still believed in love and happily ever after. He meant those words now.

"You're a real bastard when you want to be."

"So I've been told."

"Bastard When You Want to Be" added itself to Henri's mental "Songs to be Written" folder.

Some of the anger left Lucas's snarl. "How is he? Will he press charges?"

"As well as can be expected, and no. Deep down, I believe he feels he deserves to be treated badly." *Please, let him call Dr. Worthington.*

"Anything I can do?"

Anger brought bile up Henri's throat. Anger at Charles, anger at himself and Lucas for not protecting Sebastian, and anger at his own dad for not being much of a father. "He won't let me help him, why would he let you?"

"What have you offered?"

"Money. A place to stay."

"Give him what he needs."

"He needs money and a place to stay." *And me.*

Lucas spoke calmly, the way he had the day they'd met, offering the voice of reason. "Those are the same things Charles offered. What he needs most is a career and a way to earn his own way in life. His dignity."

"And how can I offer him that?"

Lucas's harsh exhale wafted through the phone. "Remember how I told you I'd approached his mother with a project idea?"

"Yes?"

"She was interested at first, but in the end turned it down."

"What was it?"

"A contemporary take on *Phantom of the Opera*."

"Remakes are a dime a dozen." Even Henri had seen one or two.

"This one's placed in modern times, and based in an inner city."

Oh, really? A mental image flashed through Henri's mind of The Phantom in a high-rise office building instead of beneath a theater. "Go on."

"The phantom is an aging rocker, disfigured in a car wreck. He hides out in his apartment all day, and only ventures out at night. A young singer moves into his building. He takes her under his wing, but never shows her his face."

Phantom of the Opera, another secret obsession he'd never reveal to the world. Damn, but Henri had crushed on the latest movie phantom. Ah, the fantasies he'd had... which now coalesced into a clear image of him and Seb in the starring roles. "Can she be a he?"

"Why?"

"Who do you see as the phantom?"

"Why, Sebastian, of course."

Oh yeah. Ideas whirled around Henri's brain. "No, it's me. Sebastian is the singer. And there has to be roles for everyone in my band."

"I don't know, Henri. What would the public think? No one's tried anything this ambitious since The Who filmed *Tommy*."

"They'll think whatever they want to. Isn't that the beauty of the theater, to set the stage and let audiences' imaginations take them where they want to go? If they want to make this homo-erotic, let them. If they want a buddy story, that's okay too."

"I don't know, Henri."

"Make it happen. But I'm not mentioning the project to

Sebastian until you've got the story in hand. Oh, and backers, though I'm willing to put up the money."

"Your name alone will get interest." Lucas sounded fully on board—and fully awake—now. "Let me see what I can do."

"You make it happen. And Lucas?"

"Yes?"

"Be here first thing in the morning for your son. He needs you."

Henri hung up and crept back into the room to take his place beside Seb. For years he'd been surrounded by folks with their hands out, wanting more, more, more, more, more. Seb wanted comfort and Henri's arms around him. If that was all he'd take, Henri would give whatever he could. "Everything's going to be all right," he whispered, pulling his sleeping lover to his chest.

TWENTY-TWO

HENRI WOKE to an empty bed and a confused manager knocking on the door. Fuck. No telling where Seb had taken off to. He needed protection from Charles. No easy thing to do if he wouldn't stay put.

"Where is my son?" Lucas demanded.

"I couldn't exactly keep him against his will."

"I planned to tell him." Lucas stopped and leaned against the doorway. The light fixture wasn't anything out of the ordinary, yet he stared at it anyway.

Henri raised a hand and Lucas flinched. Maybe Lucas had the same reasons to recoil from a raised hand as Sebastian. He didn't need any more shit. Henri placed his fingers gently on his manager's shoulder and lowered his voice. "I know."

Lucas slowly exhaled, dragging his fingers through his hair. "Why'd he leave?"

"Because he's hardheaded and determined to make it on his own. Lucas, are you familiar with many people in the opera world?"

"A few, not many."

"Do what you can to make sure he succeeds."

"Of course." Lucas pressed his hand over Henri's. This man was Sebastian's father. Right now he wasn't a manager. In days to come Henri might be staring at him across a dining room table full of holiday trimmings.

If they managed to talk some sense into Seb.

One thing at a time. "Any word on the house?"

"It's yours."

"No, it's Sebastian's, if I can convince him to take it." Too bad Henri couldn't take a month off to focus solely on Sebastian's problems. The Christmas holidays loomed, Thanksgiving having amounted to dinner with his band in a greasy-spoon diner while on the road. Would Sebastian accept the house as a Christmas gift? No, probably not.

"Once you get your script together for *The Phantom of the Parking Garage* or whatever, I want you to call a press conference." Henri turned away. Too much intimacy made him nervous these days, unless he counted Seb.

"Any particular reason? You just did one a few weeks ago."

"Not for me. For Seb. If you can find him."

———

WHAT A disgrace. Dozens of reporters flocked to Henri's press conferences—six measly newshounds showed up for Sebastian's. The man deserved better.

"Mr. Unger, is it true that alcohol and drug-abuse problems led to your dismissal from *Othello*?"

Henri glared daggers at the asshole who'd dare imply such a thing and pulled his cap down tighter on his head. Getting recognized wasn't an option. *The Sebastian Unger Show* didn't need upstaging.

"Stress-induced illness led to my *withdrawal* from the role," Sebastian replied. He sat with his shoulders back. To those unfamiliar with him, he might seem confident. To Henri, he appeared a pale shadow of himself. Still, he hadn't taken acting lessons for nothing. "You have my word, if there'd been any other way, I wouldn't have given up the role of a lifetime."

There! Take that! Only, Henri wished like hell Sebastian would tell the truth, how an abusive patron pushed him from the limelight he'd fought hard for. He searched Sebastian's face and found no traces of bruising—likely the result of a skilled makeup artist.

The questions wound down, mainly of a harmless nature like, "What's next?" to which Sebastian replied, "We'll have to see. Il Divo made the break from opera to popular music. Maybe I'll learn from them."

Finally, the woman Lucas had once planted in Henri's question-and-answer session raised her hand. "Mr. Unger, is there any truth to the rumor that rock musician Henri Lafontaine wants to collaborate with you on a musical based on *Phantom of the Opera*?"

Chaos reigned. Henri's work here was done. On his way out he stopped and hugged Lucas, who waited in the wings to change Sebastian's life. "Who's the reporter?" he asked. He liked having a member of the press on their side.

"Her name's Sharon Mulcahy." Lucas let loose a grin. "If and when I finally get to be a father to my son, I plan to introduce them."

Henri gave Lucas a sidewise glance.

Lucas' grin grew wider. "In six months, she's going to be his stepmother."

"You sly dog, you!" Henri thumped Lucas on the back. "Congratulations."

"Thanks. Anyway, Sharon knows people in New York,

Friends of the Opera, who have one hell of a lot more pull than Charles. She's going to pay a visit. And I'm about to have a long talk with my son."

"Good. I need to get back to the band, but if you or Seb need me, call."

Lucas nodded, more solemn than Henri had ever seen him before. One way or another, Sebastian would make the headlines, while Charles circled the drain on his way down.

———

Hi, Bro! Merry Christmas! Wish you were here. I caught Mom going through some of your old things with a wistful smile on her face. And Dad talked about that Christmas when you were little and knocked the tree over. They miss you. Give them time. They don't like admitting they were wrong, but they'll come around.

I got accepted to UCLA! I'm not sure yet what I'm going to do, but there's no reason why I can't go to college and do some modeling, is there? Love you!

Smooches,

Jenni

P.S. Have they caught the crazy guy yet? And how's your boyfriend? You never told me his name. I want pictures of you two.

Henri glanced up from his laptop to stare at the wall with blurred vision. The area behind his heart tattoo squeezed. Right now Jenni would be opening her gifts. She'd squeal over the new iPhone and iPad, and he'd quietly sent an extra message with the *Physician's Desk Reference*.

One day she might be a doctor… or a model. As long as she'd made the choice herself, he'd accept whatever she decided.

He discarded several more e-mails, until finding one from Lucas.

Merry Christmas and expect an interesting message from Elason Recordings soon. They've got a solid track record with some up-and-coming bands. As you're soon to find out.
Lucas
BTW, have you heard from Sebastian? I haven't heard from him since telling him the news.

———

"No, DAMMIT," Henri replied to his laptop. Where the hell was Seb? Was he celebrating Christmas with friends, hiding out somewhere? Or had dickwad Charles gotten to him? His chest tightened again. What a fucked-up holiday.

He wandered through a lonely house, heavy with the scent of holly and pine. Garlands hung over the doorway to his living room, festooned with gold-and-white ribbon, glittering gold baubles hanging from the creation. A tree stood by the glass doors leading out to the patio, echoing the theme of green, white, and gold, clear lights shining from the branches.

The decorations didn't stop when he left the house—his housekeeper's obsession with the holidays extended to the topiaries around the swimming pool, and pots of holly lined the walkway. The display should have been pretty, and would have been, had someone else been there to enjoy the woman's efforts.

What a big fucking monstrosity of a place. He'd only bought the mishmash of glass and chrome at his mother's insistence. It didn't feel like home. No, home was in the Colorado Rockies. Still, if his sister took him up on the offer of a place to stay, she and her friends might enjoy the pool, not that he'd ever used the thing.

His bandmates were with their families, and he'd even given Arnulfo the day off. There'd been no signs of the stalker since the dead roses, and no proof they'd even come from the same guy who'd drugged him.

His next appointment with Dr. Worthington wasn't until next week. For all he'd accomplished in his life, where had he taken a wrong turn that led to spending Christmas alone?

He looked out over his neatly groomed lawn. Except for the recently added decorations, the place showed no character at all. If he stayed here, he'd need a landscaper. Roses. He'd plant roses. And gladiolas.

His cell phone rang and he stared at the name on the screen. His heart skipped a beat. Sebastian! "Oh my God, Sebastian! Where are you?"

"A cab dropped me off at your gate. Can I come in?"

"You're where?" It had to be a joke. But no, a familiar shape stood beyond the wrought iron gates, waving. Henri bounded up the walk and fumbled with the keypad, typing in the code to remove the metal barrier. Then he was in Seb's warm embrace, in front of his house, for the world to see. At the moment he didn't give a damn.

Nothing mattered but the man in his arms. Here, safe! After a moment he registered Sebastian's shiver. "Let's go in."

Sebastian hesitated, staring up at the imposing reminder of the differences in their paychecks. "Maybe I should go."

"It's a house," Henri said, "it's not really a home. It will be if you come inside."

Seb glanced around the foyer as they entered, but there wouldn't be any motion from the other rooms to attract his eye —they were alone in the house. "I take it you didn't patch things up with your family."

Did Henri detect a note of accusation? "I'm working on it."

Sebastian raised a skeptical brow in answer.

"No, really! I am. That's why I've agreed to open for Hookers and Cocaine—as a sign of good faith."

The brow rose higher. How Henri had missed that simple gesture. Sebastian knew him well.

"And to show them up." If Henri succeeded without his mother's help, maybe then she'd learn to respect him.

"That's my Henri." Sebastian's smile seemed almost cheerful if not for the rainclouds in his eyes.

Broken. A broken man. Ah, to be the glue to piece him back together again. But Henri must move slowly. One wrong move could send Sebastian running again. "I'm afraid I'm alone here today, and I never learned to cook. Want to order takeout?"

"I didn't come here to eat—I came here to see you." Sebastian wrapped his arms around Henri, asking a question with his eyes. Henri answered by meeting him halfway. Sebastian moaned into the kiss, hanging on so tightly Henri fought to breathe.

Henri clung to his lover. If he let go, Sebastian might suddenly disappear. The warmth against him pulled back. He took a deep breath and opened his eyes. Seb's beautiful face filled his vision. Seb. Here. Now. "Go into the living room. I'll get us something to drink," he said, and then he made short work of his errand, his ear trained for a door slam.

He returned to find his guest inspecting the gold record above the mantel. Henri had been proud of the shiny claim to fame once upon a time. Now he wished he'd hidden the damned reminder of unpleasant memories under the couch. "A Matter of When." The story of a man in a relationship so bad he'd kill himself to escape. Not the kind of message Sebastian needed to hear.

He placed two cups of tea on the coffee table.

"You've done well for yourself," Seb commented.

"I've made mistakes along the way." The biggest being letting Sebastian walk away the last time they'd been together. Losing his old band might have been the biggest *blessing* of his life.

"Haven't we all?"

Suddenly, the clouds blew away, clearly showing the disparity in their lives. Somewhere around his second album, Henri had taken the trappings of his career as his due, neglecting his body and his voice. Seb was a slave to his passion—so much so that he'd become a slave in truth to a manipulator. Years ago, before he'd clawed his way to the top, with his mother pushing him every step of the way, Henri might have done the same thing.

Rising on his toes behind Sebastian put Henri at neck-nuzzling level. "I'm glad you're here." In the corner a Christmas tree glittered. Henri hadn't turned on the lights. "You like Christmas?"

"I used to. The carols, the gifts. You haven't truly appreciated the season until you've experienced an opera house Christmas. They throw outstanding parties." Seb leaned back against Henri, taking on a more serious tone. "Sometimes Mom and I went home to spend the holidays with Grandma. There's a big hill behind the house where I used to go sledding. Since Mom died...." All alone. No one to spend the day with. Just like Henri.

Henri enfolded Seb in his arms. It was better this way, holding his lover from behind. Seeing tears in the man's eyes might break his heart. "Did Lucas talk to you?" He better have, or he'd hear from Henri.

"He did. And I don't know what to think. He used to visit when I was a kid, but he never stayed long. I always got the impression there was more between him and my mother than met the eye." His back shook with his laugh. "Funny thing is, I used to dream about them getting married and him being my stepdad. Isn't that a riot?"

Pressed against Seb's back, Henri felt his sigh as much as heard it. "But I also can see her doing what he said she did—pretending I'm someone else's for the prestige and acceptance. Calling herself Sebastian Unger's fiancée opened a lot of doors.

"For years there's been speculation, people whispering behind my back about how I didn't look like my fath.... Sebastian Unger. My whole life is a lie. Lucas doesn't see a reason for me to go public, but I'm tired of lies and deceit. Hell, I don't have a career left to ruin, why should it matter?" He gave a pained-sounding chuckle.

What the fuck? Sebastian lived for his music. And he wasn't a quitter. "Sure you have a career. Didn't the reporter tell you?"

Seb whirled in Henri's arms. "The bullshit about you in a musical? I've heard a lot of wild tales over the years, but that's the most creative."

"It's true. Lucas first pitched the idea to your mother years ago." Sebastian winced at the mention of his mother. Henri would have to take care until the recently reopened wounds began to heal. "I've asked him to update the score for the two of us. That meets with your approval, right?"

"A show? A Broadway show? And you with no experience?"

Ouch. "I didn't say this would be a Broadway show, Sebastian. I'm thinking bigger." Sebastian's reaction wasn't encouraging. "I'm planning a movie."

"You're out of your mind. A movie? You're planning a movie for me and you?" Seb's face fell. "What's in this for you?"

Poor untrusting Sebastian. Not that he'd been given much reason to trust lately. "Can you imagine the exposure I'd get? This will overshadow anything I've ever done with Hookers and Cocaine."

"Yeah, especially if it bombs. Don't you think this is a pretty big risk to take?"

Gee, show some faith, why don't you? "It won't bomb. I won't let it. And my band's fully on board." If they weren't, there were plenty more musicians in the world. But the misfits he'd pulled together had his back. Now to add the key player.

After a few moments of silence, Sebastian ventured a barely audible, "You're sure you want me?"

"More than you'll ever know." *And in more ways than one.* "In fact, the deal's contingent on you agreeing to the role of Chris."

Sebastian quirked up one side of his mouth and shook his head. "Okay. If I can't talk sense into you, send me the script."

"Send it where?"

"Um… that might be a problem."

"No, it's not. I have plenty of room."

"I told you...."

"I have four houses, two I haven't been to in months. No telling what housekeeping's been up to. I normally rent out those two, but they're currently empty. I'd like you to stay here with me, but if you'd rather not, you have your choice between three other homes—as a favor to me, of course. Free rent—you act as caretaker when you're there."

Lowered brows had to mean, *man thinking here.* "Where?"

"Besides this one, I own a cabin near Lake Tahoe and a condo in Dallas—don't ask, I honestly can't remember why I bought it—and..." Should he tell Seb or not? Better to be honest. "...a lovely two-story in Evergreen, Colorado on lots of land." He waited, the ball firmly in Seb's court.

Sebastian stepped away. Henri missed his heat immediately, though the room wasn't cold. "You bought my house from Charles."

Chin up. You did a good thing. "Yes."

"Why?"

"Some assholes were going to buy it, sell off your family's things, tear down the house, and build a resort." Okay, maybe he'd been too honest.

Sebastian scowled. "This isn't your fight, Henri."

"But I love that house. And the grand piano."

"Henri…."

This situation called for a little *more* honesty. "I love you, Seb. This probably isn't what you want to hear right now. You've got your life to get back together and want to do that on your own. I understand. Believe me, I do. I stood in your shoes not too long ago. If not for you, I wouldn't be where I am right now."

"What you feel is gratitude and pity. Nothing more." Resignation pushed back the hopefulness on Sebastian's face.

"Maybe. If gratitude and pity cause butterflies in my stomach whenever I hear your name. If gratitude and pity make my heart do cartwheels when I see someone who sort of looks like you. Seb, I'm writing sappy love songs. The guys are freaked out, but Tessa loves them."

Resignation turned to shock. "You love me?"

"Yes, and I understand if you can't say the same right now. You don't have to. For years I've been too busy being famous to realize how few genuine friends I have." Fists balled at his sides, Henri pled his case. "You taught me what to look for, believed in me without worshipping me for something I took for granted. You get me, Henri, Henry, or whoever the fuck I am. Besides, you've done something for me no other human on the planet ever has."

"What's that?"

"Made me tuna fish sandwiches. C'mon, let's take this to the kitchen. I'm starving." Although Sebastian held his hand, he didn't say the words Henri longed to hear. Maybe he never would.

———

"WHO's THAT one from?" Seb pointed to a brightly wrapped package under the tree.

"Tessa." Henri shook the tiny box, the kind a ring or pin might come in. It rattled. He ripped the paper and lid off to find a packet of crystals. "For luck and protection," the card said.

Steve the stylist included another cross, along with a clipping from a fashion magazine depicting models dangling crosses from their belt loops, along with snippets from various fanzines showing the legion of Henri's fans who now copied his style. A "Season's Greetings" card held the written inscription, "Told you."

Henri had sent his family vouchers for an all-inclusive resort in Cabo. Their card lay face down on his dresser. He couldn't bring himself to look at the picture of the three of them smiling in front of the family tree without him, but couldn't throw the reminder of happier times out either.

Jake sent a vintage Stones T-shirt; Michael, a book on the evolution of rock and roll; and Colton gifted Henri with a reproduction samurai sword.

"That is so cool!" Sebastian held the sword aloft to admire the workmanship while Henri unwrapped an oddly flat package from Lucas. Oh shit. He slid the gift under the couch before Seb noticed. Seb's yawn offered a perfect out.

"It's getting late. Why don't I get you settled in?"

Sebastian placed the sword on a nearby chair. "I suppose I could use a shower before bed."

Henri tuned out the gasps and "ohs!" while showing his lover the rest of the architectural nightmare he wouldn't call "home." They trudged up a willies-inducing curved staircase, the acrylic steps giving the illusion of walking on air. Garlands on the handrail lent a more solid appearance. Who the fuck thought invisible stairs were a good idea?

For the first month or so after moving in, Henri had enjoyed the glass outside wall of his room, which, at night, afforded a good view of the lights of LA. Times had changed. Who might even now be sitting in the bushes across the street, with binoculars trained on his every move? He shuddered, closed the blinds, and turned away, only to see himself in a wall of mirrors. Whoever'd built the place must've owned a massive ego, if the mirrors throughout the home were any indication.

A bed big enough for four took up a small fraction of the floor space. Funny, Henri had been more comfortable in the modest double bed with Seb in Colorado. At least he couldn't see through the floors up here, where acrylic gave way to marble.

Sebastian stood in the middle of the room, mouth open, slowly turning. "Oh my God. I've never seen a room quite like this one."

Henri found his dwelling hideous. How odd to hope Sebastian liked the place. "Does that mean 'oh my God, I love it?' or 'where's a wrecking ball when you need one'?"

"It's... it's not you." A wrinkle formed between Seb's brows. "Or is it?"

"It's not. It never was." The wrinkle smoothed. "It's something my mo... manager talked me into."

Like Sebastian's room, no pictures adorned the walls—Henri never figured out how to hang them on glass and mirror tiles. If not for the magazines and other effects stacked on any available surface, his room might have had even less personality than Seb's.

Now wasn't the time to point out Seb's lack of luggage. "The bathroom's through there if you want to take a shower, and there's a robe hanging right inside the closet. I'm going to clear up downstairs and be right back." Henri kissed Sebastian, holding on perhaps longer than necessary. Sebastian. Here in his room. But for how long?

He trotted back down the ghastly stairs, ears tuned for running water, and retrieved Lucas's gift. A picture, in a tarnished silver frame. A woman who must have been Seb's mother held a chubby-cheeked infant in her arms—an infant with soft copper fuzz on his head destined to darken into Seb's now-auburn locks.

No telling how Sebastian would react to seeing what just might be a father's way of giving his blessing. Oh shit! Seb's father! Henri reached into his pocket for his cell phone to tell Lucas Seb was safe. Hell, where had he put his phone? He patted his pockets, but no phone. When had he last seen it? Oh yeah, when Seb had arrived at the gates. But he couldn't recall seeing it after then. He must have dropped the thing in the yard.

While he'd entertained Seb, night had fallen. His house-keeper kept a flashlight in the pantry, but no matter how hard he searched, Henri couldn't find his phone.

No problem. He kept a spare in his bedroom.

He returned to the living room. Seb must still be in the shower. A few presents remained under the tree. His new recording studio had sent champagne, along with news Lucas had hinted at: "Ice Inside" had scored the fifth spot in the weekly top-twenty countdown. Nice!

Various other music types had sent gifts of wine and food. He'd eat the food and regift the wine. He didn't need temptation in the house—other than Seb.

He didn't receive even a card from any of his former band-mates, not that he'd expected them. Still, Seb's presence made this the best Christmas in recent memory.

The ornaments glittered a bit brighter; the sappy carols Sebastian insisted on playing lightened the mood. Sebastian appeared in the doorway, towel wrapped around his waist and voice as decadent as ever. He did justice to a rousing rendition of "Joy to the World." Henri joined in on harmony, their voices merging, becoming one. The song ended. Sebastian said, "Merry Christmas, Henri."

"I have a gift for you."

"You shouldn't have. I didn't get you anything."

Yes, you did. You showed up. "You can owe me. Have a seat."

Sebastian perched on the edge of the couch, one brow raised and his legs open enough for Henri to hope for a cough or sneeze to reveal all. Okay, no perving on Christmas.

"I hope you like it." Henri handed over the professionally wrapped package. His own wrapping skills sucked big-time.

Always meticulous, Sebastian peeled the tape off the paper and slowly unwrapped the gift, a Christmas gift strip tease. Finally, he opened the paper to peer inside. "You got me an e-reader?"

Was that a good reaction or a bad one? "You said you like paper novels, but I figured, as much as you travel, this might be easier to carry around more books."

Sebastian scrolled through the preloaded listing. "*Hitchhiker's Guide, Stranger in a Strange Land.*" He glanced up at Henri.

"Uh…. I didn't know exactly what you liked beside sci-fi, so I tried to give you a variety."

"*Lord of the Rings. Hunger Games?*"

"It's a good series. Or so I'm told." Henri's face heated clear up to his ears.

"Thank you. You shouldn't have."

"'You shouldn't have, I'm charmed,' or 'you *really* shouldn't have'?"

"You shouldn't have, I'm charmed. Thank you." The thank-you kiss was worth every moment of agonizing over book choices.

"I got you something else too." Henri handed over another package.

Sebastian stripped off the paper on an entire case of choco-late bars.

"I stole one from you back at the house. I paid you back—this is interest."

Sebastian threw back his head and laughed. A good sound, a genuine sound. "Henri?"

"Yes?"

Sebastian stared at the present in his hands. "Would you take me to bed?"

"Are you sure?"

"Yes. Even before I managed to escape Charles, with you I let myself dream. I didn't think of my career, or even the consequences. I wanted you. I pretended you wanted me too."

"I did want you. Do, I mean." And he'd spend however long Sebastian would let him proving it.

———

SEBASTIAN'S NAKED skin glowed in the low light of a bedside lamp, dark whorls of hair adding interest to his body. His chest pushed against the sheet, and Henri lowered the fabric for a better view. His cock throbbed.

He climbed up on the bed, leaving his clothes in a pile on the floor, palmed Seb's stomach, ran his fingers through dark curls, and paused to tease the pink nipples peeking through the chest hair. With a light touch he ran a finger down Seb's long nose and lower. Sebastian puckered his lips to kiss the fingertip as it wandered by. Down and down Henri stroked, over a bobbing Adam's apple, zigzagging across Seb's sternum, and lower, to seize the drop of fluid at the tip of Seb's dick. Henri brought the offering to his mouth and sucked away the moisture. Another drop formed. Henri licked it away and settled on his side to suck in earnest. Sebastian maneuvered him, pulling, pushing until the warmth of his mouth welcomed Henri inside.

Fingers danced across Henri's buttocks, left unadorned of artwork for the time being. Sebastian cupped the globes of Henri's ass in his large hands, working him to the beat of a song known only to Seb, vibration from his humming shooting fire to Henri's groin.

Seb was here. In Henri's bed. No telling when he'd leave again. Henri opened wide, putting Sebastian's open throat lessons to good use.

Suddenly, cool air shocked Henri out of his approaching bliss. "Stop! I'm about to come!" Sebastian shouted and pushed Henri off his cock. "What do *you* want?"

The uncertainty in Sebastian's eyes ripped at Henri's heart. No telling if Charles had ever given the man a choice.

Henri didn't hesitate. "I want you in me."

A quick trip to the bathroom yielded what they needed, and Henri saved time by preparing himself in front of the sink. He'd never been one to require a lot of preparation, as noted in his song "Fuck the Foreplay"—banned in thirteen countries.

He paused a moment in the doorway, enjoying the vision of Seb in his bed. Instinct took over—no thinking needed. Henri slid over Sebastian. Skin against skin. Breath mingling in a kiss. Someone moaned. Sebastian bucked, rubbing his erection against Henri's. Seb. His beautiful Seb.

His normal brand of condom strained to accommodate Seb's larger width. Time enough to restock later.

Henri rose up in the bed, positioned Sebastian, and hissed at the burn of the wide head pressing inside of him, stretching him. Teeth pressed tightly together, he blew out a breath. Pleasure. Pain. Mingling. Fullness. Ecstasy when Sebastian brushed against the one perfect spot deep inside.

Movement. Barely registered by a mind overloaded, nerve endings tapped to the limits. He rocked, pressing Seb harder against his prostate, and reached down to cup his cock. No stroking. Not yet. Tonight must last.

Up and down, side to side, he took his lover into his depths. Perfect. He rode out shockwaves and shuddering chills, his breath coming in gasps and pants. Sebastian gripped his sides, helping him keep the tempo. With a surge of his hips Sebastian buried himself deep, only to retreat and return.

Again and again and again. Henri lost the battle to resist temptation and enclosed his cock in one hand, holding tight but not moving. Seb's motions rocked them both, forcing a groan from Henri.

Flutters began deep in the core of his being. He raced toward the finish, fingers gliding over his flesh, aided by his own precome.

Sebastian's thrusts grew harder, more insistent. Henri impaled himself on the cock breaching his body, savoring the sweet ache heralding his orgasm. Pleasure slammed into him with hurricane force. He'd have fallen if not for Seb's hands guiding him. "I'm coming." His guttural growl barely sounded human.

In response, Sebastian picked up the pace yet again, moving at frantic speeds. "Oh God, oh God," he chanted.

Henri let go, mind bursting into a thousand glittering pieces. He came to rest in the crook of Sebastian's arm, vaguely recalling Seb's roar of completion. In a moment he'd get up, stagger to the bathroom for a washcloth, and wipe away the evidence of their passion. In a minute. Definitely not now.

One perfect moment, secure in his lover's arms. All he'd ever wanted.

TWENTY-THREE

EMPTY BREAKFAST plates littered the nightstand. Sebastian drained his coffee cup and placed it amid the pile. Seemed he'd loosened up his neatness. Then again, no one would scream at him for not immediately cleaning up the mess—may Charles rot in Hell.

"I want you to hear something." Henri padded across the bedroom floor naked, toes squeaking across cold marble, so different from the hardwood of Sebastian's home. He preferred the hardwood. After adjusting the stereo and inserting a disk, he stood, arms across his chest, to study his lounging guest.

The pristine white sheets of Henri's bed enhanced Seb's coloring, bringing out the copper highlights in his hair. "What are we listening to?"

"You'll see." Recently, guitar players had blended together in Henri's mind, but from the first chord of the recording, he recognized Michael's distinctive flair. If only Margo hadn't ditched him years ago.

Jake followed behind Michael; two different musicians with

different styles circled each other musically and came together in a meeting of minds. Together the newfound accord welcomed Colton's keyboarding, and then Tessa's bowls, the haunting ring adding a touch of the odd that fit perfectly with the song.

A male voice sang, "Ethereal. She's ethereal...."

"That's not you," Seb commented.

"No, it's not." He said no more. Head cocked to the side, Seb listened. The song wound down, the musicians dropping off until only Tessa remained. Henri hadn't even provided backup. The last note held. Voice a mere whisper, Tessa sang, "She's ethereal," her silken tones evoking the words she uttered.

Sebastian smiled. "Gorgeous. Is this some new band you've discovered?"

"No, it's my band, showing what they're capable of without me."

"And you don't mind?"

"Of course not. They're talented in their own right. I don't mind giving them the spotlight on occasion." Something he'd never done with his old band.

Sebastian snorted. "You'd never make an opera diva."

No, Henri supposed not. "I've got something to show you now."

He turned on the big-screen television he seldom watched, never being home much, and sat next to Seb on the bed. He clicked the remote. The song started again, this time with Henri singing lead.

A tree's branches swayed in time with a swing rocking back and forth. Tessa wore a flowing green dress, and elf ears peeked through her hair. Flowers decorated corkscrew curls. Behind her and the swing, Michael appeared in silver, giving her a gentle push. He faded in and out of sight, a nod to his accidental Starman persona. Up in the tree Jake plied his trade, a lute magically moaning out the bass line, while Colton, dressed as a medieval knight, lounged beneath the branches.

"The theme wasn't my idea." Henri had questioned the whole concept at first. What kind of video was this for a serious rock album? Tessa loved it. Tessa, the heart and soul of Mismatched Delusions. The nurturer. She wanted this video with elves and fairies? Henri would deliver on a silver platter, as would the rest of the band.

The camera focused on the fairy maiden, following her across a meadow. Wand in hand, she seemingly played the swaying flowers towering above her, the sweet music of her bowls emanating from their petals.

A boat ferried her across a crystal lake, the faces of her band-mates reflected momentarily in the looking-glass surface. The song ended with her lying in the boat, hand folded over her breasts and eyes closed as she whispered, "She's ethereal."

"Wow, reminds me of 'The Lady of Shalott.'" Sebastian had been lying back with his head on the pillow. Now he sat on the end of the bed, staring at the TV screen. "That's gorgeous."

"Thank you." Time to take a chance. "You said you wanted to rebuild your life on your own, but I have a huge favor to ask of you." More than a favor. Henri simply didn't trust anyone else with this all-important assignment.

"What?"

"You heard the raw version, with Michael singing."

"Yes."

"This is his song, not mine." Henri took a deep breath. "He should sing on the video and on the CD. Not me. Can you help him?"

"I'm not a music teacher. I'm too young, too raw. I could recommend someone."

"I don't want anyone else. And it's more than teaching I'm hoping for. Michael's extremely shy and will need lots of convincing of how talented he is. I'm not going to get what I want from any old teacher. I believe I will get the kind of coaching he needs from you. What do you say? I'll pay you, of course."

Blood rushed to Sebastian's face. "Oh, this is another way to sneak me a handout, is it?"

"No. It's an honest business arrangement. I appreciate what you've done for me, and want you to work with Michael, as a trial. If everything goes well, I'll ask you to take on Tessa and Jake too." As good as they were now, under Sebastian's instruction, they'd thrive.

"What about the other one. Your keyboardist?"

Some things even a musical genius like Sebastian couldn't fix. "He's a lost cause, vocally."

Sebastian lay back on the bed, tracing the rose on Henri's chest. After a moment he smiled. "He won't be if he listens to me."

Hallelujah!

They curled up in the bed. Never before had Henri been so comfortable in this room. He sifted his fingers through Seb's chest hair. A chime brought the foreplay to an early end.

Seb jumped. "What's that?"

"The gate." Damn the timing. Henri punched a button by the bed. "Yes."

"Dude, open up. We brought you Christmas dinner."

Oh shit. Jake.

———

Of course, Ms. Ethereal herself didn't even slow down at the front door. She nudged past Henri and beelined for Sebastian. "Hi, I'm Tessa, and, oh my God, Henri, the house looks awesome!"

Henri couldn't recall ever being so outmaneuvered. No choice but to face fate. "I'd like you to meet my... friend... Sebastian." He should have worked out details a few minutes ago, before the band walked in. Was Seb his friend? Boyfriend? Significant other? Henri sure as hell wouldn't settle for "fuck buddy." No way, no how. The fact that the larger Seb now wore some of Henri's too-tight clothes spoke volumes.

Tessa squealed and bounced up and down. Colton saved a vase from her elbow with a lucky grab. "Oh my God! You're Sebastian Unger. I loved you as Rodolfo in *La Boheme*."

Tessa loved opera. No surprise there. She loved everything.

Michael nudged Henri to the side. "Coming through." He carried a foil-covered pan. "Kitchen or dining room?" The scent of turkey and dressing trailed in his wake.

"Dining room." Might as well finally get some use out of a table for twelve.

"Hi, I'm Maggie. You have a lovely home." A pretty blond followed on Michael's heels, carrying a cardboard box. Looked like Michael had a girlfriend.

Jake stepped through the door. "Wait up, Mags." Okay, Michael hadn't gotten lucky.

Colton steadied the vase before following the others, a bulged-out bag hanging off one shoulder.

Colton stepped through the front door. "I've got green bean casserole." Huh?

Henri did a double take, eying the Colton in the doorway and the one now entering the dining room. Oh shit. Someone had perfected cloning and hadn't told him.

"Yo, Parker," green bean casserole Colton bellowed. "Did you meet Henri?"

The first Colton turned around, shouted, "Hi, Henri," and resumed his march through the house.

No one but Tessa dwelled much on Sebastian's presence, too busy hauling food from the cars to the dining room.

"Tessa!" Michael called. "Find plates and silverware."

"Oops. Duty calls. See you guys at the table." She scrambled away. Sebastian grabbed the wobbly vase she hit before it fell. He examined the bottom and rubbed a finger across the marble table. "Velcro. I'd suggest Velcro."

The band had met Sebastian. Sebastian had met the band, and the world hadn't stopped spinning. Meteors hadn't destroyed the earth. Yet.

Clinks, clanks, a *crash* and one "Oh shit! I hope that wasn't real china," summoned Henri to the dining room. Having never cared to own such a thing, he certainly wouldn't miss the brown ceramic bowl lying in pieces on the floor. Good riddance.

Sebastian responded to a tearful Tessa before Henri. "Here, I'll get it." Sebastian knelt to pick up the pieces.

"I'm sorry, Henri!" Tessa scrambled around on the floor beside Seb.

Henri joined them in retrieving tiny shards. "You're not hurt, are you?"

"I'm okay." She sniffed. "But the bowl isn't. I'm so sorry. I'm such a klutz!"

"It's okay, Tessa. It's a bowl. I have plenty of those, and they didn't cost a small fortune like the ones you play." Actually, his mother had paid a couple thousand for the monstrosity. Henri couldn't find it in him to care. Perhaps Tessa's playing left her with a special affinity for bowls in general.

With a festive tablecloth hiding them from view, Sebastian met Henri's eyes. Something in their coppery depths hadn't been there before. Under the guise of reaching for the same broken pottery, Seb clutched Henri's hand for one brief moment.

"What?"

"Tell you later," Seb replied.

Because of the joint effort of the band members and their assorted "plus ones"—or perhaps in spite of—soon the table filled with a holiday feast. Turkey, dressing, gravy, cranberry sauce, green bean casserole, corn, and rolls lined up in various dishes. "You didn't have to do this," Henri told them. "I said I was okay spending the holiday alone."

Colton (or was it Parker?) said, "Yeah, but you didn't handle the 'alone' part well, so why trust you to manage feeding yourself?" He glanced from Henri to Sebastian and back again, a smirk on his lips. No use telling him, *"He's just a friend."* For all his Bruce Lee delusions, his powers of observation otherwise worked fine.

They sat down at the table, Jake with Maggie, Colton with his brother, gangly Michael with petite Tessa. "Why didn't you bring someone?" Henri asked Michael.

Michael's face purpled and Tessa gave a tinkling laugh. A cough barely disguised Michael's, "I did."

"Where?"

Tessa laughed again. Oh. Oh!

Tessa and Michael? Someone needed to be the voice of reason. "Will this affect the band?"

"Dude, where did you think 'She's Ethereal' came from?" Michael picked up Tessa's hand and kissed her knuckles.

Tessa nodded at Sebastian and then focused on Henri. "Not all *affects* are bad. You've been hanging around the wrong bands."

A "Hey, pass the green beans" from Jake ended relationship conversations and started the feast.

No one questioned Sebastian's presence in Henri's house or life. Instant acceptance. Whatever capacity he filled met with the band's approval, apparently. Henri relaxed. "Sebastian here is the reason I can now hit a high C."

"Oh, that must have been a wild night." Colton snorted, and Jake guffawed at Michael's casual comment.

Henri buried his face in his hands. Sebastian patted his back. "You have your hands full with these folks, don't you?"

"Yes."

The sniggering died. After a while Michael asked Sebastian, "You're a vocal coach?"

Tessa answered for him. "He's a star performer with the North American Opera."

"I've asked him to work with us, refine our sound." Henri hadn't considered mentioning future plans yet, but why not take advantage of the moment? Michael might not be open to the idea of working toward replacing Henri's vocals with his own on the "Ethereal" video before its release. He'd recruit Tessa to help convince the guy.

"Can you help me?" Michael broached the question on his own. Good, better for him to accept the challenge voluntarily. Those lyrics needed Michael's vocals, especially since he'd written the song for Tessa.

Sebastian fit right in to the group, wrapping a huge hand around the back of Henri's neck. "If I can get him to stop huffing like a marathon runner in the middle of a line...."

Either they'd already decided Sebastian was Henri's lover and didn't care or his status didn't matter. Period.

After dinner an enthusiastic Michael disappeared into the study with Sebastian. "Loo, loo, loo, loo, loo, loo, loo, loo," reminded Henri of his first week at Sebastian's house, what seemed like years ago instead of months.

As they were leaving, Tessa rose up on her toes to whisper in Henri's ear, "You have our approval. He's a keeper." She pecked Henri on the cheek and climbed onto a chair to repeat the process with Sebastian before joining Michael by the door.

The band left, leaving Henri with Sebastian in the foyer. "Earlier you said you'd tell me later. What did you mean?"

Sebastian took Henri's hand. "There's been too much going

on in my life to consider adding someone on a permanent or semi-permanent basis. And I'd sworn not to use you as a crutch to prop me up while I regain my footing. But seeing you there, not caring about an obviously expensive broken bowl and more concerned for Tessa and her embarrassment, it finally hit home what a decent person you are."

Now there was an accusation Henri didn't hear every day. "Sebastian. I've been in and out of rehab for years. I was front man for a band called Hookers and Cocaine, for crying out loud, and for the first few years tried to live up to the name. I'm anything but a good person."

"Yes, you are." Mimicking Michael's earlier gesture with Tessa, Seb brought Henri's fingers to his lips. "And in that moment I realized something."

"What?"

"I've always dreamed of someone like you."

Best Christmas gift ever.

TWENTY-FOUR

LADY GAGA? Really? Henri followed the strains of "Bad Romance" straight to his kitchen. Sebastian danced across the floor, bumping the refrigerator door closed with his hip and belting out the song.

Henri leaned quietly in the doorway, admiring a relaxed Seb. Finally he asked, "How'd it go with Dr. Worthington?"

Sebastian came to a full stop, regarding Henri with wide eyes. His momentary fright disappeared. "Fine. She helped me see my relationship with Charles in a different light. I know it up here...." He tapped fingertips against his temple. "Now to learn it here." He tapped the area over his heart.

"That's good. You also were doing one hell of a job with a rock song."

A lovely flush crept up Sebastian's cheeks. "Char... my patron scoffed at me listening to anything but classical or opera, calling popular music a waste of my time." He studied the sandwich in his hands. "I hid your CDs when he visited."

"You listened to my music?" Sure, Henri'd found the evidence, but they'd yet to discuss the matter.

"Yes. And I used to envy you. Instead of singing someone else's songs, you created your own. I imagined how you'd be… someone so unlike me, never letting anyone push you around."

"But I'm not like that. My mother controlled my life, like Charles controlled yours."

Sebastian raised his gaze to meet Henri's. "Yes, and now we're both free. Would you like a sandwich? And I could really use some help backing up Ms. Gaga." He smiled.

———

"How's HE doing?" Lucas sat at the dining room table, in the same spot his son had occupied during breakfast.

"Pretty good, considering. Look, he has a lot on him, but he's seeing Dr. Worthington. He'll be okay."

"Sharon's New York friends are working on a way to expose Charles for the asshole he is, while keeping Sebastian out of the line of fire. Has the bastard contacted him?"

"No." Henri would kill him if he did.

Lucas nodded, running his finger down his coffee cup handle. "I have a lot of making up to do."

"Why not forget what can't be changed and work on the future?"

"I want to be a father to my son." A world of pain dwelled in Lucas's eyes.

"He knows. Give him time."

"Has he had any luck finding a new company?"

"Not yet. He's auditioning now with a group out of LA."

"Sharon's friends…."

"Sebastian wants to succeed on his own." Damned the luck.

"Stubborn, like his mother."

Did Henri detect pride in Lucas's tone?

After a sip of coffee, Lucas changed the subject. "Any word on your stalker?"

"No. Maybe he's given up and gone away." Henri could only hope.

"Maybe. Even so, I think we should consider beefing up security for your tour."

More security, following him around. Or rather, following Sebastian, though the man might be upset to discover Arnulfo keeping a discreet but watchful eye on him. Charles could be anywhere.

Lucas opened his computer bag and pulled out his laptop. "While it's booting up, take a look at this." He slid a magazine across the table. "Enough bad news. Here's something you might like."

Henri stared at the latest edition of *American Drummer*. Oh, wow! Tessa had made the cover. Resplendent in her fingerless gloves and dressed entirely in lavender up to the tips of her glitter-frosted hair, she posed behind her drum kit, seemingly in motion even in a photo. The headline labeled her, "Little Drummer Girl." About time the band members got their own accolades.

Lucas's smile turned grim. "I'm glad you're sitting down." He tapped a few keys on his laptop, then turned the screen toward Henri. "A friend brought this to my attention."

Had an offer from *Rolling Stone* come through? "Henri Lafontaine's Biggest Fan," the website proclaimed. Images of Henri filled the page: shirtless and sweaty onstage with Hookers and Cocaine. Damn, Tessa was right. He had looked a bit ragged, with his flyaway hair and grungy jeans.

He focused on a post made the previous day, judging by the time stamp.

At first he didn't find anything wrong with the beautiful

landscapes portrayed. The mountains, hazy in the early morning. A walking trail. A log and stone two-story house, Seb standing on the porch. Oh shit! Where had those come from? More pictures, taken from a tour bus window… his old band. His new band. His sister's last birthday party. His family.

Oh God! The air suddenly left the room. "The motherfucker got my cell phone. He's been here!" And likely knew about Sebastian. Crap, crap, crap, crap, crap. "I need to send this link to Arnulfo and Detective Shepard."

"Already done." Lucas studied Henri, face grim. "You be careful." *And look after my son* remained unsaid.

———

SEBASTIAN AMBLED into the room. Henri minimized the fan page he'd visited far too often since Lucas's visit two days ago. Better not to cause needless alarm. Secure arms surrounded him. He could get used to this. "You're coming to the concert tonight, aren't you?" Taking on the world worked better with Sebastian at his side.

"Wouldn't miss it."

Good. Tonight, not only would the fans get one hell of a performance, if all went according to plan, they'd hear an exclusive new song. Henri melted into his lover's arms, enjoying the calm before the storm. Sebastian hadn't mentioned leaving, and he also didn't "loo, loo," throughout the day. Which would be worse, him leaving to pursue his career, or him giving up on his singing altogether? Singing was Sebastian's world. Henri couldn't imagine him without his opera.

Time enough to worry later; right now he had a band to shame and a psycho to evade.

———

LUCAS CHATTED with Margo. At an elbow nudge from Sebastian, Henri waved. So far his mother hadn't blabbed to the press about his coming out, though the widening of her eyes and slight twitch of her lips when she regarded Henri standing so close to Sebastian equaled her adding one plus one and getting two gay musicians. Now wasn't the time to let Sebastian in on the "I'm in love with a man" conversation he'd had with his family. Not talking about his folks meant not mentioning his parting shot. Margo fluttered her fingers and disappeared backstage, no doubt to hover over the dregs of Hookers and Cocaine. Two-to-one odds said her new lead singer wouldn't show.

"Remember," Lucas said, "no matter who gets star billing, the audience paid their money to see you."

If only Henri could convince himself. He huddled backstage with his band to shouts of "Henri, Henri!"

"Tonight we kick ass and take names," he said, considering them each in turn. "And Michael?"

"Yeah?"

"Tonight, fifth song? Slide in 'A Matter of When.'"

"But we've never done that one in public before."

Henri grinned. "It's high fucking time, if you ask me." Not only would the song blow his old band's version out of the water, Henri's secret weapon even now settled on the front row. Henri joined Tessa's preconcert ritual, bouncing on the balls of his feet, adding a bit of "loo-, loo-ing" to the mix. Calm down and warm up at the same time. Win! And the best part? Henri didn't need pills to get him out on the stage tonight. Tonight, thanks to Seb's teaching, the band joined him in vocal warm-ups.

Tessa had clothed herself in peach lace and chiffon, bringing to mind Stevie Nicks back in the eighties. She rocked the style. Colton wore a silk dashiki over his jeans. At least he wasn't channeling Bruce Lee. Henri and Jake both wore jeans and T-shirts. No fucking way would they wear leather and be mistaken for members of the headlining act. Michael's button-down shirt and khaki pants had become "Starman's" trademarks.

Tessa gave him an appraising glance and a wink.

Somewhere in the throng of chanting humanity sat Seb… and possibly a deranged lunatic psychopath. Had to take the good with the bad. Technicians hooked them into mics, making last-minute preparations.

Mismatched Delusions took to the stage, except for Michael, who hurried into a side room for his part of the show.

The crowd rose to their feet for "Ice Inside," cheering Henri on when he hit and held the high C note. Damn. The lights, the music, the cameras, the fans. Seb. Life didn't get any better than this. At this moment, the entire fucking world revolved around the stage.

Finally, the moment Henri had been waiting for. The lights faded down until only a lone spotlight shone on him. He strolled to the edge of the stage, where he'd been told Seb was sitting, and held out his hand. In the bright light he couldn't make out his lover. He started singing, hand still extended.

"Where have you been?"

Nothing. Henri motioned for his band to repeat the line. He said aloud, "Again," into his mic for Michael's benefit.

"Where have you been?"

Again, nothing happened. Holy shit? What now? Just when he'd made his mind up to continue solo, Seb's powerful tenor replied:

"Dove sei?"

A hand gripped Henri's, and he pulled Sebastian into the spotlight. "Ladies and gentlemen, Sebastian Unger!" Hooting and catcalling followed, but whether it was because the crowd recognized Seb or merely acknowledged him as special to Henri was anyone's guess.

The band kept the beat going while Henri and security

helped Sebastian onstage. Henri picked up on the second line, stepping close to Sebastian to hand him a mic:

"All my life spent lonely."

"Tutta la mia vita in solitudine." Damn, but Sebastian sang like an angel. The crowd agreed with their screaming and clapping.

"I know you're out there."

"Lo so che sei là fuori da qualche parte."

Henri's words were no longer a song. They came straight from the heart. Music and sweat poured out of him in equal measure.

"The one I've waited for."

No lover's caress ever thrilled like Seb's "La persona che aspettavo."

Henri altered the next line, changing "I know I'll find you" to "and now I found you."

The words blended with Seb's "Lo so che ti troverò."

Henri's "It's just a matter of when" and Sebastian's "E' solo una questione di tempo" mixed with perfect accord. The music blended into the background, and Henri sang his love song to Sebastian. Sebastian might not return that love, might never return the love. Henri loved enough for two.

After the song Henri hugged Sebastian tight and helped him off the stage. No way in hell could the next act compete with what they'd delivered. No matter what the critics said tomorrow, tonight Mismatched Delusions rocked. From what he could see of the audience, not a single spectator remained seated.

At last the set ended and Henri took his bow, then turned to bow to each of his bandmates in turn. They joined him at the stage edge. Even Michael appeared in the flesh. They clasped hands and bowed as one.

Henri dashed off stage. Moments like this called for Sebastian to share the glory.

A veritable sea of reporters and cameras lay in wait. Henri surged on, counting on Lucas to field the questions. What a clusterfuck. Where was Seb? He glimpsed russet curls down the hall and picked up the pace.

Holy shit. Seb stood backed up to the wall while Charles sneered. Nose to nose with Henri's lover. "Oh hell the fuck no!" Henri charged.

"Henri! No!" Tessa shrieked.

Arms wrapped around him from behind. Jake rumbled, "Don't ruin your moment. We got security for this."

Henri twisted in Jake's grasp, searching out his bodyguard. "Arnulfo? That man shouldn't be backstage. Get him the fuck out of here." How the hell had Charles gotten in anyway? Was he following Seb?

"Go to the dressing room. We got this." Michael headed off down the hall with Sylvia in hand.

Time slowed down. Sebastian's hands against Charles's chest, pushing, his scream of "Never again!" Holy fuck! He fought back. He finally fought back! Hallelujah!

Henri weighed the odds. No, he didn't need the bad press of taking out Charles in front of witnesses. Sebastian didn't need any bullshit either. He breathed a sigh of relief when Arnulfo inserted himself between Seb and the dick of a former patron.

With his band clustered around, forming a human shield about Sebastian, Henri spun on his heel and charged for his dressing room. If Seb wasn't there in five minutes, he'd go find the man.

Hey! Why so dark in here?

TWENTY-FIVE

HOLY SHIT! What the fuck happened to his head? A bump slammed Henri against a hard surface. Damn! He rocked violently from side to side, an engine's vibrations reverberating against his back. A trunk. He was in a trunk, riding over some god-awful rough road. Where the fuck was he?

His shoulders ached from having his hands secured behind him. Trussed up like a Christmas turkey. And cold! What the hell happened? He'd headed to the dressing room, the lights were off. He groaned, the pain in his head making itself known. Another bump jolted his shoulder. Whoever did this would have hell to pay. He wriggled his fingers toward his pocket for his phone. Damn, he'd been onstage. He never took his phone onstage. Not that he'd get the tape off his mouth to talk.

Rolling to the left didn't help—he'd been packed in pretty tight, with little wiggle room. The emergency trunk latch remained out of reach, taunting him. So close and yet so far away. Gasoline fumes burned his nose.

Where the hell was he and where the hell were they going? And please, please, please, let Arnulfo be hot on their tail.

The car slowed, jostling over rugged terrain, and finally stopped. From outside came an off-key version of Hookers and Cocaine's number one song, "A Matter of When":

"Got a date with a bullet, got a date with a gun...."

Jeez, the guy couldn't sing. He clunked around the car, opening and closing doors, stomped a few feet away, and dropped something on the ground. Would Henri be next? Should he try to scream or pretend to be out cold?

Finally the trunk lid popped open. "Oh, you're awake. I hope I didn't hurt you too bad." Holy fuck. He'd recognize the bastard's voice anywhere, even after all these months.

Henri couldn't make out the man's face with a flashlight shining in his eyes, but he jerked away from the fingers probing his injury. Damn, there had to be a fist-sized goose egg on the back of his head.

"Aww... don't be like that. You made me do it. If you'd gone with me last time, I wouldn't have had to come back."

Sure, blame the victim.

Blame the victim, make him pay....

Fuck, not now! I am not writing a song called "Blame the Victim." Not, not, not.

The fingers inspecting his bump trailed down his cheek. "I know what you need, probably better than you do."

My bodyguard with a gun in his hand?

"I have every one of your songs, and I've listened, really listened to what you were saying."

I was in a band called Hookers and Cocaine. Nobody should've listened to me.

"You tore my heart out with 'Lonely.' But don't worry, I'm here now. You'll never be lonely again." The guy stepped back, and a bit of illumination cast him in silhouette at the same moment woodsmoke assaulted Henri's nostrils.

The guy wouldn't shut up. "And then you came out with 'A Matter of When.'"

Actually, "A Matter of When" had come first, but now wasn't the time to argue with the crazy person, not that Henri stood a chance with his mouth taped shut.

"I wanted to help you but didn't know how." Crazy Psycho Fan from Hell rambled on, reaching around Henri to pull out various unidentifiable items. He paused long enough to lean in, nose inches from Henri's. "After you wrote 'Walk Through Fire' I figured it out."

He grabbed Henri's arms and hauled him from the trunk. Crackling, dead grass broke his fall. Henri "oomph!" and "owwww"ed behind his tape gag as he bounced over rocks and sticks toward a bonfire, the guy dragging him by the legs. Ow! His shirt caught on something. He left a chunk of fabric behind. Flames cast gold shadows on a ring of twisty shapes. Trees. Tall ones. A breeze blew smoke right at him and he coughed, perhaps more violently than necessary, hoping to win sympathy points.

His abductor knelt down beside him. "I love you. The tabloids tried to say you were with women, but I know better. I know it's a man you were singing about. And I've figured out a way to get you away from him forever, the one you wanted to escape in 'A Matter of When.'"

"A Matter of When" referred to escaping my controlling mother —I know that now—not an abusive lover, you shithead!

"I wouldn't hurt you. I'd treat you better."

Then how about untying me and letting me go?

Instead, the most unstable fan on the planet turned his back and tossed a branch on the already blazing fire. At least Henri wasn't cold anymore.

"Lonely" described the ache and longing of needing someone

to love. Though at the time he'd written the lyrics life had been good, there had been something missing, noticeable only with the entrance of Sebastian into his life. "A Matter of When" spoke of getting out of a bad situation at any cost. But what did "Walk Through Fire" have to do with anything?

Oh shit. *Life going up in flames, I'd walk through fire for love.* Oh, holy hell, no.

His host disappeared and reappeared a few moments later, gas can in hand. "It may hurt a bit, but the pain won't last long and you don't have to be afraid. I'm going with you."

No! No! No! No! No! Henri struggled, screaming against the tape over his mouth. *Dear God, we haven't talked much lately, but please don't let me die tonight. Not like this.*

I'll be a better person. I'll stop lying about who I am. But please don't take me away from Seb. He makes life worth living.

Sirens split the quiet night—too fucking far away. They'd never make it in time if they didn't hurry, and as rough as the roads were, they'd have to drive slowly. And no telling if they were even coming for him, or if they just happened to be in the neighborhood, bound for somewhere else.

The fan hummed while he sprinkled more gas on the fire. *I can't die like this!* Henri added, *I'll patch things up with my family* to his plea bargain with the higher power.

The fame, the wealth, the trappings of his career—he'd trade all to return to Seb. They'd work things out, they'd find a way. Nothing mattered but being with Sebastian—everything else faded into details.

Sebastian, Sebastian, Sebastian. The world revolved around Sebastian. Oh, God. Jenni! Sebastian and Jenni. He couldn't leave them.

With his captor's back turned, Henri grunted, groaned, and managed to get his bound-together legs underneath him. Escape wasn't an option. He'd stall until help arrived. The crackling fire covered his sounds and he hopped away, arms behind him. He fell face-first with a thud. Pain lanced through his cheek. He glanced toward the fire. Crazy Boy hadn't heard. Henri scrambled back up, pins and needles jabbing through his legs. *Shake it off. Run!*

With running out of the question, he hopped, leaning against trees for support. Fire lanced through his chest from lack of air. Breathing through his nose didn't help. The sirens came closer.

Crazy Boy turned around. "Henri?" He searched the surrounding brush. "There's no need to run. I'll take care of you!"

That's what I'm afraid of. Henri stood still, braced against a sapling to keep from toppling over. His kidnapper stomped his way through knee-high dead grass. A flashlight beam swiveled from side to side. Fuck. Heading right for Henri. "I know you're here."

No shit. Where else would I be?

The flashlight's beam slipped by, illuminating trees and... nothingness. A few yards away the land dropped off. A known devil pitted against a mystery ledge.

If I get out of this I'll never, ever write depressing lyrics again. It's sunshine and roses from here on out. Tessa will be happy. And she can wear her damned fairy costume to every fucking concert. Sorry, Lord, do I need to give up cussing too?

He froze. The beam flashed over him, stopped, and returned. *Don't see me, don't see me!*

"Oh, there you are." Backlit by a now-raging fire, Henri's worst nightmare appeared as evil incarnate, blackness against the light. Sirens no longer shrieked in the distance.

Henri stared at the fire. His funeral pyre. Certain death or the unknown? He took a deep breath. *Sebastian Unger, wherever you are, I love you.* He plunged through the trees and over the edge.

———

"MR. LAFONTAINE?"

The voice came from a million miles away, from a shadowy shape swimming into Henri's field of vision.

Hands lifted him onto something solid, jostling him more violently than the car trunk. Voices. Garbled words.

"I'm still alive," he tried to say. A crackle and gurgle came out. Tape. Why was there tape over his mouth?

"Henri?" A familiar voice. Arnulfo.

Henri raised his hand to have it clasped into a welcome grip. "Henri, you're hurt. We're getting you out of here." More jostling. Someone forced his eyelids wide to shine a light inside. Arnulfo let go of his hand. Henri waved his fingers. *Don't let me go! Stay with me!*

Yelling in the distance. A stinging in his upper arm. A gunshot. Quiet. Blackness.

———

SUNLIGHT STREAMED in through the window, filtering through a veritable garden of flowers. A riot of color lined the windowsill: carnations, gladiolas, varied displays that must have cost a fortune… and a single red rose. He didn't need to read the card to figure out who'd sent the gift. Sebastian. While everyone else's displays spoke of money, Sebastian's spoke from the heart.

His head ached, as did one arm, and his left cheek stung.

"Oh good, you're awake."

His blood ran cold. Margo. He turned his eyes toward the woman who'd given him life, perched in a chair by the bed.

Instead of perfectly styled hair, she'd pulled her tresses back into a simple ponytail. No cosmetics hid the effects of her years. It'd been a long time since she'd looked like a mother. Now her resemblance to the woman who'd once sat up with him all night when he was sick made his heart ache.

"Where...."

"Oh, Ree...." She hadn't called him Ree since he was seven years old, nor had she enfolded him into such a heartfelt embrace, jarring his painful arm. He bit down on his lip to keep from shouting. What was a little pain against a heartfelt hug? Margo... Mom... jumped back. "I'm sorry! I forgot how badly you were hurt."

Maybe he hadn't been as quiet as he'd hoped. "No, it's okay." They stared at each other. So much needed to be said to close the gulf between them. The hell with it—he'd made promises he intended to keep. "Hi, Mom." He offered the words as a truce.

She responded, "Hi, son." And then she smiled. One day they'd have a long talk—right now they were family again. "I sent your sister home to take a bath and get some rest. And your dad's not been on his job long enough to take much time off, but he dropped by earlier."

"Dad got a job?" Whatever drugs they'd given him must be good. She couldn't have actually said *Dad got a job*.

His mother gave him a sheepish smile. "Part time, but we're hoping for full time soon, after he's proven himself. It's not easy to find work without an established history."

"And you've been sitting with me? How long?"

"You were brought in the night before last. We'd wondered where you went after the concert. The police wanted to talk with you as soon as you woke up, but I won't tell them if you don't want me to."

She fussed with his pillow, voice emerging a bit shaky. "How are you feeling? You gave us quite a scare."

Running, or rather, hopping. Falling. Agony. "Details are fuzzy. What happened?" He licked his dry lips and his mother raised a plastic cup, complete with bendy straw, for him to suck down the sweetest water he'd ever tasted. Who was this woman and what had she done with Margo?

"From anyone's best guess, you were conked on the head, hauled out of a window, thrown into a car, and taken to the woods. You jumped into a ravine to get away. You've got a broken arm, scrapes, bruises, and a possible concussion. We were worried." She sat the cup down on a table by the bed. Tessa could play that cup. And the table. It'd be a good backup to the ringing in his ears.

"What about the guy?"

Margo—no, Mom—searched Henri's eyes. "He shot himself."

"Dead?"

Her gaze fell on the fingers twisted together in her lap. "I'm afraid so. The officers might tell you more, but that's all I know."

Safe. Henri was safe. But a human life was too great a price to pay. While in rehab Henri had met many people who were out of their minds, most on a temporary basis. He shuddered. What made a man plan to burn someone, and himself, alive?

"You've got a lot of people wanting to talk to you, but until you woke up, the doctor only allowed one at a time, and family."

Time to find out how much she meant her change of heart. "Where's Sebastian?"

"He's in the waiting room—refuses to leave. You meant it when you told us you were in love with a man." A statement, not a question.

"Yes."

"Is Sebastian the one you told us about?"

"Yes."

"I thought it might have been a phase, a kid experimenting,

or you drugged up and not caring who you slept with back when you'd sometimes sneak a man into your room while on tour." A touch of bitterness crept into her tone, gone the next minute. "You know what this'll do to your career?"

"I don't care." At least she hadn't said, "What this will do to the family?"

"I didn't think so. I'd be lying if I said this is what I'd wish for you—" Henri started to object, but his mother continued. "—because it won't be easy. There will be haters, those who'll try to drag you through the mud."

He snorted. Ow! His head hurt. "I've got haters now."

She didn't deny the truth.

"What's your opinion?" Her thoughts shouldn't matter after all they'd been through, but they did.

She glanced up from her hands, eyes so much like Henri's own staring back at him. No contacts marred their similarity. "I've had a lot of time to think over the past few weeks, especially while sitting in this chair, wondering if you'd ever wake up, and what I'd say to you when you did. At some point along the way I stopped being your mother, didn't I?"

No need lying about the obvious. "Yes."

"Then I've lost my right to a say in the matter. Though I hope, in time, I can win back some maternal points. I miss my boy." His arm tingled where she placed her hand. "You're not coming back to the band, are you?"

"No."

"Probably for the best. I'm not cut out to be both your mom and manager."

"You got me my start." Might as well give credit where due.

"And pushed you even when you didn't want me to. I'm glad you're making your own way in life. I suppose the doctor needs to check you out now that you're awake, and your man is dying to see you." Lines formed around her eyes when she smiled. "I heard you two singing. He's got an incredible voice, and you sounded so good together."

Damn, but he'd gotten some good drugs, to hear his mother say such things. "I think so."

"And if his worry is anything to go by, he loves you deeply."

Really? "I hope so."

"Can I be a selfish manager bitch one more time?"

"Just once." And not a single time more.

"Is it true about you planning a rock-and-roll remake of *Phantom of the Opera?*"

"That's the plan."

"Is there a role your sister could have? She needs the exposure."

Oh, this might be fun. "Speaking of 'exposure,' can I cast her as a nun, in a habit that goes all the way up to her chin?"

Margo sighed. "If you must."

———

DETECTIVE SHEPARD entered after Margo left. Not Sebastian, damn the luck. "I won't take much of your time." He handed over a photograph. A smiling young man in cap and gown, clutching a diploma, stared back at Henri. His heart clenched. The guy appeared a wide-eyed innocent, unlike what Henri assumed a lunatic should look like.

"That's him." Henri handed the photo back. No need to drag the horror out a minute longer than necessary.

"His name was Roger England, a loner and IT specialist who worked mostly from home and didn't go out much, according to his landlady. The proverbial 'such a quiet young man.' He'd moved from New Jersey just before his first encounter with you. His apartment was filled with concert memorabilia, posters, magazines. Turns out he was a big fan. He'd also been treated for depression and schizophrenia. We found several unfilled prescriptions in his apartment."

Wrinkles formed on Shepard's forehead. "We recovered four full and one empty gas can from the site, as well as rope and duct tape, the same inventory we'd found in your hotel room. He also left a note at his apartment, confirming what you believed he'd planned. It seems Mr. England had been in the hotel a few days earlier, working on the door locks. Apparently, he'd programmed himself a master key and bribed his way into the party after your show."

"And he's gone now." He'd never really be gone. Henri saw the man's face every time he closed his eyes.

"Yes, he's gone."

"Can I ask you something?"

"Sure."

"Did he have a family? Anyone to miss him?"

"None that we've identified."

"Lonely."

"Huh?"

"He said he began to identify with me after I released the song 'Lonely.'" If that's what lonely did to a man, Henri never want to be alone again. "His inspiration for our being together forever was 'Walk Through Fire.' I suppose I'd better be careful what I write from now on." Henri held out his hand for the detective. "I appreciate what you've done."

"Will you be returning Officer Reyes to us now?" Shepard took Henri's hand in his, giving a firm shake.

"Not unless he wants to go. It's come to my attention that I need someone running security for me. Particularly if next year's Grammys go the way I hope." He tried for a grin, but stopped halfway. Ouch! "I promised only to kiss him on special occasions."

For the first time in their acquaintance, the hard-nosed detective smiled. "I'm sure he finds that reassuring. Now, if you'll excuse me, I have murders to solve. It's been a pleasure working with you. Perhaps we'll meet up again someday, under better circumstances."

"Maybe we will." Henri made a mental note to send concert tickets to Shepard's precinct. As long as Charles remained a threat, he'd keep Arnulfo around.

"One more thing," Shepard said before he left. "We found video equipment at the site. He'd planned to film the whole thing. We've watched the site for accomplices assigned to retrieve the camera after... well, you know. So far we've turned up nothing. He appears to have acted alone, counting on someone to find the evidence eventually."

Henri settled back onto the hospital bed, breathing deeply and releasing tension he only now noticed he'd held. He lost his sympathy for his abductor. The asshole had planned to burn Henri alive, and himself, live on camera. Sick fuck. He almost called for Shepherd to come back.

Soon Henri would have to face the press, his manager, his band, and the world. But first....

"Can I come in?" Sebastian peered through the partially opened door.

Henri smiled. "Get over here." He held out his unbroken arm.

Seb sat in the chair by the bed and leaned into Henri's hug. "I thought I'd lost you."

"I'll never let anything come between us again. I promise." Sebastian didn't need horrific details. He had enough problems to worry about.

They sat quietly, Sebastian running fingers and lips over Henri's face, carefully avoiding cuts and scrapes. Finally he said, "If I said I might be falling for you, would you think it's the worry talking?"

"Is it?"

"No. I've been pretty much smitten since the first time you returned after our month together. You came back. I didn't think you would."

"And kept coming back. I'll always come back for you. Always." Smitten. Not the same as "I love you," but close enough.

"But...."

"No buts."

"Yes, buts. What if the press finds out about us?"

"Sebastian, when I was lying tied up on the ground, preparing to meet my end, I made a promise that nothing would come between us ever again."

"What about your career?"

"What about it?"

"What if you lose your fans?"

"I won't lose them all. And I'll gain new ones. But in the end, it doesn't matter. I could lose my entire career. As long as you're with me I won't care."

"You mean that?"

"I do. What about you? The opera world may not be as accepting as rock fans."

Sebastian chucked. "Opera types are usually pretty open-minded. And if not, I'll find a new job."

"Doing what?"

"I can always apply as kitchen help." He ran his lips along Henri's. "I'm told I make a pretty good tuna fish sandwich."

"That you do. But I'm thinking that real soon, neither one of us will have much to worry about, jobwise."

———

SEBASTIAN LAY curled up in bed, his hair fanned out on the pillowcase. "Come to bed, Henri."

"I will in a minute, after I check my e-mail." Henri stared at the laptop's screen.

Henri,

I'm now afraid of my future wife. Sharon's "New York friends" are forces to be reckoned with. They gave Charles a choice: resign from the Met's board or be booted and have every plaque or brick with his name pulled from every opera house he's ever touched.... They remember "little Sebastian" hanging out in Annette's dressing room and are out for blood. Oh, and did I mention they're friends with Charles's wife? Even opera can't compete with the real-life drama currently playing out in New York.

The legal age for consent in Colorado is seventeen, and the opera traveled, which means federal law takes precedent over states'. The federal legal age of consent is eighteen. Charles will soon be answering a lot of questions.

I don't know how you talked him into it, but I'm glad Sebastian pressed charges. He needs closure. Please take care of him.

Lucas

Henri would hold Seb's hand every step of the way to giving Charles what he had coming.

TWENTY-SIX

HENRI STARED out the window, watching fluffy snowflakes fall. The scent of woodsmoke no longer gave him the screaming shivers, and he warmed himself by the fire Sebastian had started in the fireplace. White covered the trees and mountains. Spring would arrive soon. Until then, Henri intended to enjoy a winter wonderland in the Colorado Rockies.

Arms wrapped around him from behind. Safe. Loved, even if Sebastian wasn't comfortable enough to say "I love you." He would, one day, once he considered himself an equal again. Baby steps. Dr. Worthington called them baby steps. Holding Henri, kissing him, acknowledging his love with all but words. Good enough for now.

Henri wanted the words, but didn't truly need them. The tuna fish sandwich and cup of tea resting on a tray near the piano spoke volumes. God, he loved this music room. Seb's office.

"I still won't accept this house from you," Sebastian murmured against Henri's hair. His goose egg was gone now, the only remaining traces of his ordeal a few greenish-yellow bruises and a broken arm.

"I'm not giving it to you. You have to earn it." Compromise: let Sebastian earn his own freedom. Right now Dr. Worthington relayed the words through Henri. Hopefully the doctor imparted the same words of wisdom to Sebastian personally.

"And how do you propose I do that? This house is worth about two hundred years' worth of tuna sandwiches."

"By starring in *Phantom of the Bronx*."

Even Sebastian's snorts were melodic. "A starring role won't equal the price of this property. I insist on earning my own way in life."

How many years had Henri waited to hear someone utter those words, and not latch onto him simply for his wealth? "Oh, you'll earn it, all right. Remember how hard you worked with me last summer?"

"Yes."

"Before production begins, I need you to work with the band —and my kid sister. I'm warning you, she can't hold a tune in a bucket."

"And how about you?"

"Me?"

"It's been a while. Need a refresher?"

Henri grinned. "I might. How about a few open-throated exercises?" He spun in Sebastian's arms and knelt. If they were going to spend much time in this house, he'd need throw rugs to cushion his knees. Lots and lots of throw rugs. And pillows. Hell, maybe they needed to move the old settee and install a fold-out couch.

He unzipped Seb's pants and fished his already half-hard cock out of the opening. The purpled head beckoned Henri's tongue. A swipe across the slit made Sebastian moan. Ah, what sweet music. Henri dove lower to suck his balls, while stroking Sebastian's shaft with his hand. Seb's legs trembled.

Bracing the shoulder of his bad arm against Seb's thigh, Henri bobbed up and down in earnest on Seb's spit-slicked erection, wrapping the other arm around Seb's legs for support. Sebastian hissed, pumping his hips in time with Henri's sucking.

Henri ran his tongue around the head, softly nipping with his lips. What a beautiful cock—thick, veins bulging. Tasty. He wrapped his lips around the head, swirling his tongue over the tip.

Hands under his armpits urged him to his feet. Sebastian wound his arms around Henri and joined them mouth to mouth. He led them in a slow tango, tongues keeping rhythm while he danced them closer and closer to the settee. Piece by piece Seb removed Henri's clothing, starting with his T-shirt.

He kissed a path down Henri's ink-stained torso and sat down to open Henri's jeans and slide them down his legs to pool around his ankles. Lifting first one leg and then the other, he removed Henri's socks and shoes. Outside the wind howled and snow formed drifts against the trees, but here Henri found warmth, love, and a peace of mind he'd never known before.

Stark naked, he strolled across the floor and closed the blinds. Not that Henri expected spies, but one couldn't be too careful, and though Arnulfo was loyal to a fault—and footsteps overhead spoke of his whereabouts—Henri had scandalized the man enough for one lifetime by answering his hotel room door in his birthday suit a few times.

He returned to settee, where Sebastian lay stretched out and naked. "I think I should warn you, even after you earn this house back from me, I have no intention of leaving. That is, unless you want me to. Ultimately, the decision is yours. It's your house."

"It's too big for one person. But it works fine for two. Particularly with the extra room for the band members I'm supposed to train."

Henri climbed onto the settee, straddling Sebastian, catching his erection between their bellies. Sebastian's cock nudged his entrance. Sure hands skimmed up his sides, grabbing his shoulders and pulling him down for a kiss. This wasn't comfortable.

Grabbing Seb's throw from the settee, Henri stepped back and arranged the frothy fabric on the floor as best he could one-handed. Sebastian finished the job and sank to his knees. "C'mere." He held out his hand to Henri. Henri lay down, allowing Sebastian to position him facing the fire.

Sebastian spooned against him from behind. "I'd always hoped one day to make love in front of this fire."

An image came to mind of Sebastian and Charles in this spot. Henri pushed the thought aside. Whatever Seb had done with the man, it wasn't making love. And thanks to a restraining order, Charles would never darken their door again. Henri rested against the comfort of Seb's body, angling back to press against Seb's stiff cock.

A laugh rumbled against Henri's back. "Is that a hint?"

"No, it's a demand. We rock gods can be demanding. Don't say I didn't warn you."

"Duly noted." Seb nibbled the back of Henri's neck. Catlike, Henri turned and lifted his chin to encourage the attention.

Flames crackled in the hearth and in Henri's heart. Slick fingers worked his opening, to be replaced by something larger and latex-covered. He shoved back, biting his lip against the stretching. Damn. Just damn.

Sebastian slid inside him, inch by inch, forward and back, until fully seated. He wrapped one arm around Henri's waist, idly running his fingers up and down the length of Henri's shaft. Henri wriggled, getting more comfortable and putting more pressure on the right spot inside of him. He sucked in a breath and huffed it out slowly. He wanted to roll Seb over, climb on top, and fuck them both senseless. Every nerve, every atom of his being shrieked *more, more, more, more, more!*

In this Seb called the shots, and his wildly beating heart against Henri's back said he needed as much as Henri did. And yet, he hesitated.

"If you're afraid of hurting me, you don't have to worry. I'm fine," Henri assured him.

"It's not that." Sebastian's breath gusted against Henri's bare shoulders, sending a chill up his spine.

"Then what is it?"

"I've never known a perfect moment before. I want to pause and savor."

Henri twisted as far as he could, bringing his lips to Sebastian's for a brief kiss and imprinting the moment in his mind, as Seb must be doing. He tightened his inner muscles.

Seb groaned and bucked against Henri. "You don't play fair," he griped. With slow but sure strokes, he sealed their union. Seb, inside him, wrapped around him, loving him, erased memories of any who'd come before. Sebastian. His Sebastian, stroking him in time with their loving.

Slow, unhurried, Seb kissed a path across Henri's shoulders, nuzzled his ear, nibbled an earlobe, and bit lightly where neck met shoulder. He picked up the pace, moans deepening as he neared climax.

Henri rode each stroke, breath caught in his throat at the perfect, perfect stretch, the rub of Seb's cock against his prostate, the firm grip around his length.

"I'm going to come." Sebastian closed his mouth around Henri's shoulder, rhythm faltering, and released into Henri's body. Pulse after pulse, his cries of release harmonized with Henri's earthy groans.

Though his tempo grew erratic, Seb continued to stroke

Henri. Henri added his hand, gripping Sebastian's fingers and controlling the speed. "Ah, ah, ah!" He bowed forward, clamping down on Seb's hand as he came.

At last they lay slack against each other, complete.

Tomorrow they'd set the wheels into motion for their future, whatever their future might bring. They'd soar or they'd fall, but they'd do so hand in hand, and the world be damned.

Words weren't needed. A subtle clasp of Sebastian's hand meant "I love you." Henri returning the gesture meant "I love you too." A kiss to the shoulder meant "I'll always be here for you," and a kiss to the knuckles replied, "I know."

Henri dozed and awoke to find himself covered with a quilt, Seb's arm serving for a pillow. He'd never been so content. As he drifted off to sleep again, a piano melody formed in his head. He hummed along:

One perfect moment,
Of one perfect day,
Of one perfect life….

"I'm a sap."
"But you're my sap." Seb hugged him tighter.

TWENTY-SEVEN

TWANG, TWAAAAAAANNNNNNG, Sylvia sang, working her magic with Michael's fingertips on her strings. Holding true to his onstage persona, he appeared as a shadow against a wall, illuminated by a car's headlights, larger than life on a movie screen.

Henri, playing a disfigured has-been rocker, half his face hidden in darkness, crooned, wooing his on-screen love with sweet words. Sebastian, as the talented young singer, Chris, warily glanced right and left, searching parked cars for his phantom mentor, the one who coached him, nurtured him, yet never showed his face.

Chris intoned, "Where are you, why can't I see you?" in a tenor that would soon bring the world to its knees. The sound man knew his stuff: Seb's voice seemingly echoed off the walls of the set.

A low keening answered him, an unseen Tessa speaking through the new Tibetan bowls Henri'd given her as a gift.

Closer and closer the phantom and Chris came, until finally, the scarred rock star and unblemished protégé met face to face for the first time.

"I am ruined," Henri sang, against Sebastian's "Beautiful to me."

Together they raised their voices, their locked gazes full of meaning. "Meant to be, meant to meet, meant to share our music."

The credits rolled. Behind Henri his mother sniffed. "That is so sweet."

Henri turned to Sebastian, seated beside him. "He is, isn't he?"

Applause filled the theater, and as the lights rose, so did the audience. From Henri's other side, Lucas murmured, "You've surpassed any hopes I had." He wiped at his eyes with the back of his hand. Henri wrapped him in a one-armed hug. Chances were Lucas still saw Annette on screen, reflected in their son. Lucas reached past Henri to clutch Sebastian's hand. Sharon clung to his other. "I am damned proud of you both."

Sebastian didn't speak. He merely beamed at his father and new stepmother. The newness of suddenly having living parents hadn't worn off yet.

"Are you ready?" Henri asked.

Seb nodded. Lucas stepped aside to let Henri and Sebastian out of the aisle. Back pats and compliments followed them from the theater to a pack of waiting reporters.

"Mr. Lafontaine, what made you decide to produce a musical?"

"A good script, a good cast, and the need to challenge myself and my band." Lucas had drilled him on possible questions, and Sharon—in black this time—hovered near the back of the group to get the last word in.

Tessa, Michael, Jake, and Colton fanned out behind Henri and Sebastian, joined by Jenni and Henri's parents. They still had issues to work out, but Jenni openly hugged her brother. Despite his threat, she'd appeared in the movie as a helpful shop girl, not a nun.

"Mr. Unger, do you intend to pursue an acting career or can we count on seeing you back on the opera circuit soon?"

Sebastian eyed his father, who'd forbidden him to jeopardize his career with a name change. "Please, call me Sebastian. The future is yet to be determined. Right now, I'm earning my keep as a vocal coach, and collaborating with Henri on his upcoming album."

The reporter turned his attention to the band. "Congratulations on your Grammy nominations for Best Rock Song and Best Rock Performance by a Group. What's next for the band?"

Henri handled the question. "We'll finish writing, take our new material to the studio, and start touring."

Another reporter stepped up. "Is it true Hookers and Cocaine are going through more changes?"

Henri donned his best "surprised" face. "Really? No, I hadn't heard that." What he had heard was that after his band's stellar performance as their opening act, the crowd left when Henri did.

After a few more innocuous questions, Sharon asked, "Mr. Lafontaine, some have said that the characters of Chris and the phantom are gay, and the ending song marked the beginning of their lives together. Was that your intention?"

The closet door opened. Henri and Seb stood at a crossroads. Henri glanced at Seb, who smiled. Now came their moment. "Actually, the beauty of the story is the audience can read into the subtext what they will. If, for instance, you'd like to imagine Chris and the phantom chugging beers and watching a Cubs game on TV, so be it. If, however"—he winked at the nearest camera—"you want to imagine the two main characters holding hands and ambling off into the sunset together, that's your right. Imagine the ending as you want to."

Henri laced his fingers with Seb's, and the sidelong glance and half smile he threw his lover wouldn't leave much doubt which ending would become reality. He and Seb had remade their lives. Being happy together was now, not "A Matter of When."

LYRICS BY EDEN WINTERS

A Matter of When (New Version)

Where have you been?
All my life spent lonely
I know you're out there
The one I've waited for
I know I'll find you (and now I've found you)
It's just a matter of when

A Matter of When (*Date with a Bullet*—Original Version)

Got a date with a bullet,
Got a date with a gun,
No matter what I do,
One day it's gonna come
You say that you love me
But you only speak in lies
Put me down every minute

And I gotta say good-bye
'Cause got a date with a bullet
Got a date with a gun,
And every day that I stay with you
The closer that day comes
Got a date with a bullet,
Got a date with a gun,
No matter what I do,
One day it's gonna come
It's just a matter of when

Ice Inside (Original Version)

Ice inside where her heart used to be
Though she hides it well so none can see
With a smile on her face she fools passersby
I know her well, I see the lie
They only see what she wants them to see
But she can never hide the truth from me

She feels so warm when she acts the part
He can't see the icicle she has for a heart
He feels complete when she's by his side
But there's ice inside, there's ice inside
He only sees what she wants him to see
But she can never hide the truth from me

Some may believe
Some won't care
Deep within, she hides despair
Lonely with her lover near
The pain is more than she can bear
There's ice inside, there's ice inside

Ice inside where her heart used to be
Though she hides it well so none can see
With a smile on her face she fools passersby
I know her well, I see the lie
When she stands before her mirror at night
Only I can see the ice inside.

ABOUT EDEN WINTERS

You will know Eden Winters by her distinctive white plumage and exuberant cry of "Hey, y'all!" in a Southern US drawl so thick it renders even the simplest of words unrecognizable. Watch out, she hugs!

Driven by insatiable curiosity, she possibly holds the world's record for curriculum changes to the point that she's never quite earned a degree but is a force to be reckoned with at Trivial Pursuit.

She's trudged down hallways with police detectives, learned to disarm knife-wielding bad guys, and witnessed the correct way to blow doors off buildings. Her e-mail contains various snippets of forensic wisdom, such as "What would a dead body left in a Mexican drug tunnel look like after six months?"

In the process of her adventures she has written fourteen m/m romance novels, has won several Rainbow Awards, was a Lambda Awards Finalist, and lives in terror of authorities showing up at her door to question her Internet searches. When not putting characters in dangerous situations she's a mild-mannered business executive, mother, grandmother, vegetarian, and PFLAG activist.

Her natural habitats are airports, coffee shops, and on the backs of motorcycles.

Keep up with Eden and Rocky Ridge Books by joining the newsletter.

edenwinters.com
Edenwinters@gmail.com

ALSO BY EDEN WINTERS

Settling the Score

Small-town mechanic Joey Nichols gets dumped hard, but novelist
Troy Steele can help him find his way to revenge, and past it to love in
this Lambda Award Finalist/Rainbow Award Finalist story.

The Angel of 13th Street

Noah Everett devotes himself to getting rent boys out of the life, but doesn't count on Jeremy Kincaid finding his home in Noah's heart in this Rainbow Award Finalist novel.

Diversion (Book 1)

Lucky Luckylighter, an unlikely drug enforcement agent, and his partner Bo Schollenberger get together while solving their first case in Book 1 of this Rainbow Award-winning series.

More From Rocky Ridge Books:

The Dark Angels Series

Hot rockers from Z. Allora—With Wings is the first in this four-book series, flavored with yaoi and full of men falling in love.

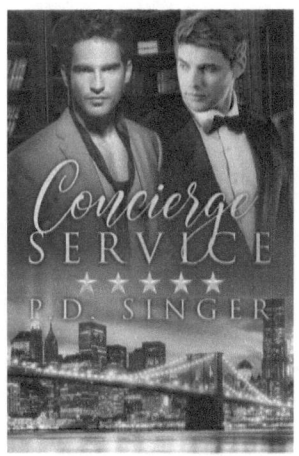

Concierge Service

Joshua Hannes, concierge at the swanky Vivaldi Hotel, can

find anything from a dye job for a purse dog to sold out theater tickets, but he's unprepared for billionaire Craig Ridley's request for a friend.

————

Keep up with Eden and Rocky Ridge Books gang by joining the newsletter.

www.ingramcontent.com/pod-product-compliance
Lightning Source LLC
Chambersburg PA
CBHW052026240626
47153CB00006B/1970

* 9 7 8 1 6 2 6 2 2 0 8 3 6 *